PENGUIN BOOKS

BLUE IS
THE COLOUR
OF HEAVEN

Richard Loseby was born in Port Moresby, Papua New Guinea in 1963. He grew up in Australia before moving to New Zealand at the age of eight. In 1980 he ventured into advertising as a copywriter, working in London from 1985 to 1993 before returning to Auckland as a senior writer at DDB New Zealand. Richard is married with two children. This is his first book.

ACKNOWLEDGEMENTS

To the men of Hezbollah and Jamiat-i-Islami, particularly Nebi Mohandaspoor, I owe my sincerest gratitude for allowing me to share their lives. To my family and especially my mother for enduring the months of not knowing; to Sue and Brian Shoosmith for their friendship, outrageous hospitality and the loan of a Northamptonshire cottage in which this book first took shape; to all my friends in New Zealand and England for their constant encouragement; to my colleagues at DDB and to Philippa Gerrard and Bernice Beachman at Penguin, my appreciation extends beyond these few words.

PENGUIN BOOKS
Penguin Books (NZ) Ltd, cnr Airborne and Rosedale Roads, Albany,
Auckland 1310, New Zealand
Penguin Books Ltd, 80 Strand, London, WC2R 0RL, England
Penguin Putnam Inc, 375 Hudson Street, New York, NY 10014, United States
Penguin Books Australia Ltd, 250 Camberwell Road, Camberwell,
Victoria 3124, Australia
Penguin Books Canada Ltd, 10 Alcorn Avenue, Toronto,
Ontario, Canada M4V 3B2
Penguin Books (South Africa) (Pty) Ltd, 24 Sturdee Avenue, Rosebank,
Johannesburg 2196, South Africa
Penguin Books India (P) Ltd, 11, Community Centre, Panchsheel Park,
New Delhi 110 017, India
Penguin Books Ltd, Registered Offices: Harmondsworth, Middlesex, England

First published by Penguin Books (NZ) Ltd, 2002

1 3 5 7 9 10 8 6 4 2

Copyright © Richard Loseby, 2002
Author photograph Francois Maritz

The right of Richard Loseby to be identified as the author of this work
in terms of section 96 of the Copyright Act 1994 is hereby asserted.

Editorial Services by Michael Gifkins & Associates
Designed by Mary Egan
Typeset by Egan-Reid Ltd
Printed in Australia by McPherson's Printing Group

All rights reserved. Without limiting the rights under copyright reserved above,
no part of this publication may be reproduced, stored in or introduced
into a retrieval system, or transmitted, in any form or by any means
(electronic, mechanical, photocopying, recording or otherwise), without
the prior written permission of both the copyright owner and
the above publisher of this book.

ISBN 0 14 301821 3

www.penguin.co.nz

BLUE IS THE COLOUR OF HEAVEN

A journey into Afghanistan

Richard Loseby

PENGUIN BOOKS

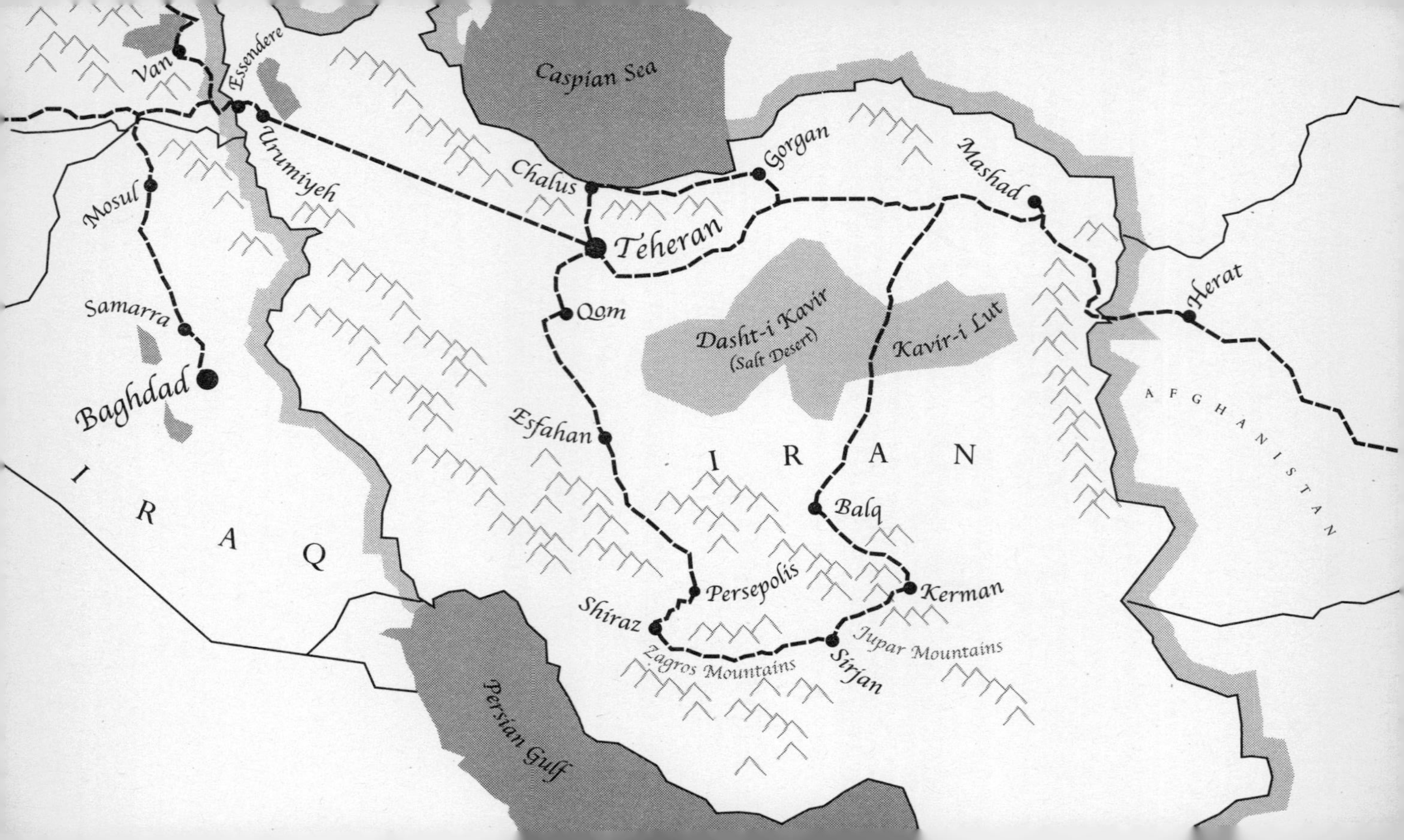
Caspian Sea
Van
Essendere
Urumiyeh
Mosul
Samarra
Baghdad
Chalus
Gorgan
Mashad
Teheran
Qom
Dasht-i Kavir
(Salt Desert)
Kavir-i Lut
Herat
AFGHANISTAN
Esfahan
IRAN
IRAQ
Balq
Persepolis
Kerman
Shiraz
Sirjan
Jupar Mountains
Zagros Mountains
Persian Gulf

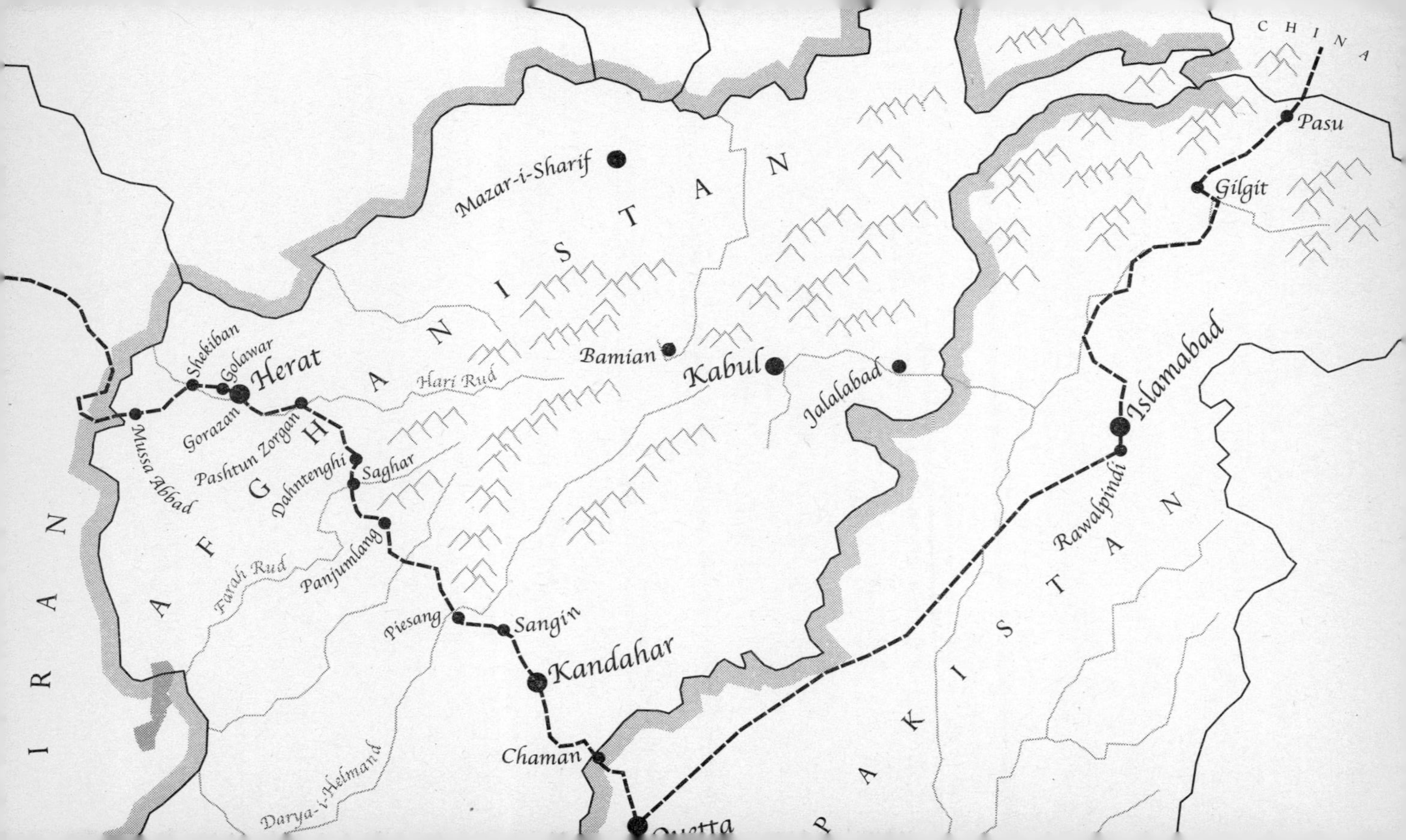
CHINA
Pasu
Gilgit
Islamabad
Rawalpindi
PAKISTAN
AFGHANISTAN
Mazar-i-Sharif
Bamian
Kabul
Jalalabad
Hari Rud
Herat
Golawar
Shekiban
Gorazan
Pashtun Zorgan
Mussa Abbad
Dahntenghi
Saghar
Panjumlang
Farah Rud
Piesang
Sangin
Kandahar
Chaman
Darya-i-Helmand
IRAN

To Elisabeth

With a Heart of furious fancies,
Whereof I am Commander.
With a burning spear and a horse of air,
To the Wilderness I wander.

With a knight of ghosts and shadows,
I summoned am to Tourney.
Ten Leagues beyond the Wide World's end,
Methinks it is no Journey.

Tom-a-Bedlam

Auckland, New Zealand, September 2001

'What colour is it in heaven, Daddy?'

I look up from the newspaper that is plastered with photographs of the World Trade Centre collapsing under the weight of terrorism. My bright-eyed son Thomas is looking at me on the window seat with all the curiosity of youth, clutching a Thunderbirds toy and watching CNN from the sofa. He returns to the images that depict scenes of more devastation. I cringe because I hadn't realised the TV was still on. Death pervades the sitting room and I'm the guilty parent, corrupting my child's innocence. I reach for the remote to let normality resume. The thick black smoke clears and the sun suddenly shines through the garden doors. Tangled metal is replaced by twisted climbing roses and a lemon tree.

'Come on, Tom,' I say, trying to change the subject and putting away the paper. 'Let's go find Isobel.'

He gets off the sofa and on the way past the piano bumps his head on the thick wooden leg. Not badly, but it's enough to cause a tear or two. I crouch down and place my hand on the growing lump, willing it to go away.

The little cottage we live in is growing smaller as the children get bigger. One of these days we're going to have to move somewhere that doesn't present as many obstacles to anyone under three feet tall. Old Broadwood grand pianos are beautifully made, but they tend to take up a bit of room. We'd be more comfortable in a villa; one with double bay windows and a return verandah wide enough for scooters and skateboards.

'Better?' I ask, taking my hand away.

He gives it a good rub and nods back. There's a red mark, but the bump has receded.

If only the pain of the last few weeks could be so easily remedied, then perhaps Afghanistan might have been spared the horror of being dragged into yet another war, this time not one of its own making. The phone had already run off the hook with *friends asking how I felt about the New York terrorists, the Taleban government, Osama bin Laden. Each time I had pointed out that people like this did not represent the average Afghani; in fact far from it – most of them weren't even Afghans. The people of Afghanistan were proud and honourable, no more bent on the destruction of Western civilisation than you or I. They just wanted to go back to their lives, I would say. After over two decades of conflict they had grown tired, fighting off an invader who lurked outside the walls. No wonder they had been overtaken so easily by the one from within.*

I turn back to my boy.

'Well,' says Tom, not prepared to wait any longer for an answer to his question. 'I hope it's a really pretty colour. Sort of like . . . blue maybe.'

'Could be,' I reply. 'It could well be.'

ONE

In Sofia, with the British Ambassador and his wife, I was invited to join a final dinner party on the eve of their retirement. The other guests were a mixture of British embassy people and high-ranking Bulgarian officials, including an old bull-necked General and a young, attractive interpreter. The Bulgarians, however, were the dominant force, and their ruddy faces beamed in anticipation of the excellent meal to come.

The residence was all elegant staircase, creaking floorboards, long echoing passages and high-ceilinged rooms, richly decorated with the ambassador's personal collection of *objets d'art*; souvenirs from his other postings. He and his wife, who were old friends of my family, had lived all round the world but Sofia was their final assignment. Now they were about to exchange the big house for a small cottage somewhere deep in the English countryside. It was a hectic time, but even so, on hearing that I was passing through by train from London, they had generously invited me to stay.

It was February. Snow was drifting down outside and collecting on the window-sills, while in the dining room a log fire crackled away in the grate, burning brightly and casting shadows out across the floor. I sat half way down the long table, opposite the General who, having left his gold braid behind, wore a suit instead of a uniform. He looked smart in a military way, but not comfortable.

'I am told you are a traveller,' he growled. 'It is a profession?'

'Of sorts.'

'Do you travel in my country now?'

'Not this time,' I replied. 'I'm headed further east.'

He interrupted with a click of his tongue.

'Muslims,' he said disparagingly. 'I do not care for them much,' and he looked away to eye up the pretty interpreter.

The man on my left was Bulgarian also, of slender build, with thick black Balkan hair and a jutting chin. He was younger than the others, in his early thirties perhaps, and had his eye on the girl as well. But for the moment he wanted to hear more of my plans and took up the conversation where the General left off.

'You have heard the news of course, about Iran.'

Less than two days before, Iran's Ayatollah Khomeini had slapped a *fatwa* on the head of Salman Rushdie for his book *The Satanic Verses*. Now it seemed the whole world had gone mad. Muslim demonstrations in London's Regents Park, book burnings in Pakistan, idle threats from far-flung Islamic countries and the breaking off of diplomatic relations between Britain and Iran. My chances of travelling any further than Turkey, of getting into Iran as I had planned for months, were now severely jeopardised.

'I'm hoping it'll die down quickly,' I said.

He nodded doubtfully and frowned at his empty wine glass, willing one of the staff to notice. Then he looked up and asked, abruptly, 'Why do you want to go to Iran? The border is closed. No one can get through.'

He was right, of course. The entire country was a closed shop – had been ever since the Islamic revolution in 1979, when the corrupt regime of the Shah had been finally deposed by the return of Ayatollah Khomeini. I could still remember the television news bulletin showing the Ayatollah arriving at Teheran airport on an Air France flight from Paris. There was little sign then of the bloodshed that would soon follow: the enforcement of Koranic law, the eight long years of war with Iraq, the purges and pogroms against those who did not conform. Since then, the war had ended but nothing else had drastically changed.

'I want to find out something,' I said. 'Or someone, perhaps.'
'An Iranian?'
'Not exactly,' I replied.
'You are not sure?'
'It's a little difficult to explain.'

His persistence made me uneasy. The truth was the journey was not just about Iran. In fact Iran was only the first stage in a rather more ambitious quest. In the grand scheme of things, it was the initial stepping stone, a testing of the waters; without it all my plans for the future would come to nothing.

Just then the meal arrived. A toast was made and I watched the General drain his glass in honour of the Queen, then turn his attentions towards the plate in front of him. My young Bulgarian friend was not quite so distracted, however.

'Tell me then,' he said. 'You say Iran is only the beginning. If you make it that far, what next?'

'There is another idea.' I decided to come out with it. 'Something I have toyed with for many years and would like to see come about.'

'And?' he said.

'I want to cross into Afghanistan.'

He put his knife and fork down abruptly and stared. 'You are serious?'

'Completely,' I replied.

'And for a long time you have wanted to do this?'

I nodded.

'Ever since I was eight.'

TWO

As a child in Australia, I remember my father knowing a few things about Afghans. Like the Aborigines, he would say, they were tireless walkers. They knew how to ride a camel and a horse if need be. They also wore baggy trousers tied up with rope and enormous hats on their heads like piles of laundry.

What was surprising was that he had met one in the branch of the Bank of New South Wales where he worked – had even helped him set up an account because 'the poor bloke hadn't the foggiest'. The Afghan had wandered in one day with no money, only a handful of uncut precious stones; rubies and emeralds in fact, washed down from the high mountains of Afghanistan during the rainy season and deposited on my father's desk in a ragged leather pouch. The gems were legal tender, of course; these were the days when opal miners regularly arrived clutching their hard-won earnings. In the end the bank had authorised a loan and the Afghan had gone out west with his camels to start up an outback haulage business. The Silk Road had come to Australia.

What we didn't know then was that Afghans had been arriving by ship for quite some time. With their remarkable beasts of burden in tow, they had come to work for the Australian Railways who, in their march across the outback, were encountering problems getting supplies to the workforces. To the average Australian the qualities of the camel were already well known. The film *Arabian Nights* had been a big hit in the nation's cinemas. Any man could tell you that a single camel train could cross the desert and deliver enough food and water for fifty men. It was hardly a revelation then that the Afghans came to be in such demand.

But I became fascinated with my father's story. The Afghan, our particular Afghan, with his long legs that carried him at great speed over huge distances, his odd clothing and his camels – these stirred an already wild imagination. The Afghan, as I pictured him, had blue eyes set like jewels in a smiling brown face, and hair as black as pitch. The trailing end of his hat, which I soon learned to call a turban, fell down the entire length of his back and he walked with a jaunty step. He was always cheerful; nothing troubled him too much except perhaps for the kookaburras that laughed at him from the branches overhead, and the strange tracks of the kangaroo which he had undoubtedly never seen before. Sometimes when I was dropping off to sleep, he would come and stand at the foot of my bed in the dim light, his head nearly touching the ceiling, to tell me stories of his homeland – of mountains that scraped the sky and deserts no man could cross. On one such occasion, he produced a tiny blue flower bud that opened its petals before my very eyes. It was a gift of protection he said, and he placed it beneath my pillow. But in the morning, as in a dream, the gift was gone.

Once a year, in the summer usually, my sister and I were taken to see our grandmother in New Zealand. I liked her because she was warm and kind, and always a great source of knowledge on the distant lands that surrounded our family history. Our ancestors had travelled warily across central Europe from Bohemia in the seventeenth century, avoiding the many conflicts of the time, eventually landing upon the shores of England. Then after an uncertain period of time, they set sail for the promised lands of the antipodes.

But my grandmother's favourite story was of how, in 1918, our grandfather won the DSO at the tiny Belgian village of Courtrai. Against the tide of an advancing German army, he and his company had held their line, repelling attack after attack until reinforcements could arrive. It was always the same tale, brilliantly told and never the worse for repetition. So real was it that her living room would seem to reverberate with the very explosions she described. There was the high-pitched whine of artillery shells overhead, the rattle of machine-gun fire, the flying shrapnel, and a vision through the smoke of a lone figure leading his men into battle.

My grandfather's photograph was set on the wall above her favourite chair. He was dressed in full uniform and his face was stern, gazing steadily out from under the peak of his officer's cap. Throughout much of his career he had also been a collector of old military ballads, lines of verse composed by soldiers in long-forgotten fields of battle: Waterloo, Omdurman and the Crimea. But there was always one that fascinated me. Through its stanzas I learned of the untamed wilderness of Afghanistan, and the folly of those who tried to take her by force:

> *Kabul town's by Kabul River,*
> *Blow the bugle, draw the sword.*
> *There I left my mate forever,*
> *Wet an' drippin' by the ford.*
> *Ford, ford, ford o' Kabul river,*
> *Ford o' Kabul river in the dark!*
> *There's the river up and brimmin', an'*
> *There's 'arf a squadron swimmin'*
> *'Cross the ford o' Kabul river in the dark.*

Back at home I often pressed for news about the Afghan's whereabouts.

'Is he coming back?' I would ask. 'When will we hear?'

Despite the lack of information, however, my interest in the Afghan and his country grew ever stronger. He had opened my eyes to the world map, though with an obvious bias. I sometimes had trouble finding Alaska but never Afghanistan. It was wedged between Persia and Pakistan; half mountain and half desert, a world of mystery and magic.

I also knew from my elderly aunt that Afghanistan was scarcely bigger than New South Wales. She reared racehorses in the countryside south of Sydney, and lived on her own in a big white house surrounded by ghost gums. The house was filled with what she called 'interesting junk'. Amongst these pieces my favourites were ranked: a stuffed iguana from Ecuador, a bird-eating spider from the Philippines, and a set of Aboriginal throwing spears which I used to stalk her six golden Labradors.

My aunt was also the proud owner of an immense wall atlas that all but completely covered one end of her library. It was under this great chart that I would sometimes sit, tracing the passage into our lives of the strange wanderer from the east. His path was like an indelible line that inched its way down from north-west Afghanistan to the pink countries of our Commonwealth. There was Kabul, Kandahar and Herat; Afghan cities which rolled off the tongue and were committed to memory. But always I came back to Herat as the beginning of the Afghan's journey, perhaps because it was also called the 'City of Gardens'. Somehow I felt that it was here the Afghan would have his home.

Eventually, we did hear something about him. My father returned home from work one day and announced that the Afghan's loan had suddenly been paid off and the account closed. It was thought he had struck it lucky while trekking over the Blue Mountains and had stumbled across gold under a Coolabah tree; huge great nuggets the size of a man's fist. More than enough, I remember thinking, for him to live in the lap of luxury for the rest of his life. He wouldn't have to work for the railways any more – perhaps he would even decide to go back home to Afghanistan, although the thought of this always left me feeling sad. Australia might never again see the passing of his kind.

My father alone understood these fears. He listened carefully, as grown-ups do to their children's dreams, as I explained how I would one day go and look for the Afghan. This delicate information he acknowledged with a wary look over his shoulder, just to make sure no one else was listening, and then with a knowing wink he promised to come with me when the time came.

I never forgot that promise and neither, I think, did he.

My father had travelled in his day. As a young man he had journeyed to the Americas and the Pacific Islands, and I recall there was a photograph of him taken in the early morning light, leaning against the railings of an old ocean liner, gazing out at distant horizons. His friends called him Blue, because he had red hair and because this was Australia. It made him stand out in a crowd, something with which he was never quite comfortable. He was genuinely quiet and thoughtful; not a demonstrative person. 'Blue Loseby,' they would say, 'is a good man.'

Our weekends and family holidays were nearly always spent at the beach. He would put me on his broad back and swim way out beyond the surf, until all sight of land was lost behind the great blue breakers of the Pacific Ocean. 'You have nothing to fear,' he would say calmly, and of course I believed him.

In this private place which was all our own, he taught me how to swim and tread water, how to negotiate the rips and ride the waves. But the most important lesson of all, he had said, was simply learning how to let go.

'The sea will carry you, son. If you let it.'

Not until years later, after growing up and seeing how the world worked, would I truly understand what he had meant. For him, the sea was a metaphor for life itself, the ever-changing ebb and flow over which one had no control. To fight it, like swimming against a rip-tide, he once warned, was to invite almost certain calamity.

My father also had a wonderful smile which set everyone at ease. I remember that smile now more than anything else. It came from deep within the man; someone who had tried to walk an honest path through life. People liked him and trusted him; they relied on him greatly at times. Perhaps the strain over the years was too much; even though he was still relatively young, in the end his health suffered.

Doctors came and went, baffled by an affliction that refused to respond to their treatment. During one winter he was in and out of hospital for a long time. Finally he came home in the spring for good, and I counted the days until we would swim in the sea again. I thought it was just a passing illness, something he would quickly shrug off. It never occurred to me that we were soon to lose him. When they discovered the cancer, it was all too late.

The suddenness of his death, only days after my fourteenth birthday, made it all the more difficult to comprehend. There was a sense of total and irretrievable loss; the loss of a close friend, and then nothing. No thought, no understanding, no feeling. The finality of it all was unbearable, so I blocked off the pain and refused to believe in separation. In a way, I suppose, it was like going to sleep. But what brought me round was not the slow awakening to reality, but another quite separate shock altogether.

In December 1979, thousands of Soviet troops invaded Afghanistan, and almost immediately the injustice of this barbarous act ran parallel with the unjust nature of my father's death. The two events became intrinsically linked. The fact that both my father and Afghanistan had ceased to exist was unacceptable. I began to believe they were simply locked away somewhere, and an idea formed in my head that in one I would find the other.

My father wasn't gone. He lived on in a mountainous realm of a distant country; a land of mystery and magic, where I would one day go and find him, smiling and waving with the Afghan by his side.

THREE

I left the soft life of Sofia and plunged east into Turkey. I had a tight budget to worry about, but besides the recent events in Iran there was little else for me to concern myself with for the time being. My old khaki bag was light and felt easy on the shoulder. Its only precious contents were an old but trusted Pentax camera, some film, and a small silver-coloured heart which had been sewn onto the inside by Elisabeth – the girlfriend I had waved goodbye to at Victoria station in the early hours of a grey Monday morning. Time was on my side, however. So I hitched rides with Turkish truck drivers and started to learn the rudiments of their language.

From Istanbul I worked my way east along the Mediterranean coast, through Ephesus, Fithiye and Tarsus, before heading up towards the mountainous Kurdish regions nearer to Iran. Against the advice of a local leader in the village of Kahta, near Malatya, I climbed the Nemrut mountain alone at night, wrapped in a thick coat and knee deep in fresh snow, to sit on the summit with the ancient Commagene gods and king, waiting for the sun to rise. I ventured up into the icy mountains of Zap above the Iranian border, and was escorted back down again by Turkish soldiers. I watched the village football team of Hakkari beat the town of Van for the first time ever, and joined in the celebrations afterwards. Once I was even invited to a Kurdish wedding where they defied a Turkish decree and played their own national music long into the night. Kurds were always flouting the law, though they had good reason to.

In Mardin, a town on a rock above the plains of Mesopotamia, I was shown photographs of a village in Iraq where the Kurds lay dead in the streets – gassed, young and old, by Saddam Hussein, the Butcher of Baghdad.

The pictures belonged to a young Kurdish student whose parents lived in the sprawling refugee camp hundreds of feet below, while he shared the roof of the town's Koranic school with a family of peregrine falcons. He was a karate enthusiast, who woke every morning at dawn for prayer, then spent twenty minutes cutting, chopping and drop-kicking invisible foe. He was training, he said.

'For what?' I had asked.

But he had only smiled, and with consummate ease, sliced the air in front of my face with his foot. Here it seemed, was another willing recruit for the Kurdish resistance: the Pesh Merga, Those Who Face Death. But he was a shrewd and intelligent recruit. He did not try and bombard me with political doctrine concerning the Kurdish state. Even when I asked what he thought were the possible solutions he remained tight-lipped. He would only ever say one thing: that I should try to go and see Iraq for myself.

Iraq and Iran had been fighting each other for eight years, a war which had only recently stopped. Their two capital cities, although many hundreds of miles apart, had regularly lobbed missiles at each other. At the very least, Baghdad would be an interesting subject for later comparison with Teheran. The only question mark concerned Iraq's border with Turkey, and whether or not it was open to the likes of me.

From Mardin I went back westwards to the Iraqi embassy in the Turkish capital of Ankara, an overnight journey by bus which saw me sandwiched between the window and a huge Turkish wrestler who called himself the Mad Mullah, a name he had used more in Germany than in his own country. He was a congenial sort, not the type you could imagine trying to break someone's back or biting the head off a budgerigar, though these things were apparently his stock in trade. The only other bad habit he had was practising his moves while asleep, so I crawled out from between the window and the wrestler to lie in the aisle.

Ankara appeared next morning out of the grey gloom of a rainy day. Its streets were filled with sad-looking people on their way to work, and the traffic noise was irritatingly loud after the quiet of the mountains. The embassy was found quite easily after following the directions given to me by an information bureau. They had said to look out for the ugliest building in the block, and they were right. It was a ghastly concrete place encircled by high walls and security men with pocket-size machine-guns. Inside, the Iraqi officials were even less friendly. They sat behind their wide desks beneath portraits of the glorious leader Saddam Hussein, and said no, absolutely out of the question, was I crazy? Only pilgrims making the Haj to Mecca could have a visa for Iraq. However, back outside and around the corner, I became entangled in just such a bustling, impatient queue of Turkish pilgrims bound for Saudi Arabia and the holy city of Islam. Their passports were being liberally stamped with Iraqi transit visas by a small man in a grey suit. The crowds were making him uneasy. He didn't like the pushy Turkish women prodding him and yelling in his ear. He dearly wanted to go to lunch. In the rush, somehow I received a six-day permit.

FOUR

The Iraqi face on the other side of the glass is looking straight at me. Narrow, nervous eyes above a bushy moustache.

'Sex magazines?' he whispers.

I say nothing, out of disbelief.

'Sex magazines?' he mutters again, and this time a hand comes out and jabs anxiously at my bag on the concrete floor of the border post, while the face looks over at the other Iraqi customs officials standing a short distance away.

I am dumbstruck, a condition he takes to mean he isn't being understood properly.

'English?' he says, frustrated. 'You speak?'

I find my tongue and put it to use.

'Yes, I . . .'

He puts up his hand as a colleague passes by. When the man is safely out of earshot I am beckoned closer and whispered to again. But by now I have realised what is going on.

'No, no!' I say. 'No magazine.'

The face looks crestfallen, and then, realising he is vulnerable, a look of disdain enters into his eyes. The change in tone is remarkable. He rises to a level of sanctity where I am the decadent, salacious party, not he. My passport is scrutinised, obviously in the vain hope that further evidence can be found to convict me of debauchery, therefore cleansing him of his own guilt. The visa is correct, however, and with an officious bang, the stamp is added.

Entry permitted, ZAKHO, IRAQ, 10.4.1989.

It is not what you might call a wonderful first impression, but I am determined to put it behind me as a chance incident. As the darkness creeps in, shrouding the watchtowers up on the surrounding hills, I catch a ride with a petrol tanker to the city of Mosul, about forty miles inside Iraq, where I can rest for the night. The driver is an obese Turk with chubby fingers. He says he has ten children, all big and healthy like him. I tell him I have none.

He roars happily. 'If your woman is no good – get another!'

Along the way, torchlights suddenly begin to wave frantically at us from the side of the road. They are local villagers, he explains, hungry for the apples which the other drivers occasionally smuggle through. He thinks this is a tremendous joke and repeatedly slaps his thigh to emphasise the point. They have all their oil, yet nothing so much as a common fruit!

'Crazy Arabs!' he chortles, and the flab under his chin wobbles like jelly.

In Mosul, I manage to get a room in a small hotel on the edge of town, not far from the River Tigris. The Turk dropped me off several miles back along the main north/south road, and I had walked for an hour or so before finding it. The streets are dark and almost empty of traffic, with only a few neon signs hanging over a single row of shops. Directly above one of these is the place which offers a bed for the night, and I go up to find an unshaven Iraqi looking after the bookings. He has just one room remaining which turns out to be dirt cheap, but the walls have been drilled through with tiny peep holes that look into other rooms. I have slept in rough places before but the seediness of this turns my stomach.

I undress in the dark and lie on the bed, listening to the guttural tones of a language unknown to me, blaring from a television somewhere. There is no window, only a large fan on the ceiling to keep the air circulating. I am almost asleep when there comes a knock on the door.

He is young and drunk. Something has spilt down the front of his dirty white *dish-dasha*, the ankle-length Iraqi shirt. He sways in front of me while his eyes try to focus on a point above my head. Finally he manages to convey his purpose by pointing to the opposite wall at a framed picture of a small boy. Then he sticks his hand on his crotch and leers. I slam the door in his face and lock it again, propping a chair under the handle for good measure. My feelings towards Iraq are rapidly beginning to slide.

First thing next morning, I am travelling south over the dull, flat, featureless desert, together with yet another Turkish truck driver. He is heading for Baghdad with a load of spare automotive parts after staying the night at the same hotel in Mosul. Sayid Ahmad is thirty-three, a thin, wiry man with grease-covered hands and a grease-stained face. Even in this heat he wears a string vest under his grubby white shirt – clearly visible through the material. He does not care for Arabs much, and he smiles at their pure white *dish-dasha*; like women's dresses, he says. But this is only his second trip into Iraq. The first had been ten years ago, before the Iran/Iraq war broke out. His father is Iranian; Ahmad is an Iranian name, and so he had stayed well away from Iraq.

It is not surprising, given his background, that Sayid feels the way he does. The relationship between his ancestral home and that of its neighbour has, throughout recorded history, rarely risen above open hostility. In the beginning, around 1000 BC, the Assyrians rose to power in this fertile basin of Mesopotamia and swept all before them: Egyptians, Babylonians, Medes, Palestinians, Syrians and Persians. Roughly four centuries later, the great empire foundered upon the sea of its own decadence and corruption, giving the Persians an opportunity they could not resist. Their ruler Cyrus the Great conquered all of Assyria and more besides, until his own empire also crumbled several generations later. Mother Nature had done her best to separate the two lands. She had seen what was coming: the jealousies that mineral wealth would bring, and the differences in religion. She had put in place the Persian Gulf and a high mountain range. But in the end, human perseverance won out and they had been at each other's throats ever since.

For the whole day we journey along an almost dead-straight road that passes only the occasional settlement. Most are no more than roadside pit-stops, brick sheds selling puncture repairs and Coca-Cola from ice-filled barrels; the overriding sentiment is that Northern Iraq is an empty place. Finally, at sunset, the outskirts of Baghdad begin to appear. Shopowners are closing up their stalls for the day, carrying inside the few goods that provide their living. Some children are kicking a ball around a dusty square, and a goat is obliged to play goalkeeper, tied as it is to a stake between the posts. All of a sudden, as we come in out of the desert, there are power lines and palm trees – silhouettes against the orange glow of evening, and from a minaret unseen comes the familiar call to prayer.

Close to what seems like the city centre Sayid drops me off and I find myself near the tree-lined banks of the Tigris again, the same brown river which has flowed down from Turkey and through Mosul. We have both come a long way, although its sense of direction is undoubtedly better than mine. It flows past with a confidence I envy, heading south to join with the Euphrates and eventually pour into the Persian Gulf.

Opposite where I stand is a dark street, narrow and somewhat dingy, fronted by wretched shops, low houses, and a hotel. In the entrance a number of men are sitting on wooden stools. They all wear the traditional long shirts in various shades of white, and each man has a chequered *kefiyah* over his head, held in place by a thick black ropeband. They are talking and listening to a radio without much interest.

A young lad shows me up to a room that looks down onto the street. There is an iron hospital bed in the corner and a fan on the ceiling. Someone has tried to cheer the place up with a colourful poster of Kuwait stuck to the wall. The room smells of mothballs but at least it is an improvement on the one in Mosul. Having changed some money back at the border, I pay the lad the few dinar he is asking and am left alone to kick off my boots and lie exhausted on the bed. It dawns on me then that I haven't really slept properly in days. Baghdad, I tell myself, can wait until morning.

FIVE

The temperature has already risen into the early eighties by the time I go out for breakfast. The sun is a fiery ball over the rooftops. The fronds of the palm trees hardly stir. At the far end of the road a steady stream of traffic is passing, while in the other direction lies the river and the smell of baking bread. I venture down there and watch the old men in the tea houses, sitting on short wooden stools, smoking their pipes and playing backgammon beneath portraits of Saddam Hussein. The floors are either bare concrete sprinkled with water to keep the dust down, or cheap linoleum.

In one such place a grand old gentleman with hennaed hair introduces me to a kind of herbal tea made from the leaf of a mountain plant found only near his childhood home. He speaks a little Turkish and English, and politely lets me win a few games at backgammon. He points out the gun emplacements on the other side of the river and we talk about the war.

'It was like this,' he says, throwing the dice onto the board. 'God's will and good fortune helped us win.'

I keep quiet, feigning agreement, for the truth was that neither Iraq nor Iran won anything. In eight years of conflict, both sides eventually lost whatever ground they gained. More than a million people died in pursuit of a draw.

I ask him about the missiles from Teheran, but he says Baghdad has fared better than the other cities to the south and east. Basra, for instance, the main port on the Shatt-al-Arab waterway, bore the brunt of Iranian attacks. Now it is being rebuilt with Western aid. This he somewhat euphemistically calls progress.

'You will go to Basra?' he asks.

'No.'

'No?'

He cocks his head to one side.

'I don't have that much time, unfortunately,' I reply.

'Time! You are a young man, you have time! It is we,' he says, looking at the room full of old men, 'it is we who have no time!'

His name is Farouk and I see him on several occasions during the short time I am in Baghdad, much of which is spent along the Tigris. One evening he takes me to meet his old fisherman friends who, in time-honoured fashion, still bring their catch to the shore each evening to cook over the fires. The big fish are slit open from head to tail and then impaled upon sticks that lean over the flames, while the men discuss politics late into the night, prayer beads rattling with thoughtful concentration until, one by one, they drift back to their homes. Farouk also promises to take me to his own home, although when an invitation fails to appear I leave it at that, thinking perhaps that my presence in his home will attract the wrong kind of attention. His position is understandable. Baghdad is essentially a feared city. However, one morning a knock sounds on the door of my hotel room and there he is, in a white long-sleeved shirt and brown trousers, asking me to join him for the morning. A car is waiting downstairs and we drive several miles beyond the city to a small village near the river. His house is nestled in amongst some palm trees with a view of the water, and we sit in wicker chairs on the wooden terrace, eating dates and drinking tea. He reminisces about the days in Baghdad, as the owner of a string of grocery stores, before the war with Iran.

'You see!' he waves a hand over the property. 'See what I have built!'

He goes inside the house where a bookcase stands against the wall, and after rummaging through a pile of papers, returns with a framed black and white photograph. It is an old picture of a simple hut made of sun-dried mud brick. Outside it is a man and his wife with their six children. Their ragged clothes tell a story of hard work in the fields. He points to the tallest boy and then sticks a finger in his own chest.

'This is you?' I ask.

He nods proudly, a smile spreading across his wrinkled face.

The photograph was taken in 1924 when he was twelve. Of his brothers and sisters, only two are still alive. He tells me his father died in 1958, the year the monarchy was overthrown by the Ba'ath Party and its future President, Saddam Hussein.

'We should have seen what would happen,' he sighs.

Exactly what he means by that, he doesn't say. Nonetheless it is clear where his allegiance lies. To his country – yes, but not completely to its leaders.

We sit on the terrace until just before noon, at which point he studies his watch for a little longer than is necessary and I know it is time for me to go. We get into the car again and start back to the hotel. It is hotter now than ever, even with all the windows down. The voice on the car radio apparently says a heatwave is coming.

'It's going to get worse?' I ask.

'Oh yes,' he replies softly. 'Things will get a lot worse.'

But I have a hunch he isn't talking about the weather any more.

―

With just two days left I go north to the town of Samarra, back towards the Turkish border. In the hotel – a terraced building of dormitory rooms overlooking a meat market – a group of anxious young students go wild over a newspaper they see in my bag. It is the national Turkish newspaper, the *Hurriyet*, and the object of their excitement? A picture of a girl, in Istanbul, in a T-shirt.

Samarra is a small place, with the golden dome of a mosque at its centre. It possesses a single main street lined with the usual array of shops, banks and restaurants, mostly selling rotisserie chicken. But beyond this, a kind of village life prevails. It has character, which is a lot more than can be said for Baghdad. The streets here are all paved, but there are more donkey carts than cars. It is quiet and unpolluted.

Later in the afternoon I walk out further from town, past a line of gigantic Saddam posters. The first shows Saddam Hussein as the warrior, leading the troops into battle. The second is Saddam the devout, kneeling in prayer. The third and fourth have Saddam as the family man, surrounded by children, and in the fifth he is weighed down with medals.

At the end of the road is the great Mosque of Samarra. Said to be one of the largest in the world, it is in fact an open area of parched earth the size of a football field, surrounded by towering walls of ancient sun-baked mud brick. Near the entrance stands the lofty minaret, looking like the tower of Babylon, but best known in archaeological circles for having a spiral staircase on the outside.

From the top, the remains of the ancient city are visible several hundred yards away, and beyond that, the reed banks of the Tigris. Here the river has widened. Smaller channels cut through the floating islands of reed stalks, and an old wooden motorboat is making its way lazily downstream under a cloud of oily smoke.

Had I possessed the powers of second sight, that cloud might have grown to an immense pall, blackening the skies to the south. The ground at my feet might have shook with the pounding of explosives being dropped on the chemical plants nearby, while overhead, the vapour trails of allied aircraft would have been unmistakable. To remark to a passing Iraqi that in less than two years he would be at war with Kuwait and her allies would have provoked a cry of incredulity.

'Kuwait! They are our brothers! Arab against Persian – yes! Arab against Israeli – of course! This is the way it has always been. But in this time, Arab against Arab? Never!'

As it is, I can see nothing but the boat, its owner and the river in simple harmony. Iraq has only just found peace with Iran, ending a long and futile conflict. Basra and other cities are rebuilding. No one wants to fight any more. Saddam Hussein is leading the people into an age of peace and prosperity.

From Samarra there is no time left to journey further afield, nor have I much inclination to do so. I continue on by bus, back towards the cool mountains of Turkey, back towards my rendezvous with Iran. As a kind of parting gesture, I visit the medieval Arab city of Hatra in Northern Iraq, and then the ancient ruins of Nineveh – no longer proud capital of the Assyrian empire. But both are sad and empty shells in the middle of the desert, surrounded by high wire fences and jealous Iraqi excavators who search my bag for stolen antiquities.

I cross the border back into Turkey, arriving at the village of Essendere, in the final days of April.

SIX

Essendere was the back door to Iran, a remote border post which was just a ramshackle collection of concrete buildings hidden away in a narrow, wooded valley in south-eastern Turkey. A stream flowed down from the snow-capped mountains, down through the middle and on into Iran.

On the Turkish side, abandoned cars with Iranian number plates sat anchored to the spot, their tyres ruptured. Eighty yards away across no man's land, a high wall bearing the stern-faced portrait of Iran's Ayatollah Khomeini marked the frontier. Beneath it, a bearded sentinel paced silently back and forth.

I was there to reconnoitre an idea.

The Rushdie affair, now almost three months old, had not helped my chances of entering the country, especially through the main border post at Dogubayazit, several hundred miles to the north. I had an Iranian visa – a transit visa for just one week from the embassy in London – but I couldn't be sure they hadn't cancelled it. In Dogubayazit, the Iranian authorities might throw a fit and tear the page out. But in a distant spot like this, would they know or even care?

My passport went round the Turkish officials drinking tea on the steps of the customs house. One of them eventually agreed to escort me over the line. He buttoned up his jacket, adjusted his cap and knocked the dust from his trousers. As we left Turkish soil, he noticed the Iraqi visa in my passport and inhaled sharply through his teeth.

The buildings straddling the road on the Iranian side were of white-washed concrete with blue wooden doors and a mess of electric cables above. On the right, beyond the buildings, a line of willow trees trailed their branches in the stream. It was swollen with snowmelt from the mountains, fast-running and rustling the reeds.

As we approached the line I heard a door slam and then, fifty yards away, an Iranian in a dark blue uniform exited one of the huts, spoke to the bearded sentinel who swung the gate open for him to pass, and then strode purposefully towards us. We stopped short and waited politely, sensing that he didn't want either of us treading on his home soil. Evidently our business was to be conducted under the full gaze of Khomeini's towering portrait.

The conversation that followed was in the language of the border; a mixture of Turkish and Farci beyond my comprehension. I stood by helplessly as my passport was flicked through by the Iranian official and the visa for Iran scrutinised – several lines of embassy scrawl in Persian being the object of his attentions. After a short while the book was closed and handed back. There were more words between them and I detected some sort of disagreement. The Iranian was acting superior to his Turkish counterpart, much to the latter's growing distaste. Finally, seemingly washing his hands of the matter, the Iranian turned on his heel and went back through the gate.

I didn't need to ask. It was obvious the answer had been an emphatic 'no'. On the visa it was written, by the embassy in London apparently, that entry was permitted through Dogubayazit only. My heart sank. My plans began to darken and fade into hopelessness, because it was almost certain the authorities at that border post would turn back a lone traveller from London in these sensitive times. As we walked back to the Turkish side I quizzed my companion on the available options, and at first he just shrugged his shoulders unsympathetically. But once we were back on the steps of the customs house, surrounded by his own colleagues and perhaps roused by their questions, he began to warm slightly to my plight. He was the kind of man who had resigned himself to do a boring job. Now my situation was becoming something of a challenge to him. The officiousness and curtness of the Iranian had upset him too, that much was clear, and it seemed he was seeking a reprisal. Perhaps my success at Essendere would be his revenge?

He chewed on a sugar lump thoughtfully and slurped his tea.

There was a consulate, he said, an Iranian consulate far away in the northern Turkish town of Erzurum. It was a ten-hour bus ride but maybe, just maybe, they could change the visa in my passport. There was a great nodding of heads by the group gathered on the steps, and further directions on what bus to take. In two days, they reckoned, I would be back. Everyone agreed the consulate was a wonderful solution. No one there liked the Iranians much. They all wanted to see me through Essendere, without even bothering to know the reason why.

SEVEN

It was a ten-mile walk back to the dusty little village of Yuksekova, where I had already provisionally booked a room in the local guesthouse. But the time was getting on and I was uneasy about walking in the dark so close to the border. All the road signs were ridden with bullet holes, although whether they were made by the military or Kurdish revolutionaries was unclear. However, I was saved the fate of finding out when a mini-bus full of young Turkish soldiers stopped to pick me up a mile from the border. They were in a jubilant mood. Three ragged men were sitting on the floor of the vehicle, handcuffed to the seats. They were Iranian Kurds, caught in the mountains trying to cross the border illegally into Turkey. Unfortunately, and probably because of my presence, the soldiers wanted to show off and play tough. They demanded money from their captives and when none was forthcoming, they dropped the butts of their rifles onto the prisoners' fingers.

These three Kurdish men, so eager to escape from the land of the Ayatollah, had seemingly traded one form of tyranny for another. Worse still was the thought of what would happen to them now that they were caught. Being Kurdish in Turkey was bad enough, but being illegal as well was simply compounding their problems. I tried to find out, but the young soldiers merely laughed and left me guessing. When we eventually arrived in the town, they bundled the hapless Kurds into the police station on Yuksekova's only street and locked them up.

That night, however, the manager of the guesthouse invited me to dinner in his small office.

'Good Iranian tea,' he said after the meal. 'The best!'

He was a Kurd, naturally. Yuksekova was a typical Kurdish village in eastern Turkey. His name was Nusret. He was young and well dressed, of middle height, with dark hair swept back and parted in the middle. He prided himself on his appearance, and because the streets were so dusty he was forever wiping his leather shoes with a handkerchief.

Long after the other guests had retired to bed we were still talking about the state of the country, the girls in Istanbul, his forthcoming wedding, the weather, anything – until the real reason for waiting up arrived at the back doorstep.

As soon as the knock came he was off down the hall. A few minutes passed. I could hear murmured voices, and a door being hurriedly unlocked. Only briefly I glimpsed an exhausted looking group of men and women entering a room at the rear of the building. The men carried heavy bags and one of the women cradled a small child. It was wrapped up tightly in the colourful folds of her dress. The door was closed. I waited, but there was no further sign of either them or Nusret. I finished the tea and went up to bed, content in the knowledge that not all Kurdish Iranians who smuggled themselves over the Turkish border were caught.

I made the journey to Erzurum by bus, all 300 miles of it, although the long trip was to be repaid by the unexpected co-operation I received from the Iranian Consulate General. He loved the letter I showed him from the Geographical Institute. It was fake, of course; the organisation was completely fictitious, but the letterhead and its contents looked entirely convincing – written in flowing Persian script by the owner of an Iranian bookstore in West London. The chairman, Sir Winston Scott, had been the creation of my girlfriend, and it was her signature in his name at the bottom of the page. It pleased the Consulate General greatly that such a fine institution would send an emissary to his country, especially in this year, the tenth anniversary of the great Islamic revolution.

There was no mention of Salman Rushdie. He instructed his assistant to make the necessary alterations to the visa, allowing entry through Essendere. We shook hands and traded pleasantries. Then he dropped a bombshell. At the border, I would have to exchange US$150 at the official bank rate, which for all intents and purposes was as good as giving it away, and that I could ill afford. The official bank rate was ridiculous when compared to the black market. At the government's Melli bank, one dollar was worth only seventy rials, while on the street in Teheran I could expect over a thousand. That much I had learned from Nusret at the hotel in Yuksekova, but when I tried to protest the Consulate General took my passport and pointed to another indecipherable line in Farci at the top of the visa.

'It is written,' he said apologetically.

And that, for the moment, was that.

I returned south to Yuksekova and sat with Nusret in a *chay salonu*, drowning my sorrows with tea. He asked me if I wanted to cross the border at night, through the mountains. But to do so was a costly business and there was no guarantee of success.

'No, Essendere is still better,' I told him, remembering what had happened on this side of the border to the three Kurdish men. They were still languishing in jail across the street from where I was presently sitting.

Nusret took off a shoe and inspected the leather closely, giving it a quick shine with his sleeve.

'There may be another way,' he said thoughtfully.

'Yes.'

'The visa. We could change it again.'

His idea was a wonderful piece of lateral thinking. The visa had been altered once already at Erzurum. It bore an impressive consulate stamp in the middle. Any further changes would obviously look as if they came from the same place, with the same authority.

Back at the guesthouse that evening, an ordinary black ink pen was found to be identical to the one used by the consulate. Under a single lamp we sat round the desk in Nusret's office, as he practised the few pen strokes that, he promised, would make me exempt from the rule. Farci is not an easy language to script. A single line out of place can change the meaning of a sentence or render it incomprehensible. Even the humble dot has an important part to play, and so it was that no effort was spared in our grand deception. Advisers were brought in for consultation and heads nodded in agreement until finally the forgery was complete. Nusret even went over the consulate's faint scratchings, making them more like his. To my eye they were exactly the same.

EIGHT

Out on the road the next day, past the bullet-ridden signs that pointed to Iran, past the straight lines of poplar trees, I started walking back to the border post of Essendere for the last time. The sky was a cloudless blue and a sudden wind was kicking up miniature dust storms along the way. I settled into a rhythm and thought about the days to come.

All of my plans for Iran and Afghanistan hinged upon getting a visa extension in Teheran. At present I had just one solitary week. Enough time, the Iranian embassy in London had said, to cross the country to Pakistan and get out. That was all they were concerned about, while my main objective was to stay as long as possible. Afghanistan depended upon having enough time in Iran to find the Afghan resistance, without whose help any venture into that country would surely end in disaster. Information on their whereabouts had come to me through various people in London, and it was thought that at least some of the rebel groups had safe houses or headquarters hidden away in the Iranian city of Mashad, near the Afghan border.

Exactly where in that city was another matter, although that was something I could sort out later. My immediate concern was that the 'transit' nature of my visa might rule out any chance of an extension in the first place.

Around mid-afternoon I had reached a mountain pass and was heading down into the valley again. The road twisted and turned, grey and devoid of traffic, past clusters of tall, rounded boulders. It was cool at this altitude. Pockets of dirty snow sat in the hollows and beneath the ridges. On either side of the road, patches of green were beginning to show through the brown tundra.

At one stage, an army patrol appeared far below, spaced well apart and walking in single file across the valley floor. I sat behind a rock and waited until they were out of sight before continuing the rest of the way down. It was my intention to sleep near the border that night, in the bushes beside the stream which flowed into Iran, so that I could cross over in the early morning and make full use of the day. Doubtless this would not have been permitted in such a sensitive zone.

Roughly quarter of a mile from the frontier, where the scrub was at its thickest along the river bank, I found a suitably grassy clearing and spent the rest of the day in hiding. Darkness came early as the sun dipped behind ice-capped mountains, making my position even more secure. I finished off some bread and a few dried apricots, then curled up on the ground wrapped up tightly in my green poncho, listening to the stream gurgling past. Over in the east, where all was dark, Mars appeared and was soon followed by a thin moon that travelled ever westwards across a blue-black sky. Its dim light illuminated the valley, sparkled on the water, stars reflected in the sea, reminding me of the ocean. I was thinking of tomorrow, of the future, and in my tired state, of what it would be like to float into Iran beneath the wires, undetected. Then I must have slept.

When I woke again it was to the sound of a car horn nearby, then the sudden sweep of bright headlights and the roar of an engine passing. It was pitch black and very cold. I had no idea what time it was. I sat up and looked around. The car had already disappeared into the night, its driver probably one of the Turkish border officials on his way home. But his use of the horn intrigued me. Who was he signalling to? It didn't make sense. Out here, who else was there?

Suddenly it dawned on me, and I ducked down as a line of soldiers passed only feet from my hiding place. In the faint light they were just silhouettes, but they were silhouettes with guns and the closest I could have reached out and touched. Hardly daring to breathe, half expecting the shout of discovery, the glare of light, the volley of shots fired wildly, I waited and watched as each slow, silent step took them further and further away. Several anxious minutes passed before I dared to sit up and look, and only then could I afford to relax. Up on the dark hillside, flashes of torchlight told me they were climbing up out of the valley.

At daybreak I washed in the stream and put a comb through my hair and beard. I carefully concealed again about US$250 in cash for the black market later. Then, after collecting my things together and generally trying to smarten myself up for the occasion, I started off along the road for the border.

But it was very quiet. The abandoned cars were slumped in their corner still. The two guards stationed on either side of the line faced each other across the great divide with apparent indifference. In the new sun, a red-combed rooster clambered quickly onto the roof of the customs hut and watched me with beady little eyes as I sat on the steps, basking in the warmth. When the Turkish officials did eventually arrive they were a little surprised to see me so early, but this matter was forgotten once the visa and consulate stamp were pointed out. There were smiles all round, especially from the official who had escorted me across the border the time before. He could hardly contain his excitement. He gazed at the Iranian border huts with a small gleam in his eye. It was going to make his day to watch me walk across, and happily this moment was not long in coming. With all the formalities completed, I said my farewells and crossed over no-man's-land, under the dour gaze of the Ayatollah, into the Islamic Republic of Iran.

The senior Iranian officer seated across the desk from me shook his head and pointed to the consulate writing in my passport with a look of disgust.

'Who wrote this?' he grunted in English. He was not the same man I had seen the previous time. I was stuck with this ignominious character, whose navy blue uniform was half undone, and whose breath smelt of something putrid. He was a big man in a small room and he wasn't in a good mood. Something was annoying him. He scratched at his armpits and sat on the edge of his chair.

I explained to him, somewhat nervously, that the consulate of his country had been responsible.

'Bah!' he said. 'The writing is terrible. The last few words are almost unreadable!'

I took a sharp intake of breath, then let it out slowly when it became apparent that his displeasure was thankfully aimed at the low standards of education amongst his countrymen. It appeared then that Nusret's forgery, although a little clumsy, had worked all the same.

At his command I emptied the contents of my bag onto a long wooden table and stepped back. There were only a few clothes, a journal, camera, knife and poncho, but he was most interested in my collection of talismans: three lucky shells tied together with a piece of yellow string, and Horton – a marble elephant the size of a ping-pong ball.

Horton had been with me for years. When I was travelling he came along as guide and dutiful companion, and when I wasn't, he masqueraded as a paperweight in my office at home. Possessor of a simple philosophy and the wisdom of an old soul, his religion was that of wandering and his God was the God of walkers.

To distract the officer and hurry things along, I declared some traveller's cheques and a small amount of cash. Leaving my possessions, he took out some forms and started filling them in, one after the other, until a small wad of paperwork sat on his desk. I was given a pink form with the warning not to lose it under any circumstances. Then we went next door to where another set of documents were filled in. Again a pink slip was thrust into my hands along with the same dire caution, although what these forms were for I had no idea. I was settling myself in for a lengthy wait when, after a short lecture on how to behave in Islamic society, he simply told me to go.

'Is that all?' I asked.

Apparently it was. He walked off down the hall and never looked back. On this occasion, neither did I.

NINE

In huge letters of gold that almost covered one wall of the small Urumiyeh airport departure room it read: *Everyone knows we didn't start the war. In the name of Islam we were only defending ourselves.*

It was talking about the recent war with Iraq, and the equivalent in Farci was written above in letters just as large. Only partly true, it was a classic piece of finger-pointing that belonged in the playground.

Underneath, seated in a long line of orange plastic chairs, the women waited quietly, all of them dressed in black from head to toe as dictated by law. Only their eyes and noses were visible, and a few teeth, clamped over the edge of their chador to keep it in place.

The menfolk stood on the other side of the room, watching me watch their women. I stopped when I remembered that this was a punishable offence in Iran.

I had made it! To Urumiyeh to be precise, a town just a few

miles from the borderline. After a short and happy walk that morning, I had come across a military outpost where a convoy of goods trucks was just about to leave the compound. The soldier who stopped and offered me a lift proved to be a lucky find. The first thing he had said to me was 'Dollar?', and so instead of having to look for it, the black market had found me. Using a mixture of Turkish and sign language, I had then also discovered that by far the fastest way of reaching Teheran was to fly. It would cost 6,000 rials, the soldier said, an amount that, thanks to the unofficial bank, worked out to be a mere US$2.50! The bus journey apparently would have taken more than sixteen hours. With Iran Air I was going to be in the great city of Teheran before lunch.

There weren't any seats left in the departure lounge, but in an empty corner of the room stood a wooden box, about chair height, that looked sturdy enough. I began to wonder if anyone would mind me taking the weight off my feet and was about to test the theory when there erupted a terrible shrieking and howling from behind. An old man had burst away from a group of men nearby and was bounding towards me, his brown robes flying, his pure white turban bobbing up and down, waving his arms frantically. I stood up quickly and stepped aside, trying to distance myself from the scene. As he pulled the box away, the lid popped open revealing what looked to be copies of the *Holy Koran* inside, the most sacred of Muslim texts, and he, I suddenly realised, was a mullah.

The old man dragged the box to safety, then lovingly took out the books, kissing each one and touching them to his forehead. I tried to apologise but the old fellow shrunk back from me. It was useless. I had committed a major *faux pas* with a member of Iran's powerful clergy, and after only a few hours in the country!

I went outside to avoid further trouble and waited in the heat as the plane taxied in. It was 35 degrees Celsius, 97 Fahrenheit, and the sun had yet to reach its zenith. The tarmac was a shimmering sea. I looked over my shoulder through the glass door leading back into the lounge and watched the bent figure of the mullah beside his box, encircling it with his arms in a protective hug. Our eyes met briefly and his grip tightened.

How to win friends and influence people in Iran, I ruminated, is not to sit on their religion.

We flew north-east over the blue vastness of Lake Urumiyeh, then over a pale desert dotted here and there with patches of vegetation. Ripples of earth sometimes grew into mountains, but there were no clues as to what lay ahead in Teheran. Cities, I reminded myself, were all the same: bricks and cement, cars and noise, people and pollution. Yet the disturbing reality, the gospel truth which we are led to believe by our media, suggested that Teheran was no ordinary city, but a sprawling mass of religious fanaticism. The streets and avenues would be the same ones familiar from our television sets: scenes of great crowds surging forward screaming for our blood. Such a city might best be entered cautiously, giving sufficient time to peer beneath the surface and examine the shadowed corners. I wondered then whether an unhurried bus journey might not have been more comfortable, instead of having this cauldron rushing towards me at two hundred miles an hour.

The brown lands became tinged with more splashes of green as we banked for the approach. A single grey ribbon of roadway came into view, then the Elburz Mountains lifted up and trailed away into the distance, ending in a conical snow-capped peak. The first signs of urban life appeared; little dusty boxes clinging to the roadside soon gave way to larger buildings interspersed with trees and parks. And then all of a sudden, nestled beneath the mountain range, were seemingly towering structures of steel and concrete decorated with giant portraits of the saviour of Islam, Grand Ayatollah Khomeini – reaching skywards.

After all that I had heard about the 1979 revolution, when the airport was the scene of the Shah's escape and much heavy fighting, it was in actual fact a let-down. The terminal building was a ponderous structure which bore the scars of slow decay. Broken fittings were left to dangle by their wires, cracked windows remained untouched. There were pictures of Khomeini, and a poster which seemed to be celebrating the revolution's tenth anniversary with a pictorial montage of events surrounding that illustrious era: the storming of the American embassy, the hostages, the failed rescue attempt by US helicopters and the war with Iraq. But of fierce, gun-toting revolutionary guards I saw none. In fact, the official in immigration who checked my passport almost smiled at me.

I walked out into the sunshine, ignored the ranks of taxi-drivers and found a mini-bus that would get me into the city centre. The fee was a two rial coin, about the size of a ten cent piece, which was simply thrown by boarding passengers into a tin pan below the gear lever. The driver never bothered to see whether the correct money was being paid. It seemed he judged the amount by sound alone.

The traffic system on Revolution Street was perfectly clear about its position concerning pedestrian rights. It was simple: there were none. Once upon a time, before the Islamic revolution perhaps, Teheran had had pedestrian crossings, but the broad bands of white paint where barely visible now.

In the sweltering heat I had come to a place called Ferdowsi Square on one of the main avenues that bisect Teheran, where the cars, buses and trucks were bumper to bumper at sixty miles an hour. Small motorbikes used the sidewalk to get round traffic lights, and if it hadn't been for the odd tree or pole along the pavement, so too would have the wider vehicles. Sidewalk vendors guarded their wares by positioning themselves directly in front of the oncoming threat. Sometimes the bikes would swerve, sometimes they didn't. The vendors never budged.

Their goods were nearly all the same: pens, pencils, pen-knives, combs, nail clippers, matches and occasionally something like a pair of used spectacles. Cigarettes were sold in ones or twos, but rarely by the pack. As I stood watching, an orange taxi pulled into the curb and the driver got slowly out. All eight of his passengers, (and the car was an old Hillman model), seemed to purposely ignore this interruption in their journey. He sauntered over to an elderly seller and pulled out a cigarette from an open packet. A match was supplied gratis it seemed, but not once did either man notice the other. The driver lit his cigarette and sauntered back, the seller pocketed the coin and stared off into space, the passengers resumed their journey. Overcrowding had apparently forced the population to go round ignoring each other.

One conversation I'd had on the mini-bus coming into the city summed the situation up nicely.

'Teheran,' said the man in excited but broken English after he had discovered where I was from, 'Teheran is for no more than five million peoples. No more. But we have twelve million peoples living here now. There is no room for your elbows. No room at all!'

'You mean elbow room,' I had corrected.

'Elbow room! Forgive me, my English is forgotten. You have sitting room, dining room, elbow room. Yes! I remember now. But it is true, no one has elbow room in Teheran any more.'

Fortunately finding an actual room in Teheran wasn't too difficult. The Demavend hotel still had an old wooden sign in English stuck over the doorway. I saw it quite by chance at the end of a quiet street, down a narrow alleyway. Tall trees lined the roadside, shading the footpath from the sun and filtering out the traffic noise. The gutters were narrow canals flowing with clear water.

In the office I spoke with a young teenager who contemptuously put on his sandals and half walked, half slid down the hallway into a side room. Minutes later, a bald man in dark brown trousers and a light brown shirt came out. His armpits were wet with perspiration and he mopped his brow with a white handkerchief.

'Salaam Aleikum,' he said.

'Aleikum Salaam,' I replied.

I gave him my passport to look at, and the letter in Farci from the Geographical Institute. A bead of sweat rolled down his nose and dangled at the end, before dropping off and hitting the paper with a splat. Then, with a nod to the boy, he handed them back, looked me up and down once more and grunted his acceptance.

I was shown up to a small room with a bed on one side and a broken cupboard on the other. Half a mirror hung down from a piece of string on the wall to my right, but most important of all, an old air-conditioning vent squeaked away above the door. It was cool and cheap: about fifty cents.

The view from the window was of another alleyway, running into a courtyard surrounded by high walls. Every ten yards or so was a grey/green iron door which would occasionally open to reveal a small child perhaps, or a woman sweeping. Then the door would slam shut again. All the houses were like this, though it wasn't clear whether the reason was security or privacy.

But of course this was Ramadan, the Muslim month of fasting when not a morsel of food, not even a drop of water, can pass the lips during daylight, and consequently most of Teheran's inhabitants were apparently resting up indoors. Given the volume of people and traffic outside it was hard to believe it could get worse, but it seemed I was experiencing the Iranian capital on a quiet day.

On the way out, I was stopped by the sloppy youth, who wanted to know my religion. 'Shooma, Musselman?'

'Christian,' I said, and walked out past a portrait of an unsmiling Ayatollah Khomeini.

The heat was tempered slightly by a freshening breeze and the mountains, cloaked in the haze, seemed further away. The back streets twisted and turned into such a warren that it was difficult to keep a sense of direction. I passed a group of carpet repairers in the shade, finishing off a day's work, before turning right by a man-made stream. The walls of sun-baked mud bricks on either side revealed little. The occasional tree provided some shelter from the sun, but the heat was building up in that narrow lane so I turned round and went back to Revolution Street.

The stream of traffic roared past the shops, hardly slowing for the roundabout that was Ferdowsi Square. A line of people were waiting outside the Iran Air booking office, while on the opposite side of the road a huge advertisement for Canada Dry clung to the side of a building. Despite Ramadan, a trader selling a variety of nuts was doing good business, though no one was eating. The bags of pistachios were slipped in behind veils or into trouser pockets for later. Every black shroud concealed a woman, with only part of her face, hands and ankles left uncovered. The men were all in long-sleeved shirts, many with their buttons done almost right up in true Muslim fashion. Bare arms and necks, even for men, were regarded as moderately indecent. If there was any frustration built up through these clothing constraints then it was released in the way the Teherani drove and in the way some of them conducted business.

The traffic was lethal. I witnessed an accident within minutes of arriving. Apart from the yells of abuse, neither driver bothered to get out and inspect the damage. They simply carried on as usual, curses and all. The street sellers, however, were worse. Should any competitor challenge another for ground space, then all hell broke loose. With flailing fists the argument was usually settled, though I saw one old bookseller in Revolution Square become the victim of a younger man's territorial claims. It was hard to decide whether it was the heat, or the overcrowding, or the pangs of hunger which excited their fury. But one thing was certain shopping in Teheran was never dull.

There was nothing limited in the variety of things to buy, either. Seiko watches and Pentax cameras, as well as Italian leather shoes, were on open display. I even passed the grand offices of IranFord at one stage, but no sign of a showroom. It was the great irony of Iranian life, this abundance of Western goods, and a probable source of embarrassment for the mullahs in government too. The airforce defending their skies did so with American jets. But they got round it, as they did with all foreign equipment left behind after the revolution, by proclaiming that such things had been confiscated by Allah and his followers, and put to a better use. In other words the aircraft had been reborn under the Islamic faith, to fight the good fight.

On the way back to the hotel down one of the side streets, my attention was suddenly drawn to a green canvas banner hanging over a doorway. It was flapping noisily in the wind and the symbol it bore, that of an upstretched hand grasping a Kalishnakov rifle, belonged to Khomeini's revolutionary guard, the Pasdaran. A bearded man in green uniform was crouching beneath it, cradling the same automatic weapon in his lap and quietly remonstrating with a small boy who was guiltily trying to hide a half-eaten apple behind his back.

I could easily imagine the nature of the lecture: 'All Muslims must fast daily between dawn and dusk during Ramadan. This is the law of Allah, to make amends for our sins. And only when a black thread is indistinguishable from a white thread in the darkness does the fasting end.'

I went back to the hotel to rest and to wait for darkness. I was starving, but the law of God is the law of Iran, and is best not broken.

That night I found a place to eat not far from the hotel. A large fan turned lazily above vinyl-topped tables and a linoleum floor that looked as though it came from a trucker's pit-stop in midwest America. Three men were digging into a pile of rice and kebab at one of the corner tables and they paused momentarily when I entered. One of them got up after a short while. He was wearing a white apron and he went round to the other side of the counter. Behind him was a blackboard with several lines of Farci which I guessed to be the menu. I pointed at the top line.

'Chelo kebab,' he said.

I pointed at the next line.

'Chelo kebab.'

And the next.

'Chelo kebab.'

Slightly bemused, I ordered the top line and sat down at the back. Moments later, a plate of raw onions arrived, followed by a shredded salad, gherkins, yoghurt, four large meat kebabs and a pile of steaming rice with a slab of butter on top. The deluxe chelo kebab no doubt.

'Cola?' he grunted.

I nodded and a bottle was banged down on the table. It was one of the old-fashioned, shapely Coke bottles. The famous trademark was on one side and the equivalent in Farci on the other. At the bottom it read: 'Bottled in Iran'.

This was clearly Islamic cola with no Western additives.

I had started on the rice like someone who knows a hopeless task when he sees it, when a man slid into the chair opposite. I peered at him over the top of my rice mountain and swallowed.

'Salaam,' I said.

He nodded and smiled. He was young, no more than sixteen or seventeen, with big black eyes, thin wisps of hair on his chin and a slightly witless look about him. That might have been an unfair judgement to make so quickly for his next words were in practised English.

'I would like to speak to you,' he said. 'I study English. I would like to be learning from you.'

I was delighted. Unfortunately, with those three sentences he had practically exhausted his supply of English. Muhammad was the restaurant owner's son and his cheerfulness was such that I made him stay and share the meal. As it turned out, we had a highly educational and enjoyable evening which, by the end, saw us both holding great wads of paper serviettes covered in words. His were in English, mine were in Farci; mutual phonetic translations of almost everything we could see.

My determination to learn Farci was just as great as Muhammad's was to speak English. It was imperative that I achieved some command of the language, not only in travelling around the country, but for the future in Afghanistan where Farci was also widely spoken. But after only one day Teheran fascinated me. It was like a concealed room that had been forgotten for years and was now prised open. Now, more than anything, I wanted to stay and uncover what had lain hidden for so long. I wanted to dig deeper, but first I needed that visa extension.

TEN

In the morning the old man was wearing a dark suit and his snow-white hair poked out from underneath a navy blue cap. He was stooped over slightly, and he shuffled along towards me with the aid of a walking stick. From the shade of a tree I watched him approach. At the last moment he looked up and his eyes were twinkling.

'So where do you think Mr Rushdie is hiding?' He smiled, then burst out laughing and tried to slap his knee.

I was in a tiny park in north Teheran, having gone there to collect my thoughts after finding the central police station, the hopeful source of an extension, disappointingly closed for the day. The park was really no more than a garden, well shaded from the sun by tall trees and even taller buildings. Its dark green interior, however, provided a wonderful retreat.

'I'm sorry,' he said. 'I couldn't resist it. Your reaction, hmm, very amusing. Last thing you expected to hear, I suppose. You are from where? England perhaps?'

'Yes, there and other places,' I replied.

'Other places!' he said, steadying himself with his walking stick and glancing towards the park gate. 'It is many years since I spoke with someone from other places. What a shame we did not meet earlier. I've been here all morning and now I must take the bus home. Are you staying in Teheran?'

'Near Ferdowsi Square.'

'Ah, that's good,' he said, eyes brightening. 'It is on the way. Please, come.'

The old man, his face calm, his eyes smiling, appraising, spoke at length about life in Iran. There was no prompting on my behalf. It was quite clear he just wanted to talk. At the gate he hesitated and with his stick, drew back the ivy hanging across a sign that served to remind everyone of the correct Islamic dress for women. It was there to counteract slipping standards he said; to stop any funny business happening in the foliage. It was the Pasdaran's sign.

Leaving the ivy to fall back, he moved off slowly towards the bus stop.

'My young friend,' he said. 'It may be hard for you to believe, but up until the Islamic revolution, that park was full of young people: laughing, courting, falling in love.

'Today,' he shrugged. 'Today it is not permitted to look at a woman, unless she is your wife or sister. And sometimes even then they will ask you for proof!'

The bus arrived. A badge on the front grille read: *IranFord*. It was almost empty and we took a seat near the front door.

'We are all equal are we not?' he said.

I nodded, surprised at but enjoying the frank way in which he was speaking.

He continued, 'You and I, he and she. The same blood runs through our veins. Religion, colour or sex do not divide us. Only some choose to have it that way.'

The journey was not far but a traffic jam slowed us down. He went on to talk about the Iran of fifty years ago. In those days, he said, the Shah had ruled that one mullah was enough for each city.

'Now you can see how many there are.' He started coughing badly, as if the thought made him sick.

For ten years he had worked in Kurdistan, building grain silos with a British construction firm. Now he was old and dying. Once he'd dreamt of being invited back to England, but the dream was never fulfilled.

He remembered Mr Williams, the manager, who was also a Baptist minister. A good man, but one who always had trouble with the Kurds.

'Tried to convert the younger men,' he said. 'And they had come at him with knives.'

Soon after, the company pulled out of Iran, leaving him behind to get married and raise a family. In the war with Iraq, one of his sons had gone missing in those same Kurdish mountains.

His cough suddenly got worse.

'But I've had a better life than some,' he gasped.

The bus came to a stop in Ferdowsi Square. I shook his hand tenderly and jumped down onto the footpath. The doors slammed shut, the driver gunned the engine, and the old man turned to face me. Through the dusty window I could see his lips moving but I couldn't hear. He tried to slide the window open but it was stuck and the bus was pulling away. With one last effort he succeeded.

'Remember,' he yelled over the din in earnest. 'We are all equal.'

The driver shifted gear, the engine roared, and in a cloud of dust he was gone.

The following day, my second assault on the police was more successful. It started to rain gently in the morning and the wind blew the smell of it down from the mountains, but by the time I had reached the road in which the station was situated, the rain had become a downpour. Sheet lightning flashed intricate patterns across the sky. I sheltered beneath a red and white striped shop awning with two other men.

'Ay Khorda,' muttered one in prayer, as the crack of thunder sounded overhead.

The station was on the opposite side of the road and further up. Some men and women were gathered in the entrance, though the police on duty were less well protected and were already soaked to the skin. Banners bearing proclamations in Persian hung like wet rags from the ground floor window, dragged down onto the pavement by the added weight of water.

I slung my old bag over one shoulder and made a run for it, leaping over the mud-stained torrents that coursed down the roadway, eventually reaching the building with a final heavy-booted splash.

At a desk near the door, a police officer was struggling to re-assemble the machine-gun he had taken apart to oil. As in so many other places, a large portrait of Khomeini hung on the otherwise bare wall behind him. He finally succeeded, and with a triumphant grunt, slammed the magazine into place. I showed him my passport and he directed me upstairs.

In a large white-washed room, where uniformed policemen and ordinary civilians were forever running into each other, I saw a sign on a door that read: *Western Bloc citizens and Others*. Mobs of people surged past outside it, documents clutched guardedly to their chests, their faces resigned to the struggle against bureaucracy. Many more had lost all hope and their cries echoed throughout the room: 'Three days I have been here! Three days!'

I pushed my way through.

The office looked as though it had been well designed to repel invaders. The desks were at the rear with the police officers tucked safely behind them, backs to the wall. No one else was in the room so I walked over to the nearest officer. He was a thick-set man with a neatly trimmed beard and a squashed face like a boxer's. The top button on his shirt was done up and his sleeves were rolled down: the mark of a reverent Iranian. I cleared my throat.

'Salaam,' I said.

He looked up but didn't smile. I handed him my Australian passport and he studied the cover carefully.

'What is this?' he said finally.

His use of English, although broken, was surprising. But I was to discover later that nearly all Iranian police knew at least a few words.

'Passport,' I said.

He fobbed off this reply with a look of disdain. Of course he knew what it was, but that was not what he was asking. Then I realised he was pointing at the national emblem on the cover, and more specifically the kangaroo.

'An Australian animal,' I said, wondering where this conversation was going.

'Ah yes,' he said. 'Kang-gah-ru.'

His curiosity satisfied, he flicked through the pages in a practised way, stopping suddenly at the Iraqi visa. I braced myself for his reaction, but if he was at all angry it didn't show. He simply took an age to drink from the glass of tea on his desk, replacing it with great deliberation. Then without looking up, he said:

'Iraq. Good or bad?'

'Bad,' I replied instantly.

'In Baghdad there are many buildings destroyed?'

'Many.'

'Ha!' He seemed happy at this news. 'Our rockets did this. Did you know that?'

His pencil became a ballistic missile, launched from his note pad, and slammed into the table top. There were no survivors. He liked that. You could tell by the way he stuck out his tongue.

Finally we got down to business.

'What do you want?' he said.

I told him, adding that I had been unfortunately delayed in

reaching Pakistan. He found the Iranian visa a few pages further on.

'A severe stomach problem,' I lied, 'prevented me from leaving Urumiyeh.'

'I understand,' he muttered, reading the visa.

For a full minute there was nothing said between us. I listened to the muffled noises of activity in other rooms, wondering whether I would soon be forced to join some interminable queue. I pictured the rest of Iran spread out before me, waiting to be discovered: the blue-domed city of Esfahan, Shiraz, perhaps the Caspian Sea and eventually Mashad. It all seemed to hang there so tenuously.

Outside, the rain had stopped and the sun was trying hard to break through the clouds.

He grunted. 'Two weeks.'

'Excuse me?'

'You may have an extra two weeks, that is all. Come back the day after tomorrow.'

He returned to his paperwork and I walked out with these words reverberating in my head. All the worry and anxiety suddenly turned to nothing. It felt as if a great weight had been lifted from my shoulders. I could have leapt up and punched the air. Instead, I went outside into the street, smiling and humming a happy traveller's tune.

ELEVEN

Mahmoud worked in my hotel as an odd-job man and night porter. His was the thankless task of ushering in late arrivals in the dead of night, and he would often sleep inside the hotel entrance. He was a dark-haired and rather thick-set thirty-year-old; quiet and thoughtful; an intelligent man who had been taught to speak English by his parents, and through listening to the BBC World Service. While I waited for the visa we often sat in the hotel lobby, drinking tea and talking. Several times Mahmoud steered the conversation onto the subject of Turkey, and he was always asking questions about its borders, the soldiers, the currency, costs and the language. His interest, however, was not purely educational. The real reasons were all too clear. Mahmoud was marking time until he could escape from Iran with enough money and information.

One afternoon he took me on a tour of the city.

'Life is so complex here,' said Mahmoud.

This complexity was perhaps best illustrated by the unofficial black market. The centre of activity was located just south of Ferdowsi Square, where a score of men gathered with their calculators and cash-filled briefcases to do business. There was nothing secretive about it. Some dealers openly displayed US and German bank notes in the hope of attracting passing trade. But while all this was going on, a dozen police stood watching from across the road. According to Mahmoud, the government turned a blind eye while it suited them. A policy of inconsistency kept everyone guessing as to when and where the hammer would fall. Should they need a scapegoat, he said, to blame for any flagging morals, any number of law-breakers could be picked off the street and made an example of.

Sadly, all too often it was the womenfolk who were targeted. Every year, as summer temperatures increased, veils might be loosened or even a pretty headscarf worn with a dark overcoat, instead of the ugly black chador. There were those who even dared to wear a touch of make-up, although these women ran an even graver risk. The Pasdaran, who were the official watchdogs of the revolution, were known to favour summary justice, but their actions were as nothing compared to the unofficial vigilante groups who patrolled the streets and whose God-given duty it was to punish all wrongdoers.

Getting anywhere in Teheran was another conundrum. There were buses and mini-buses plying fixed routes for a few rials, but taxis were faster and only slightly more expensive. If there was an empty seat, the hopeful applicant had to run alongside, clinging to the doorframe with ten or twenty others, yelling his destination through the window, ever watchful for that nod of approval from the driver. Women were usually squeezed into the front, with as many as four men in the back. For the slim and agile, a seat was often available between the driver and his own door.

We went to Shemiran, a prosperous and pleasantly green suburb in the north of Teheran where a high concentration of Pasdaran were presumably there to remind the well-to-do Teherani just who was still boss. The walls of many buildings were daubed with revolutionary graffiti. DEATH TO ISRAEL slogans loomed large over private residences, while radios were broadcasting long speeches on moral behaviour. Above stood the Shah's old palace, home to the once all-powerful but inevitably corrupt Pahlavi dynasty. It was a monument to decadence and greed, occupied by the ghost of a deposed king and by the Ayatollah Khomeini who, if we were to believe the nation's media, had apparently shunned its many sumptuous halls, preferring instead to live in just two unfurnished rooms. Though he lived in the northern half of the city, high up on the foothills of the Elburz Mountains where it was supposedly cooler with altitude, he still sided with those people down in the south of Teheran, down at desert level, where there was nothing but hellish heat and dust. The brick buildings were all the colour of dust. Houses were unfinished. There were few trees. The south had been gradually added to by people coming in from the countryside. Later in the day, we dropped in briefly to see a second-hand bookstore selling, of all things, old copies of the *Financial Times* and *Newsweek*. One page showed a photograph of a young female athlete in jogging shorts and singlet, crossing a finish line at the Seoul Olympics. Someone had gone to great pains to black out her arms, legs and hair with a heavy felt pen.

The elderly proprietor came towards us, a wrinkled man with eyes watery from reading in bad light. He spoke briefly with Mahmoud, whom he seemed to know, then nodded thoughtfully and turned to me.

'These are the times that try men's souls,' he sighed. 'Thomas Paine, 1776.'

He took us into a padlocked back room and pointed out the

books that he said were banned by the government, but which he kept out of love. I noted down three: *The Castle* by Franz Kafka, *A Month in the Country* by Ivan Turgenev, and Tennessee Williams' *The Glass Menagerie*.

'My books,' he said, passing his fingers over the titles. 'If they take away my books I will surely die.'

We left him in his library and took a bus back to Ferdowsi. On the way I checked what I already suspected: the man was Mahmoud's father.

TWELVE

By chance, Mahmoud found a place that could fix my camera, an old and trusted Pentax that had suffered through my own clumsiness and was falling into a state of disrepair.

The shop was tiny, no bigger than a wardrobe, but the bespectacled and balding owner knew what he was doing. Mahmoud acted as interpreter. 'It was dropped,' he said.

The owner winced. 'It will cost twenty thousand rials to fix.'

I nodded. It was a fair price.

The owner examined the dent on one side. 'Where did the camera fall?'

'Outside the Imam Mosque,' replied Mahmoud. 'My friend is a visitor to our country. He is here to learn our ways.'

'Then I shall charge only fifteen thousand rials.'

'Thank you,' I said politely.

'He will also put what he has seen into a book,' said Mahmoud, 'which will be read by many people.'

'A book you say! The charge is ten thousand to our friend, and tell him it will be ready tomorrow afternoon.'

I shook his hand. 'May you live long,' I told him.

'God go with you,' said the owner.

The next day, the camera was indeed fixed but the price had risen back to fifteen. It was standard business practice.

Anyway, with everything now in order – including my passport, duly embellished with a new visa – there was nothing to stop me from exploring the country further. I had decided on heading south via the holy city of Qom, an ancient pilgrimage site for Shia Muslims and birthplace to the revolution, then to Esfahan and Shiraz before turning north-east in a wide circle. My eventual goal was Mashad, the holy Iranian city near the Afghan border, where I hoped to locate the Afghan resistance and at the very least gain information on conditions within the country. Just who was fighting who was an important question. In essence there was still a civil war going on, but the reported in-fighting between the different resistance groups complicated the matter further. One thing was clear. I would need to choose my friends carefully.

I was on the road by nine next morning. The bus rolled downhill onto the main route south towards Qom, out into an already shimmering salt-encrusted desert with the hushed whisper of an engine in neutral. The driver coasted down every slope, no matter how slight. He did it to conserve fuel and cool the engine, but knowing this failed to make the trip any less annoying, for when our glide began to lose momentum on the flat, we crawled along for a half-mile before he chose to engage a gear. The passengers ganged together with the comradeship of the hard-done-by, but all to no avail. When their pleas became abusive the driver clenched his teeth. When the abuse turned to threats, he went red in the face and scowled. Finally someone passed him a few hundred rials and we went a little faster.

At about ten o'clock we stopped to pick up a handsome family of villagers, standing on the side of the road with their belongings. They had a goat which was bundled into the luggage rack on the side of the bus. The two women, both young and attractive in their colourful dress, sat opposite me. Their menfolk went in front. After a few minutes, the nearest woman produced a baby out from under her multicoloured chador and began to chew up pieces of bread and apple, which she fed directly from her mouth to the child's. I watched this with an admiration that wasn't at all shared by the fellow sitting next to me.

'Qashgai,' he said contemptuously.

The two men in front had heard him, of that I was sure, yet they said and did nothing. Their dignity perhaps would not allow it. The Qashgai were one of the last and greatest nomadic tribes of Persia, whose annual migration to and from the mountains of Fars still continued, if only just. No doubt it was this pride which found such disfavour, verging on hatred, with at least one of the passengers. How very strange, I thought, is this low opinion that city-dwellers so often reserve for village folk. Once, in Istanbul, I had told a young Turkish student about my plans to visit the Kurdish mountain village in south-eastern Turkey. He had stared at me then with a mixture of horror and fear for my safety.

'You are crazy to do this!' he cried. 'They are nothing but filthy peasants who will steal your money. And what is there to see in these places? Ancient mosques? Ancient palaces? Ancient history? No! There is nothing for you to see.'

'Perhaps,' I had suggested, 'the ancient history lies with the Kurds themselves?'

He shook his head forcefully. Their past was filled with nothing but bloodshed. They were terrorists, thieves, cheats and murderers of innocent Turkish soldiers and civilians.

'God save us from them,' he added, 'they are also without proper sanitation!'

A few hours later, the first hint of green appeared through the heat haze and there was the city of Qom: one of the holiest places for the Shia Muslim and Khomeini's platform from which he rallied the people against the Shah. Its theological schools of Koranic learning spawned the Islamic revolution in 1979. Scholars still came from the world over to study there, and at its centre, the great golden dome of Fatima's shrine shone in the sunlight, a thousand-year-old magnet for millions of pilgrims.

I wanted to see how the Qashgai would respond to the city: with awe, or with contempt. But they left the bus well before the city gates and walked off in the direction of their distant mountains.

Qom, however, was reeling. The loss of a respected leader,

Grand Ayatollah Montahzehri, had been a huge shock. As a trusted friend of Khomeini, he had been widely tipped as favourite to eventually take over the top job. Somewhat unwisely, however, in a series of private letters Montahzehri had strongly criticised the government and its policies. When these confidential letters fell into the wrong hands, his career was over. The papers said that Khomeini cried when he heard the news. He had been forced to confine his dear friend to a lifetime of silence, barred forever from leaving his home. There were portraits of mullahs everywhere in Qom. Mullahs at prayer, mullahs healing the sick, mullahs fighting the war, leading the men into battle, mullahs lecturing the nation. It was like Baghdad and Saddam Hussein all over again. And at the toll-gate entering the city, the portraits of a hundred clergymen hung above the road. But there was always one face missing, painted over or scratched out. According to those in power, poor Montahzehri no long existed.

In the small park opposite the gates of Fatima's shrine, whose golden dome and four blue minarets rose above the flat-roofed city, I sat down in the shade of a palm tree to watch the steady stream of pilgrims. All but a few stopped to kiss the great wooden doors before entering.

Fatima-el-Masuma (the Chaste) was the sister of Imam Ali-el-Riza, the eighth Shia Imam. The story goes that in AD 816, Fatima fell ill on her way to visit him and was taken to Qom. But her illness proved fatal and she died and was buried there. In terms of pilgrimage value to the Shia Muslim, her tomb today is second only to her brother's in Mashad.

Curious to see more, I joined the jostle of human beings and was swept past the sign in English that forbade entry to non-Muslims.

The inner courtyard was wide and long, its polished stone walls reflecting the blinding sunlight. To the left stood a clock tower; at the centre was a pool. The faithful were gathered there to perform their ritual wash before prayer. The shrine itself lay immediately to the right, and on either side of the magnificent high blue-tiled archway, hundreds of pairs of shoes were stacked neatly on their wooden shelves. The men entered the shrine through a door on the left side, while the women went to the right. Through the wide doorway in the middle there were latticed walls of silver, behind which lay the entombed body.

I went no further. It did not seem proper to pry in such a sacred place. The pilgrims who had come here from great distances were the rightful and dutiful subjects. Instead, I started back towards the park, unsure of what to do next. I'd already tried to find a bed for the night and failed. Every hotel had waved me away. Even the floorspace was taken up with pilgrims.

Outside the shrine I wandered past the stalls selling small round earthen tablets: the earth of Arabia no less, from the hallowed grounds of Mecca and Medina. With one of these tablets the faithful could kneel in prayer, anywhere in the world, and still be able to rest their foreheads on the sacred soil. However, past these stalls, beyond the yellow-brick building where Khomeini once lectured, and past the groups of bearded mullahs, the question of my immediate future was suddenly and dramatically solved by the local police.

The white Hillman Hunter positively screeched to a halt beside me; its doors quickly opened and I was practically bundled into the back without so much as a word being said. It seemed they knew exactly who they were looking for. My passport was confiscated and I was taken a few blocks away and marched into the central station. It was a low building behind iron railings that bordered a picturesque garden of tall palm trees and pines.

The officer in charge moved slowly about the room, puffing on his cigarette. All my papers were on his desk. Sitting on one corner was a younger policeman, idly pushing my passport around with his pencil. I was sorely tempted to walk over and snatch it back from the malign proddings of this unshaven youth, but thought better of it. Finally the officer sat down and began thumbing through the pages. He stopped at the Iraqi visa.

'What are you doing in Qom?'

He spoke in a cool, abrupt way which made me feel that I should be more worried that I was. After all, what had I done that was so terrible?

'I arrived here this morning from Teheran,' I said. 'And I'm on my way to Esfahan.'

'Then what were you doing in the shrine?'

Now I knew for certain that someone had spotted me and given a description.

'I wasn't,' I protested. 'I was only in the courtyard.'

'You went inside the walls, is that not true?'

'Yes, to the courtyard.'

'That,' he barked, 'is also part of the shrine and forbidden to you!'

There was no more argument. He went away to photocopy my papers while my bag was subjected to a cursory search. The young policeman pulled out my harmonica and scowled. Musical instruments, I recalled, were not welcome here.

The officer returned.

'Your visa is a transit visa!' he said. 'You should not be in Esfahan or Qom. You must go directly to Pakistan.'

My heart missed a beat.

'I realise that but . . .'

He wasn't listening to me. He didn't have to; he simply turned his back and issued an order to the younger man. I thought I heard him mention Zahedan, the city on the Pakistan border. My passport was handed back. The matter was closed. I was escorted back to the same Hillman police car and taken to the bus station on the edge of town.

There were two buses on the verge of leaving. It was indicated that I should get aboard the first one, and I did so in a grey mood, watched by the policeman. There was no telling where the bus was going; I wasn't able to read the sign on the front, but my guess was that it wasn't Esfahan. The passenger in the opposite seat revealed the worst. The bus was bound for Yazd, the next city on the long haul to Pakistan. It seemed I was being deported.

The other passengers began to take an interest about this time. They were sympathetic once the details of my story were explained; heads nodded amid various murmurings of commiseration. Qom could be like that, they said. The police were overly fond of exercising their power, even on local citizens. But, said one of the passengers, if I really wanted to go to Esfahan then why didn't I slip over to the far side of the compound where the Esfahan bus was sitting, engine running?

I peered out the window. My police minder had sauntered off back to his vehicle and seemed not to be too attentive. Perhaps, I mused, he would not concern himself with checking the Yazd bus again. His duty would be done by seeing it off from a distance, surely. And besides, it was already quite full. How could he tell if there was one head missing?

Spurred on by my fellow travellers, I jumped down with my bag in hand and sprinted across the tarmac for the Esfahan bus, just in time as it so happened, for the driver had finished loading and was getting ready to leave. I bought a ticket from him and took a seat at the back. In a few moments both buses were rolling out of their respective loading bays, past the policeman who sat up in his car and took notice, but who didn't get out. If there was any query at all in his mind, it was possibly as to why so many passengers in the Yazd bus were waving enthusiastically to somebody in the one going to Esfahan.

THIRTEEN

Esfahan flourished in early Muhammadan times about AD 900, was set upon by the Mongols in the thirteenth century, and then in the fourteenth by Tamerlane the Timurid (who massacred seventy thousand Esfahani and built a tower with their heads); after which it rose to prominence in the sixteenth century as the capital of Persia under the great Shah Abbas. At that time it was boasted *Esfahan-Nisf-i-Jahan*, Esfahan is half the World, and few people doubted it.

In those days, imperial life revolved around the imposing Maidan-i-Shah (Square of the King), where the mosques of the King and Sheikh Lutfallah stood before the Royal Palace. Successive monarchs used to lounge around the marble pool on the wooden-pillared terrace, watching a game of chugan, better known as polo, while behind the throne and concealed by delicate lattice screens, the houris waited to be called.

Nowadays the polo field is a pool, the palace is suitably covered by a monstrous portrait of the Ayatollah, and the names have been altered to exclude any reference to royalty. Masjid-i-Shah became Imam Mosque. Maidan-i-Shah became Imam Square, which was all quite predictable really.

It was not until late that night that we finally arrived, and because of the hour I went straight to the Masjid-i-Shah. It was quiet in the half hour before prayer time. The stillness was made even greater by the low, almost inaudible murmur coming from a man kneeling down beneath the double-tiered *ivans* of the courtyard. A book lay open before him, undoubtedly the *Koran*; his song was a recitation of prayer. At the same time all around me the tiled patterns of dark blue, azure, green and gold came to life in the floodlight. I would have stayed for hours but for the guard who wanted me to leave.

I asked him about an Arabic inscription near the entrance, which was repeated on many of the walls. The severe look on his round, bearded face instantly softened and changed to one of joyful pride. He was like a museum curator unveiling the mystery of a sacred stone to an interested party, and he grew in stature as he spoke:

'Bismilla'hir Rahmani Rahim. La illa'heh illa'llah Muhammadu rasulu'llah.' In the name of God, the most benevolent and merciful. There is but one true God and Muhammad is his prophet.

I didn't know it then, but once I had committed this prayer to memory, it would play a significant role in my passage through the heart of Islam.

I wandered off to find a place to sleep and ended up in a small, family-run guesthouse. Normally, they said, they did not take *feringhi*, but for me they would make an exception. The room was upstairs in the dark, along a narrow wooden hallway which creaked with every step. Windows on the left looked into the trees that lined the deserted street below. A streetlight cast eerie shadows onto the bare walls. The bed was also of wood, with a thin mattress covered by a white sheet. Underneath it I could see a pair of plastic sandals, the type which are so often broken at the strap, forcing the wearer to shuffle along without lifting his feet. I checked. They were indeed broken.

In the opposite corner of the room was a heavy oak chair, ornately carved with geometric patterns similar to those found in many mosques. The craftsmanship was very good. For someone, probably long since dead, it had been a labour of love. Such furniture was not seen any more. Most Iranians sat on rugs on the floor. Their rooms were normally bare except perhaps for a television or radio – which led me to believe that the chair was very old. It felt old even to the touch, and for a few brief moments it seemed the air was filled with the sounds of the craftsman's workshop, and the pungent smell of lacquer on wood.

I slept then, curled up beneath the single white sheet, until the light of dawn crept into the room.

Breakfast was black tea and unleavened bread in a tea-house down the street. It was the kind of place I was used to by now. The floor was bare cement, sprinkled with water from a watering can to keep the dust from rising. This was also done outside on the footpath, perhaps to show would-be customers that the establishment ran a clean shop. Anyway, it worked for me. I sat down on a wooden stool against the wall and signalled to the owner, who poured the tea into a glass on a saucer. He seemed displeased, until I remembered it was still Ramadan and no Muslim would have dared to order tea after dawn. I drank up hurriedly, left some money on the table and slipped out unnoticed.

Afterwards, I took a bus out to see the famous Minar-i-Jumban (the Shaking Minarets). I had read the story about these two minarets before leaving London. For some strange reason, by climbing into one of the narrow towers and causing it to sway, you make the other minaret, over fifty feet away, also start to move. Local folklore blamed the phenomenon on the ghost of a dead sheik, buried beneath the walls. However, when I did eventually get there it was closed for renovations. Workmen on scaffolds were filling the cracks in the pale toffee-coloured brick.

Fortunately the day was saved by a passing travelling salesman. He was a huge Demis Roussos-like figure by the name of Rahim who stopped and offered me a ride. He knew I was foreign. Although my beard would have been the envy of most Pasdaran, he said my blue jeans and walking boots gave the game away.

Rahim was a man who knew what struggle meant. He bore the scars of war on his arms and legs where the shrapnel had ripped into him. After his recovery they had wanted to send him back to the front. He refused, so they locked him up in prison until the fighting with Iraq had ended. They were years that he dearly wanted to forget.

His English dated from before the revolution, when foreigners came to Esfahan by the score. He spoke at length about those times. Life had been easier for him then, but apart from his eldest son who could just remember, the rest of his children had only known a strict Islamic state. This was especially saddening for him. He had hoped that because of my presence, changes had occurred to allow the outside world back in.

It was approaching midday and he invited me back to his home for lunch. The laws of Ramadan stopped at his front gate, he said with a smile, and so we would eat well and then pray for forgiveness.

His house was fronted by the usual bare wall with a blue iron door in the middle. Through this we came to a small courtyard dotted with a few flowerbeds and a fountain that didn't work. The house was his family home, a two-storeyed, flat-roofed building with stone steps leading up to a verandah with iron railings. Both his mother and father were dead now, and this week his family were staying with a brother in Qom, so we sliced up a melon, made some tea and sat on cushions on the living-room floor. The only pictures in the room were photographs of his family.

I told him what had happened to me in Qom: the arrest, the deportation, the escape.

'Such risks!' said Rahim. 'But you were ill advised in going to that place. Only trouble comes from it.'

He went on lamenting the ruin of Persia and at one point dropped the name of Xerxes.

'The Archaemenian king?'

'One-time ruler of the known world. You have heard also of Persepolis, the ancient royal city?'

I had. Persepolis was practically all that remained of the glory that once was the Persian empire. Begun by Xerxes' father, Cyrus the Great, six centuries before Christ, it was surely one of the great works of its time. Thousands of labourers spent their lives constructing it. Their place of origin, their status, trade and salary were all recorded by the king's scribes on special clay tablets, found earlier this century beneath the fallen columns and pediments.

Rahim was adamant that I should see Persepolis at dawn. The overnight bus to Shiraz would pass within a mile of it.

'It is like nothing you have ever witnessed before,' he whispered reverently. 'Nothing!'

A few days later, his words would prove to be no exaggeration.

I stayed in Esfahan longer than expected. It was such a beautiful place, with avenues of slender white tree-trunks supporting great leafy canopies overhead. Turquoise domes housed their splendid galleries of mosaic art, and more besides – the quiet, ethereal nature of Islam's finest and most hallowed centres. The air within these mosques was rarefied, filled with centuries of devotion so strong that it could be felt upon entering.

On my last evening, however, I returned to the square via the old bazaar's dim and dusty warren of covered lanes to visit the Royal Palace. I was alone, but for a group of adolescent girls, swathed in black chador, who spied on me through the wooden latticework. Their pretty laughter echoed through the royal chambers, like that of the original courtesans perhaps. Sadly, there was little else of the past in those sad and empty rooms. The structure had been left to rot; painted panels had been angrily defaced, walls that were once coated in gold had been deeply scarred by knives, and rubble was strewn underfoot. Overlooking the square was an open, airy platform with a blue-tiled pool at its centre. Mighty columns of oak supported the heavily beamed ceiling, but the wood was riddled with termites and the view was partly obscured by the back of

Khomeini's head.

After a while, one of the girls plucked up the courage to approach me and ask where I was from.

'Ahz Inglestan,' I said.

Her dark eyes flirted with mine as she let the veil slip from her face. It was a coy and remarkably alluring move, but that single innocent gesture was against all the laws of Iran. The penalties were great, more so for her probably, and even though her friends egged her on, even though there was no one else about, she suddenly grew nervous and turned on her heels and fled. A host of black sheets scuttled noisily down the stairs and appeared moments later in the square below, walking quickly in a tight bunch, peering through their veils at the figure upon the platform. Shame, I thought. In any other country we might have had dinner.

Later that night the hours passed quickly as the bus I was travelling in hurtled through the darkness. The stony desert surrounded us on all sides, illuminated by moonlight and by the sweep of our flickering headlights. The road climbed and fell. Even in the darkness the salt glistened white here and there, as if the earth were once again a sea, and the whiteness was the foam of waves breaking over a rocky shore. Then the rocks swelled in size, until they were houses with yellow lights that flashed by our windows, briefly silhouetting the rows of sleeping men snoring inside the bus.

Here indeed was a veritable tangle of humanity. Dark-skinned southerners, olive-skinned northerners, moon-faced Mongols, Asians, Turks and Afghans; the latter were discernible by their swarthy appearances and flowing turbans – traders, every one of them from the modern Silk Road, bound for the bazaar.

Two hours before dawn, the driver pulled over to the side of the road and called me forward as I had requested earlier. He then pointed out a smaller road on the left, just visible in the darkness, which he intimated would lead me to the place called Takht-i-Jamshid, otherwise known as Persepolis.

'Kopek!' he warned as I stepped down.

The bus drove off. I stood in the middle of the road for several minutes watching it go, warily listening out for the hostile canine activity he had just spoken of, and feeling the coolness of early morning. It was good to be out of the bus again, under the stars and alone. Towards the east the sky was slowly turning to a dull grey, against which could be seen the darker jagged outline of plane trees and distant mountains. In high spirits I started walking, sensing the openness of my surroundings, and feeling almost childlike once again. In the night – was it weariness? – my emotions began to take over, and surprisingly I found myself close to tears, brought on by the memory of my father and the night he was lost to us forever. In the early hours before dawn I had woken with a start, sitting up in bed for no apparent reason, and finding myself staring at an old-fashioned clock on the far wall. The time was exactly three minutes past the seventh hour – I could remember it clearly. With the blinds drawn the room was pitch dark but I could still see that clock, and with it came a sensation of great tranquillity. There was sadness but also a wonderful feeling of release, as of a great weight being uplifted, and then I must have lain back and returned once more to sleep.

In the morning he was gone. I knew instantly from the look on my mother's face as she drew back the curtains and let the light flood in. Just after seven o'clock, she had said, and the recollection of what I had seen that night came roaring back. For some reason I did not say anything about it, perhaps because it was private, perhaps because it was also slightly marvellous. It wasn't so much the time of his death being precisely that of my sudden awakening, but for the fact that I had seen this old clock on my wall, with its ornate frame of carved wood and roman numerals, its slow tick-tock that kept such perfect time, when there has never been a clock of any kind on that wall, nor in any other part of that room.

Now, halfway round the world and so many years on I started laughing, throwing back my head and mocking death with each step. But the laughter was half-hearted and I was suddenly joined by a strange sound in the distance, the howling of a lonely desert animal.

The shadows of night were melting away and the colours of the waking earth returned. Somewhere beyond the mountains before me the sun was rising unseen, and I walked on in their immense cool shadow, watching as the dawn light appeared first in the west, striking the tree tops I had just passed and lighting one after another like candles. Then there came the dividing line between night and day, following a few hundred yards behind me across the bare earth, all the way to the steps of the city. And what mighty steps!

Five hundred years before Christ, a visitor to this royal Persian city would have arrived on horseback and ridden up the wide staircase onto the platform, there to be met by the winged lions of Darius' Gate. The king, perhaps Darius himself, or Xerxes his father, might have sat upon the throne in the palace hall, beneath white marble columns and beams of Lebanese cedar, awaiting precious gifts from the furthest reaches of his mighty empire.

But then came a visitor who was not to give at all, only take. In the third century BC the King of Macedon, Alexander the Great, captured the city and in the orgy of destruction that followed, Persepolis was put to the torch.

Now, the Darius Gate is still there, and the raised *apadana* or platform on which the palace stood. The columns are naturally fewer in number, many having fallen. But those remaining upright possess enormous strength. Bas-relief sculptures of beasts and conquered vassals appear upon doorways and walls, reading like a catalogue of vanquished peoples, recording their costume, armoury, the gifts they brought, even their hair-style. The stone is hard and fine, and on one of the two staircases beside the *apadana* these carvings are of startling quality, having spent a good part of the last two thousand years partially buried.

I have the Ayatollah to thank for my solitude. It is he who has made this a desolate, silent place at the foot of a mountain range. It is he who has driven away the whirr of cameras and the noise of tourist coaches. For here is the ancient home of the

Persian monarchy, and in the eyes of God, the Prophet and Imam Khomeini, there is no greater evil than that which proclaims itself king.

The country is quiet and empty, even the sky is a cloudless blue. Rahim was right, Persepolis has no equal and I am alone with antiquity.

FOURTEEN

I left Persepolis in the suffocating heat of midday and hitched a ride to Shiraz with a team of enthusiastic Iranian archaeologists. The car groaned under the weight of their heavy equipment stashed in the boot: several sledgehammers, pick-axes and two pile-drivers. They were about to start work on a dig beside the ancient ruins, but first had to buy food supplies in town – and explosives. The leader, a severe man with an intense stare, enquired as to whether I too was an archaeologist.

'No, I'm afraid not.'

He looked dismayed. He had clearly hoped to impress the foreign expert with the importance of his task. Persepolis and its surrounding acres of virgin soil ranked as one of the world's great archaeological treasures, and I could see that he viewed it all as his sole property. Just then the car hit another bump in the road. His arsenal of destruction clanked noisily in the back.

'Then I will tell you,' he said. 'It is very delicate work. Always so very, very delicate.'

An hour later they dropped me off in the centre of town, near the markets.

In the bazaar hotel at Shiraz, tall, thin, bearded men with long white turbans like the radiant tails of exotic birds were in constant flight up and down the stairs, taking the steps three at a time. One man was different. He was short and well fed, slightly balding on top and clean-shaven. His business clothes would not have been out of place in any London office, circa 1976. He had about him the confident air of a successful entrepreneur and his dark brown briefcase was like a constant companion. In perfect English he said he didn't like the hotel, but that it was the only one in town that wasn't full. He was used to better. His name was Ali and he was a big carpet dealer from the holy city of Mashad.

'Have you seen Mashad?' he asked me.

'Not yet.'

'Then it is settled!' he said, magically producing a card. 'Here is the address of my business there. You will be my guest!'

And with that he waved farewell and was gone, out of the door into the depths of the great bazaar.

Shiraz is the principle city of Fars, the province of southern Iran which, because it is home to the ruins of Persian monarchy, is tolerated by Teheran so long as the oil keeps flowing to the refineries and ports along the Gulf. But Shiraz remains largely unpolluted by this mineral wealth. It lies nestled in a valley beneath the Kuh-i-Barfi, the Mountains of Snow, and the town's gardens are green and plentiful. Turquoise domes and blue minarets rise above flat-topped mud houses which have stood the test of time for centuries. Some of Persia's greatest poets were born here long ago, and the ancient beauty of Shiraz survives in many an eastern verse.

I made myself at home in a room at the back of the hotel, out of earshot of the street traffic, then laid up for the rest of the day. I wanted to catch up with my journal and see to various repairs to my bag. The canvas straps had torn off a long time ago and so, every once in a while, I would make good the needlework which held them on. The result was a mish-mash of stitching in a myriad of cotton colours.

About four o'clock, once the fierce temperatures had abated, I went downstairs to take a look around the bazaar. It was spread over a wide area and divided into two halves by a road which cut through the middle. At the main entrance, a great clamouring of wood on metal rose from a line of copper-bashing urchins, while the senior members of this trade haggled with their customers over sweet tea and cigarettes. Further on the spice-sellers were sitting behind their colourful sacks of cumin and coriander and the leather-workers were hard at work with tannin-stained hands. Teaboys kept the bazaar's thirst quenched while the carpet dealers stood outside their stalls, putting on airs and maintaining their priority in the pecking order of business.

It was while I was passing just such a dignified group that I came into contact with the familiar figure of Ali again. Their ranks were split wide open as with a suitably theatrical entrance, this ebullient carpet man from Mashad stepped forward to clasp my hand firmly in his. He was just at that moment on his way to see some rugs, he said, an exercise which I was bound to find of supreme interest. Should I join him, the secrets of the bazaar were mine to discover; no better guide could I hope to find than him. Not accepting, even if I had wanted to, was simply out of the question.

Ali led me through the bustling passageways of the main bazaar to its most secluded regions, cellars both dark and ancient – owned by men of not dissimilar description. Sometimes the only light came from flickering oil lamps attached to the mud-brick walls, and any conversation was had in whispered tones. The architects responsible for constructing this place had not had privacy in mind, for sound carried a great distance along its corridors. In any event, no intruder could have crept up undetected.

The rooms were small, high-vaulted chambers about six paces long by four wide, with carpets of all description stacked along the walls, right up to the ceiling in places. Ali knew exactly what he was looking for. He had come in search of old pieces, rare items of worth to wealthy collectors in Europe, and in this search he was helped by an old bazaari, an octogenarian as bright and eagle-eyed as a man half his age. In his baggy brown trousers and ancient tweed jacket, he acted as a kind of middleman. He seemed to know everyone and they him, but more importantly he knew the prices that sellers had paid for their goods. It was insider dealing of the old kind and for his information – which helped Ali greatly – the old man was handsomely paid.

Not that Ali needed any help, mind you. He was, without

doubt, a classic of his trade, the consummate artist of the deal, a showman, a conjurer and a conman whose manner was charm itself. When a beautiful rug caught his attention, he stalked it for hours like a hunter would his prey. His greatest trick was to spend ages haggling over a completely different and quite worthless carpet, purposely paying an overinflated price for it, which delighted the seller so much he invariably let go the better rug for a pittance.

As we walked away from one of these artful deceptions late in the day, the muezzin's call to evening prayer came floating down through the corridors as if from far away, and some of the dealers locked up to go to the mosque outside. Ali was not quite so disposed. He was a religious man, he said. He believed in the one true God and the one true faith, though he admitted he was not as devout as some.

'But!' he said with pride. 'I have the best collection of prayer rugs in the whole of Mashad.'

They were his children, and he commented upon their age and significance like a happy father. When I asked which was his favourite, he answered without hesitation. It was the Afghan, a rug that had once lain for hundreds of years within the great and holy mosque of Mazar-i-Sharif, in north-western Afghanistan.

'And do you know how I came to own such a thing?'

I shook my head and watched as he made sure no one was listening.

'Mujahedeen!' he whispered.

Immediately my interest doubled.

'Two weeks ago,' he said. 'They brought it to me from Herat city. A terrible journey through the mountains and minefields, then past the border Pasdaran. But these are hard times, you know.'

That was all Ali wanted to say on the subject, but at the mention of the rebel fighters in Mashad I suddenly felt the tantalising closeness of the next stage of my journey. Part of me wanted to get going, to keep moving towards the goal. For many months it had been the focus of all my attentions and with only so much time remaining on my visa, the anxieties grew into a nagging uncertainty. How would I also go about finding the mujahedeen when they were probably intent on keeping their whereabouts a secret?

The rest of my time in Shiraz was cut short. Staying in one place was gradually becoming intolerable. As a kind of penance I went and visited the tombs of the great Persian poets, Hafiz and Sa'di, and tried to lose myself in their gardens of cypress and pine. I wandered the streets of Shiraz and stumbled across the peace and solemnity of the Friday Mosque. But all the time there was my objective, Mashad, a long way off over a very sizeable piece of desert. Its pull was tremendous, and perhaps wrongly, like the itinerant pilgrim, my eyes were beginning to see only the road leading to it.

FIFTEEN

In the morning I was travelling east from Shiraz with the driver of a goods truck. He wore a black shirt with a good-luck charm pinned to the pocket, but he drove in the middle of the road regardless. Various other charms and trinkets dangled from the roof of the cab, and a colour photograph was taped to the dashboard. He had two daughters and, by the grace of God, a son and heir.

Outside, the desert-brown landscape was changing as we climbed up into the Zagros Mountains. Soon, patches of green arable land were suddenly appearing – and down below in the valley there was a river, running fast over stones bleached white by the sun.

It was around noon that we pulled into the village which was the driver's first destination for the day. He was doing the rounds of the local hospitals and was going as far as Kerman, where I could then catch a bus to Mashad. The narrow streets were shaded by clusters of palm trees and each small house was hidden behind a wall of sun-baked mud. On one side stood the village mosque, its cool interior harbouring a number of people from the incessant, energy-sapping heat of midday. A warm wind came in gusts down the main street, whipping up the dust into swirling columns of purple brown.

We rolled up to a long, whitewashed building at the end of the street. A red crescent was painted on the roof – the equivalent of our own Red Cross. It was a hospital for war veterans, and the mentally ill.

The resident doctor pushed through the swing doors in the front entrance and was delighted when he discovered that the week's delivery of supplies also brought an English-speaking foreigner. He showed me inside while the driver was unloading. He wore a clean white coat over his work clothes and he spoke English surprisingly well, given our remote location. He was about thirty, with curly red hair and a beard which he brushed out from his chin in the manner of the ancient Persians.

'Welcome to Sirjan,' he said.

In his office there was a wooden desk and two chairs. A calendar was stuck to the back of the door and an electric fan mounted on the wall made the pages flutter. The bookcase held a number of medical journals, written in Farci on cheap paper; photocopies of the original apparently. There was also a paperback book printed in New York entitled *Clinical Psychology and You*.

'I am the only person here right now,' he said almost apologetically. 'Except for the patients of course.'

From somewhere down the hall I could hear a soft moaning, then a sudden strong smell of disinfectant wafted into the room.

'Excuse him please. It is the smell which is disturbing him.'

Eventually the moaning died but the smell remained. It was a sickly aroma which stung my nostrils and took me back to a hospital of years ago. I was not sorry when the driver announced it was time to go.

SIXTEEN

Kerman was the last major stop before the central desert. To the south towered the lofty Jupar Mountains, home to the fierce winds that baked the town in summer and froze it in winter. To the north lay the empty wastelands of the mighty Kavir-i-Lut over which I would soon have to pass to reach Mashad.

I stayed in a cheap hotel, half of which was painted blue, the other half left bare. The owner was a small Zoroastrian man who hated blue, but his wife, a giantess, had chosen the colour while he was away. He wanted red, the colour of the eternal flame so sacred to his religion. She didn't. And there for the moment the matter lay.

'Do you know the story of Kerman?' he asked.

'No.'

'About the Worm?'

―

The Worm was the legendary *kirm*, said to be of immense size. It brought wealth and prosperity to the community, and for this reason the district was called Kerm-an, 'Land of the Worm'.

The Sasanian king Ardashir was told by his astrologers that he would never subdue Kerman with force, not while the creature remained alive. Its magic was too strong.

On the strength of this Ardashir gave up his military expeditions and disguised himself as a merchant. He then procured a large number of cases, filled some with rice, others with lead and others again with armed men, then set out for the Worm's village.

He pleaded with the worshippers to be given the honour of

feeding the Worm and when they agreed Ardashir lit a great fire on which he cooked the rice and melted the lead. When all was ready, the creature devoured the rice, and when it opened its mouth for more, the king poured the molten lead down its throat. In agony, the Worm gave such an exceptional leap into the air that it disappeared from view, landed in Bam 125 miles away, and exploded with earth-shattering force.

Ardashir released his armed followers from their cases and with their aid easily subdued the votaries of the Worm, taking possession of the whole district.

He didn't realise the relevance of the story to his own situation. His wife ruled the roost, while he claimed to be king. She was the Worm. He was Ardashir. I couldn't help but feel that this time the Worm would win.

SEVENTEEN

In 1980, a short time after the Islamic revolution in Iran, President Jimmy Carter sanctioned a covert airborne attempt to rescue United States embassy personnel from the hands of Islamic extremists. The hostages had been taken during the storming of the embassy, and were thought to be held somewhere near Mashad.

Six hours before dawn on 12 November, three US Navy helicopters took off from the aircraft carrier *Missouri* in the Persian Gulf. Flying only a few feet above the waves they crept in beneath Iranian radar, refuelled at a secret base in the mountains near Kerman, and made their way unknowingly into a freak dust storm in the central Iranian desert. At some time, with visibility close to zero, two of the helicopters collided and crashed with the loss of twenty lives. The third was forced to abort the mission.

The repercussions were soon to prove disastrous. When the wreckage was found, the Iranian revolutionary press printed a story that enraged the nation. The lives of the embassy hostages were threatened, America was confirmed in the eyes of millions of Iranians to be the Great Satan, and Carter was elected out of the White House. It was the biggest operational failure since the Bay of Pigs fiasco in 1961.

Part of that same desert, where the mission ended, was spread out before me now. The flat green fields of Kerman were left far behind and soon we were travelling along a thin grey strip of roadway through bare hills, down a great smooth slope veined from the watercourses created in the rains, then onto the wide-open plains. The patterns and textures changed continuously; the colours varied from ochre to dark red to dark grey. The only thing that never altered was the baking heat. It was much more than 40 degrees Celsius outside – quite possibly closer to 50, but there was no way of measuring. It was simply hot, and the journey sixteen hours long. I knew that if I could get through this, then I could get through anything.

The bus was completely full. Townspeople and village folk rubbed shoulders with a team of white-turbaned mullahs on their way to Mashad and the sacred shrine of Reza, the eighth Imam. The mullahs sat squashed together, all wearing the same sullen expression, like mourners on their way to a funeral. Their presence, however, was unfortunate. The laws of Ramadan would have to be strictly obeyed, even though it was written in the *Koran* that travellers were exempt from the fast. In the eyes of Iran's clergy, modern travel was not thought of as sufficiently debilitating to warrant immunity from God's holy law. We could drink, but we couldn't eat.

Next to my seat at the front of the bus was a barrel of iced water and a plastic jug. Being the closest, it seemed appropriate that I should be the one to fill the jug and take it round, as was the custom. But at the command of one of these dour-faced mullahs that duty fell to another. Presumably I was unclean, an unbeliever, unfit to quench their thirst; surprisingly it annoyed me.

Muhammad, the driver, was sympathetic. He was a tall man with a big stomach which amply filled the space between him and the wheel. He didn't like anyone telling him what to do, either. With the noise of the engine to drown out his voice, he lambasted the mullahs and the government in a language I could easily understand. But the man he disliked most of all was the one who made him drive the Kerman-to-Mashad route for such a poor wage. He raised a hairy fist in the air, the salute of the proletariat. Perhaps he was a communist, but I wasn't game enough to ask.

Afternoon slowly turned into evening, and evening into a moonlit night. The road behind became as long as the road in front. At one stage I looked around and saw a layer of salt several inches thick which seemed to cover everything, smothering whatever life remained in this desert. Nothing could ever grow here, no roots would ever take hold in such soil, and as I dozed for a while next to the half-open window, feeling the hot air on my face, I started to wonder at the way in which fundamentalism was also attempting to smother Iran. Islam was a complete religion, with laws and guidance that could, like the *Bible*, be used in any community. But Shia fundamentalism was all about isolation. Its rejection of Western civilisation was understandable on the grounds of incompatibility, but even Iran's closest neighbours were sometimes frowned upon for their lack of religious fervour. The government-sponsored graffiti in Teheran had said IRAN IS NEITHER EAST OR WEST. Presumably it occupied a limbo world somewhere in between, self-contained but always having to feed off the developed nations for machinery, higher education and medicine. And because of this dependency it had become a victim of its own ideology, foiled by its own grand scheme. But then perhaps this was the sole intention. There was a lot about fundamentalism that was injurious and self-flagellation was almost common practice; before it could build, it was bound to destroy.

When I opened my eyes again it was dark outside. Muhammad was slowing down, but there didn't seem to be any reason for stopping. He was looking out his side window as we came to a halt and the engine died. Abrupt, military-sounding voices were issuing commands and beams of torchlight played upon the windows. The door opened suddenly and a man armed with a machine-gun leapt up the steps. The interior lights were ordered on. Then came an officer, a senior member of the Pasdaran, a leader of minions.

'Leave the bus!'

One by one we climbed down onto the stony ground. Beyond the beam of our headlights and the glow of the Pasdar's fire there was nothing to see except for a simple mud-brick hut and a short tower behind a barbed wire fence. We stood in the middle of a limitless void. The air was humid still, a wet heat that made the desert grit stick to our skin. They herded us over to where our baggage was being pulled out onto the road and we picked out our own to stand by. Three men standing next to me appeared to be a little more nervous than the others. They wore the waistcoat and shalwar camise of the Afghani, whose relations with the Pasdaran were notoriously bad.

Needless to say, their travel documents and my passport were picked upon and scrutinised by the officer, who then passed them onto the guards with a casual indifference. While the belongings of the other passengers were being prodded and subjected to a brief examination, our meagre possessions were turned upside down in the dust. Photographs were checked and torches shone into our faces. I felt like an animal caught in the beam of oncoming traffic, frozen to the spot, heart pounding, waiting for the blow. Instead, voices were suddenly shouting from behind; then came the rattling of bolts as a metal gate swung open and the four of us were escorted through the gate, down a concrete path and into a barracks room lit by a single bulb. There were more guards inside, asleep and snoring on the floor when we entered. Heavy, well-worn army boots poked out from under light-grey blankets. Sleepy faces looked up at us. We were told to sit down in the corner while our papers were inspected again.

The room was bare, except for a tattered poster bearing Khomeini's 'don't piss with me' expression, and a few slogans painted onto the walls that probably glorified the virtues of life with the Pasdaran. The floor was covered with a kilim carpet, and only one or two soldiers had thin mattresses. The rest made do with the hard ground. Wooden pegs hammered into cracks in the walls served as lockers for them to hang their weapons on.

The officer came and stood over me first, wanting to know about my work, family and religion, all of which I answered well enough in the Farci I had learnt so far. This appeared to satisfy him sufficiently to leave me, guessing my fate, before he turned to the other three. It was then that his manner changed from harmlessly brisk to brutal, and the tone of his voice raised to fever pitch. If the answers to any of his questions were too slow in coming, he would stick a boot into the nearest man's ribs. It reminded me of the Turkish soldiers' treatment of the Kurds who had been caught trying to cross the border near Essendere. On that occasion also, physical force had been used with routine nonchalance. Only these Afghani had done nothing wrong. They were singled out for persecution simply because of who they were and where they came from.

When the interrogation finally ended some fifteen minutes later, their papers were thrown in their faces and their baggage dumped in a pile. We were left to walk back out to the waiting bus, where the faces of the other passengers were glued to the windows, there to embark again upon our journey.

Hours passed. The cold now took its turn to make the journey uncomfortable. I dozed again as we hurtled through the night, aware only of the half-moon eerily illuminating the salt-covered desert, and of the twin shafts of our headlights that searched the way in front. When dawn eventually came, the desert lay behind us like an ocean crossed, here and there were small oases of life, and once again we rode through a habitable world.

EIGHTEEN

Like a bull's-eye at its centre, Mashed's shrine to the Imam Reza is the point from which all things radiate. Sun-struck buildings and dusty streets spread out from its great high walls, which surround an area many acres in size. And in this space there stands the golden dome of the shrine, the high arched entrance-way of the mosque, and the inner courtyards of stone over which tower turquoise minarets that shine in the sun like polished marble. Everywhere there are pilgrims, some arriving by car and bus but the vast majority on foot. Their faces are sunburnt from a long journey and many carry their possessions upon their backs. They will camp within the courtyard of the mosque and shrine, sleeping beneath the *ivans* or in the open cells above the burial vaults. Central Asia feels closer. There are Turcomen with high black fleecy hats and Mongols with wide, open faces.

The Serai Sayid was only a short walk from the shrine – serai being short for caravanserai, the market stations which dotted the trading routes of old. This serai was of a more modern variety, but only slightly. Its thick wooden doors were weather-worn and split, and the boards were held together by the original nails. It was about five storeys high, squeezed in between a shoe store and a run-down hotel for the poorest of pilgrims, on a busy road lined with trees and steel drums holding iced water for the thirsts of the faithful. On the steps of the serai, an old woman with a broom made of desert brush waged war against the dust and dirt that blew up from the street.

I went inside.

It was cool and quiet compared to the street, and the smell was the familiar, dry, musty smell of old carpets. They were piled high in every direction, with their owners close by. Afghans, Turcomen, Tadjiks and Persians mingled together. The serai, with its many levels, was going about the quiet order of a business unchanged through the centuries.

Then came a sudden voice from above.

'Salaam Richard, how are you?'

The friendly face of Ali was peering over the wooden railings. He had handed me his card in Shiraz, and had invited me to drop in.

'Come up, this way.'

A staircase led to his office which, like all the others, was an open-fronted cell looking out onto a wide terrace with an iron railing. There was no central floor to the serai as such; it was hollow in the middle with a walkway round each level. Consequently news travelled fast and as usual, Ali turned it to his advantage.

'It is wonderful,' he chuckled. 'By now the whole serai is thinking you're a big buyer from overseas. Please, do not be so quick to correct their mistake.'

I took off my shoes and sat on a pile of carpets at the back. Ali caught the attention of the serai tea-boy and in an overly loud voice ordered tea for his foreign guest. A tray of glasses filled with the hot dark liquid duly arrived, followed soon after by the first inquisitive dealer. He was a bald-headed man with an ingratiating smile who just happened to be passing. He in turn was succeeded by a more solemn fellow from the far side, then by two more dealers from the upper floor and so on. At times Ali's little storeroom was bustling with activity, which was just the way he liked it. When the procession of visitors ended at midday, it was only because the fasting month of Ramadan was now over, and nothing was going to deter these people from lunch.

Before he too went home, Ali took me a few doors down the street to the local inn. They had a room but only because it was Ali who was asking. Mashad was another holy city that catered to pilgrims first, travelling infidels last.

I washed in the sink across the hall from my bare little room, rinsed out my shirt and then held it out the window for a few minutes to dry. Then, after a short siesta, I walked down to the old bazaar near the shrine.

A street-seller lay asleep across the entrance with his wares tucked beneath him. Similarly, the darkened stores within had either a broom handle placed across the front or the owner himself lying there on the floor. One dingy cavern had for its guardian a small boy perched on a high stool, chin in hand, staring glumly at his feet.

In the long, grey vaulted ceiling, angled shafts of sunlight fell through octagonal holes and landed in perfect parallel lines upon the dusty floor. As the world turned and the day wore on, the old bazaari probably kept time by their path, knowing when it was time to start work, stop, eat and go home. If the muezzin's call went unheard, prayer times would also be there for the devout to read.

Under one of these spotlights sat a man on a chair, his white shirt reflecting the light so brilliantly in the dark stone passage that he shone like some sort of celestial being. I carried on through the shadowy catacombs, listening to the rattling of hooves upon the flagstones and the mutterings of solemn old men, drinking tea on wine-red Bokhara rugs and smoking their *naghileh*. The wheels of a passing cart stirred up the ancient dust and the air filled with the smell of cardamom. Through another entrance the bazaari were slowly returning in ones and twos. Soon the activity would again be great, but it was peace and quiet I was after, so I went out the way I came in.

It was around three o'clock when I got back to the serai. The late afternoon light was raking down from the skylights. At the back I could see a party of boys playing cards on an upturned box. They stopped when they saw me and stared as I climbed the staircase.

Ali was still out, so I went upstairs to take a look round. The higher I went the smaller the shops became. Some were no more than large cupboards with a single chair and a few rugs. On the very top floor the carpet repairers had their businesses, and it was here that I was cornered by a relic from the past.

'Groovy, man!' said the voice excitedly.

He was in his early forties with a dirty face, smeared with blue dye and framed by an untidy mass of black curly hair. He wore flared trousers, sandals and a pale blue body shirt. There was a slightly glazed look to his eyes that made me feel uneasy. Minute drops of saliva sprayed out from wet lips as he spoke, and he wiped his mouth with his sleeve. With his hand he grasped mine and for a moment I thought he was going to pinch my skin to see if it was real.

Finally he let go and said, 'It's been a long time. A real downer, man. Hey, where are all the others?'

He looked over my shoulder, hoping apparently to see a horde of colourful tourists and hippy travellers. I told him there were no 'others', not yet anyway, and his face fell briefly.

'Well, you're here, man, you're here! That's a start.' Then he burst out in another rush of decade-old English. No one had been here to tell him the language had changed since the heady, pre-Khomeini years. He remembered Haight-Ashbury, the Doors, Joplin. He dug up words and phrases that came from the era of flower children, and he recited them like incantations and mantras. All the travellers who had passed him on their way to Afghanistan and the Eastern trip, all the carpets he had sold, all the dope, the girls, the free love came flooding back.

Then he stopped smiling and dropped his voice to a whisper.

'Do you need some stuff?'

My surprise must have seemed like interest.

'It's good, man. If you want, come to me all right. I've got the stuff stashed.'

Here was another Iranian conundrum. The country that purportedly led the revolution in the Muslim world, the blossoming flower of Islam, still had a problem with the illegal cultivation of other blooms in hidden valleys.

Not wanting to be anywhere near drug dealers in a country where even petty theft got you the chop, I went to the level below and ran straight into yet another English-speaking carpet seller. Shahria was a small, straight man with blue eyes and nut-brown skin. He was a civil engineer, he said, who now taught English to middle-class Mashadi teenagers and dabbled in carpets on the side. He had lived in Australia for five good, long years and was overjoyed to hear that I too had sampled giant oysters at the Rocks beneath Sydney Harbour Bridge. To reminisce, he invited me to his house that night for dinner.

I showered in the local *hamam* across the street from the hotel and following Shahria's directions, caught a bus out to the suburbs. It was much greener. Tall plane trees lined the roadside, and the walls surrounding many houses were ivy-covered. A footpath with a grass verge delivered me to the appropriate iron gate. I knocked but there was no reply, so I let myself in. And it was like entering another world: an enclosed inner courtyard garden with electric lights illuminating lush fruit trees, roses and a trickling fountain. I knocked again on another door and this time heard footsteps and Shahria's voice from inside. But it was not Shahria who appeared. The woman was beautiful, stunning, in fact. She had long, flowing black hair and a dazzling smile. No chador or headscarf, just a slim figure in jeans and shirt. Shahria smiled from over her shoulder and uttered those tragic words to one who has just that moment fallen in love: 'Richard meet Sanaz – my wife.'

The house was spacious and modern in the style of the seventies. Hanging plants and Cubist paintings hung on the walls; the rugs were many and varied. A set of African spears stood in one corner. There was a sofa and chair with a low table in the middle and next to that on the floor, a red plastic mat with three plates, knives and forks. We knelt down to a meal of rice and chicken and talked about the hardships facing those who do not adhere to the strict Islamic rules. Like many educated Iranians presided over by the current medieval theocracy, Shahria chose to have no religion at all rather than accept the one being pushed upon him. Sanaz, on the other hand, had been raised by her father and mother to believe in Islam. But she wore the chador outside her home only to avoid trouble. They were what might loosely be called 'ordinary people', but at times it was like holding a conversation with a condemned couple facing life imprisonment. They wanted to get out, although it would take a lot of cash to buy their freedom in another country, much more than Shahria could earn teaching English. Selling carpets he hoped would be more profitable, and to this slender thread all their dreams were tied.

'What about engineering?' I asked.

'Oil rigs,' he muttered. 'Down near the Iraqi border. Long hours in the stinking heat. During the war some Iraqi soldiers overran our position and Sanaz was forced to run into the desert, pregnant. That was it for us.'

Sanaz got up abruptly and went into the kitchen. Shahria also went strangely quiet for some reason, until I noticed that the tell-tale signs of children in his home were missing. Clearly the invasion that day had taken a great toll on both their lives.

To change the subject, it was with Shahria that I first raised the question of Afghanistan. When I eventually explained the reason for my interest he was stunned.

'How do you know these rebels won't kill you?'

I tried to explain that that was exactly the point. I didn't know. I was trying to find people to talk to who did know. I told him my plans of contacting the various mujahedeen groups in Mashad.

'It won't be easy,' he said

'I didn't think it would be,' I responded.

'Do you know which group are best?'

Jamiat-i-Islami were the largest group in the Herat province, the area surrounding Herat city. And their influence was known to extend across the country to Pakistan. If I were to make it in, the only real option was to keep going in that direction, hopefully still with Jamiat.

'But there are other groups,' I added.

'Which ones?'

'Harrakat or Hezbollah,' I said.

'Hezbollah!' he exclaimed. 'Party of God people. The hostage-takers of Lebanon. Now I know you're crazy.'

I argued a little unconvincingly that Afghan Hezbollah were entirely different to Iranian Hezbollah, but he wasn't having any of it.

'Come on,' he said. 'No one walks through a war zone, especially not this one. The whole country is mined. Your chances of surviving a week are zero, and you are talking about several months. Why don't you stay here and get a job teaching English?'

If these words of warning had come from a reliable source, I might have heeded them. But as it was, Shahria scarcely knew more than I did. He was relying upon what he felt to be the case, not what he knew. So the subject of Afghanistan was dropped. Instead we chatted about Sydney, Manly beach and Fosters lager until it was time for me to go.

The days that followed were hard ones. The whereabouts of any mujahedeen group remained a mystery. Opinions ranged: they had moved, they were forced underground, they lived in the desert.

No one really knew.

On many occasions the advice was to give up and avoid the messy end foretold by all. At other times a wall of silence sprung up between myself and those I questioned. After several days of searching I had drawn a blank. The sharp edge of my resolve was now cracked and worn, added to which was the time factor. The two-week extension obtained from the police in Teheran was almost gone. Now I had to decide between giving up or returning to the capital to try for another. It seemed unlikely, even highly improbable, that they would even see me. But in the end I chose not to give up. Hope is always the last thing to die.

On the night before leaving for Teheran, I went with a friend of Shahria's to the shrine of Imam Reza. Farid was his business partner at the serai, a man of ideas and the drive to see them through. He walked quickly, spoke quickly and did everything else with a sense of urgency. The hair on his head, like that of his beard, was black and tightly curled. He was stringy in the way of long-distance runners and energetic optimists.

We went at a time which was quiet. The courtyards leading to the central mosque of Gohar Shad and the shrine were almost empty. A few ethereal shapes glided through the dimly lit entrances. A mullah emerged suddenly into a circular blaze of light, his white turban shining like an iridescent halo. Finally, when at last we passed through the great wooden doors and entered the open quadrangle, it was to the slow, rhythmic chanting of pilgrims, dressed from head to toe in flowing white robes. High overhead, the black sky was pierced by the golden dome's sharply illuminated outline. The minarets too, turquoise and silver towers, were awash with a light that overcame the stars beyond.

I circled the courtyard slowly, beneath double-tiered archways that carried ornate patterns, flowing Kufic script and Arabic inscriptions like those seen in Esfahan's great mosques, then past the shrine with eyes straining to see inside, listening at the same time to the pilgrim's meditative tones join the only other sound of the night: the doves. Up above, the mystical birds of Islam were calling softly to each other across the upper reaches, from minaret to minaret.

'You have seen enough?' asked Farid anxiously. He was nervous of being found out, though he tried not to show it.

'Yes, for now at least,' I said.

'Good. I'm hungry.'

Over a late meal back near my hotel, Farid announced that he would accompany me to Teheran. He was hoping for permission to take several bales of carpets to Switzerland at the end of the year. A licence to export, he said, could take him almost anywhere, even back to England where he had roamed as a youth, selling small tapestries to Kensington dealers.

'Tell me,' he said. 'Is it true or false that Harrods is now owned by an Arab?'

'True,' I replied.

He clicked his tongue and sighed.

'I had not realised things were so bad over there.'

NINETEEN

The train rolled out of the station at five in the afternoon in the middle of a fierce desert duststorm. The compartment was a sauna. Someone had left the window open and fine grit covered everything, including two soldiers who'd come from up the line.

Perched on my seat, watching the perspiration drip to the floor and evaporate on impact, it occurred to me we could generate our own compartment weather system, independent of the one outside. Storm clouds laden with cooling rain might roll in over the luggage rack.

I felt terrible.

'Do you know how to play Rol yor Pooch?' said Farid cheerfully.

'No idea,' I replied.

It sounded like something to do with the family dog.

'What is it again?'

'Rol yor Pooch.'

The game involved the simple process of elimination, along with a few poker skills. One team of players would conceal a small object, in our case the top off a Bic pen, in one of their hands. The opposing team's objective was to guess which hand it was in, by eliminating the ones they thought did not hold it. Saying *Pooch* meant you thought the hand was empty.

I felt Farid and I made a good team, but the Iranian army contingent proved themselves to be past masters. Eight years of war and their faces were unreadable.

We rattled on past villages the colour of the desert, their small domed roofs perhaps imitating the dome of the shrine. There were also funnels, like those on a ship, sticking up through the rooftops, all pointed in the same direction; east, the direction from which the wind came. From the train, they clustered together and seemed to suggest a host of ancient sentinels, ever watchful for danger, or hope. Then the villages ceased and we came nearer to the barren lands where the earth was rutted with the tracks of heavy machinery and pitted by earth-rimmed wells. Down below were the underground canals carrying precious water from the mountains, a construction as old as time. The skill necessary for making and maintaining these subterranean waterways was still handed down from father to son. Great importance and honour was attached to the trade.

The sun set on the left and an attendant came round with the evening meal. We had already paid at the beginning of the journey, but it was worth it. The rice was good and hot, mixed in with some chicken and a few pieces of gherkin. The chicken reminded me of Iraq, and especially Baghdad where the restaurants sold nothing but chicken. I mentioned this to Farid, expecting to get a reaction of some sort. But he just shrugged. In Iran I knew poultry was thin on the ground – eggs were impossible to find. The influx of people from the countryside into the cities had reduced the number of families working the land. Farms had been left empty and the fields untended.

Farid scraped up the last of his meal with a strip of flat bread and said, abruptly, 'I don't really like chicken. Goat is better.'

There was a knock at the door and the attendant arrived to clean away the remains. Minutes later he returned and slung in the blankets which were supposed to keep us warm once the desert temperature dropped. The soldiers said nothing; they merely pulled out their seats from the wall and wrapped up. Farid, on the other hand, wanted some pillows brought and extra blankets. He berated the attendant for his sloppy service and lost his cool slightly when the fellow slammed the door in his face. For the next five minutes he raved, working out his anger on the soldiers before raising his arms to heaven in frustration. Then he too pulled his seat out into a bed and curled up, grumbling under his breath.

Time passed slowly in the night, and sleeping was more than difficult. No one could agree on whether the window should be open or shut, so we had both at different intervals. The effect this had on the temperature within the compartment was such that it ranged from freezing to sweltering at regular intervals. There was nothing to do but sit up and look out the window at the passing blackness, although the magic of the open spaces was absent within the confines of the rail cab. We ground our way through a place that could not be measured in miles or in the features that went by, but only by time and the amount which it took to reach our destination.

Farid was still angry in the morning; he didn't say much as we rolled slowly towards the central station, past the rows of mud-coloured houses strung out along the track, each with an air-conditioning unit set into the back. But it was clear now that his mood was not due entirely to the discourteous attendant, or to the long journey, but to the importance of his quest in

Teheran. A great deal was hanging on the success or failure of his application for an overseas trading permit.

On the station platform we arranged to meet in Ferdowsi Square around midday and I watched him run off to keep his appointment with the export authorities. We were, it seemed, sharing the same boat.

That morning, traffic was heavy going north over the giant flyovers that leap-frog major intersections. The mountains were bathed in a soft light, but already fading in the heat.

The police response to my request for another extension was a predictable one.

'Why are you still here?' came the cry of disbelief from behind the desk. 'You should not even be still in this country!'

The officer was the same one I had dealt with the last time. The top button on his shirt was still done up and a mountain of paperwork still sat on his desk. I began by explaining in glowing terms how there was still so much to see in Iran, touched briefly upon the wonder and natural beauty of his country and presented him with the fake letter from the Geographical Institute. In hand-written Farci it described my journey as a search for the truth about Iran, ten years after the Islamic revolution. Unfortunately this seemed to have little effect upon his temperament. He blinked hard and I watched with surprise the anger that quickly built up on his face. An awkward silence filled the room. The other officers were watching. I waited silently, until finally he spoke again.

'I can do nothing. You disobeyed me. Now you must take this matter to the Ministry of Foreign Affairs.'

He sat back down in his chair and scribbled the address on a scrap of paper. It was evident that argument was futile.

The taxi-driver outside seemed to know the address. But when we got to where he thought it was, it wasn't there. He tried again, another place where the ministry might be, but this too proved wrong. Government departments were always on the move, he explained, as we raced the wrong way up a one-way street. We journeyed round Teheran for a little while longer before seeking the advice of a passing pedestrian, and in that way we found the right building.

The Ministry of Foreign Affairs was entered through a gate which opened out into a wide courtyard with small trees and shrubs at its centre. There seemed to be no main door with a reception desk, so in the end I picked the nearest entrance and found myself in a long, dark corridor lined with an endless row of dusty offices, inhabited by grim-faced officials. The first grim-faced official waved me on to the second, who pointed me in the direction of the third, who handed me on to the fourth. Eventually I found someone who could deal with my request, but this individual seemed to imply by the shocked expression on his face that extending a transit visa was not only unlawful, it was downright ungodly.

My patience evaporated. There was no point in going any further and possibly making matters worse. I managed to extricate myself from the situation without raising the alarm and slip quietly outside to go back by bus to the central police station. It was my only available option. Perhaps the officer I had spoken to there had had enough time to calm down.

It was just before noon when I finally arrived back at the station office to find it empty, save for a lone uniformed policeman who looked as if he was also in the process of leaving. I asked him where everyone was.

'Gone,' he muttered. 'Holiday.'

Suddenly a tiny light of hope appeared at the end of the tunnel. I explained to him my position, how in less than two days my visa would have expired, making my presence in his country illegal in the eyes of the law, and how there was now insufficient time remaining for me to reach the border. He thought about this for a while, then stretched out his hand and asked to see my passport. I handed it over, along with the fake letter. I wasn't sure whether he was seriously considering the problem or just being nosy. He looked up and asked, 'Is Australia a good friend of Iran?'

'Great friends,' I boasted.

He said, 'There is also Muslim leader in Australia then?'

'The Ayatollah Bob Hawke,' I said proudly.

'Then may Allah grant him long life.'

I nodded in respectful agreement, and couldn't believe my luck when he took out from a desk drawer a big blue stamp book and stuck a whole row of visa stamps on a fresh page of my passport, adding to each one his signature. I was asked to pay a little money. For the paperwork, he said guiltily, but I didn't argue and the money was duly pocketed. If the occasion was marred slightly, it was only because my fake letter from the Geographical Institute was taken away and photocopied, although I trusted that its inclusion within my file signified officiousness rather than suspicion.

Later, I met up with an excited and jubilant Farid in Ferdowsi Square.

'I have it, my friend, I have it!'

He was waving a few sheets of paper before my eyes and doing a little jig on the pavement. The export licence had been granted, very much against the odds evidently, leaving him free to pursue business interests in Europe. For Shahria too, his partner in Mashad, the future was suddenly looking better.

'Tonight,' he said, 'I will take the train back to Mashad. Will you come?'

I explained that there were some people I wanted to see in Teheran. With time on my hands I would return at a later date.

To celebrate we went to the Melli eating house in a cellar beneath the street. The cellar was a disused bomb shelter turned into a lucrative business. It was full of office workers and shop assistants sitting at vinyl-topped tables, mashing their afternoon meal with a mortar and pestle.

'You want Ab Ghousht?' said Farid over his shoulder.

'Whatever you're having is fine.'

'Good. Ab Ghousht for two.'

'As a matter of interest,' I asked, 'do they have anything else to eat here?'

'No, why?'

'I just wondered. Ab Ghousht then, is what all these people are eating?'

With amazement I watched as chunks of meat and potato

were pounded into a pulp using the aforementioned implements, then scooped up with pieces of flat bread. The tea was too hot to drink from a glass, so it was poured into a saucer and slurped.

During lunch I noticed a wooden box with glass sides over by the doorway. The outside was decorated with revolutionary posters and a string of plastic roses had been nailed to the edge. In the bottom of the box there were a few coins and a one thousand rial note – not a great deal of money.

'Donations?' I asked.

'For the families of those martyred in the war,' Farid said.

I looked again and noticed that someone had also pinned to the box photographs of the deceased. Smiling, happy, boyish faces captured in better times; older men looking proud in their smart uniforms; professional soldiers with blank eyes. One was a black and white snapshot of a youth laid out on his deathbed. The sheet was pulled back showing the extent of his considerable wounds, and it baffled me that anyone would want to show off such a picture in a restaurant.

I asked him whether Mashad had ever been hit during the fighting, but he shook his head. They had been shown propaganda films of the war – going well of course. Footage of the counterstrikes in the Kurdish mountains; troops with red bandannas round their heads, the colour of martyrdom, swarming over Iraqi positions; the big guns firing and destroying Iraqi towns. But of actual war and fighting – happily – they had seen nothing in Mashad.

'This is why the city is so big now,' he explained with a wry smile. 'The population grew with people coming to escape the war. They all knew Saddam Hussein's Scud missiles couldn't reach that far. But if you asked them, they'd probably say they came to be near the holy shrine.' He laughed. 'That's human nature, isn't it?'

Back at the Demavend hotel that evening I was given the same room upstairs, overlooking the alleyway. The battered air-conditioning unit over the doorway still creaked and groaned, the sheets bore the impression of a recent guest, but it was home. I went downstairs to the reception office and found Mahmoud, apparently waiting for me. He hailed a small boy from outside to fetch two glasses of tea. He seemed very excited.

'Have you heard the news?' he said quietly.

'No.'

'He is sickening. Ayatollah Khomeini lies in hospital.'

Although the authorities were adamant that the Imam had fully recovered from a recent bout of illness, it seemed there were still rumours that all was not well. According to Mahmoud, it was only a matter of time before the truth came out.

'How old is he now?' I asked.

Mahmoud looked up to the ceiling.

'About eighty-something I think, but he has a brother who is even older.'

'Longevity is probably in the family.'

'Longevity?'

He looked at me quizzically.

'It means long life.'

He paused for a moment, lost in thought and staring down at his feet. Then I heard him say in the faintest of murmurs, 'My friend, for the sake of this country of ours, I sincerely hope not.'

He looked very sad suddenly, and tired, so to change the subject I told him of my plan to return to Mashad, and it was his suggestion that I did so via the Caspian Sea, the Darya-i-Khazar, the largest inland sea in the world. According to Mahmoud it was the most beautiful sight, set in a mountainous sub-tropical region with heavy rainfall and lush forested areas. Hard to believe in such an apparently dry and dusty country, but I was so captivated with his description that I decided to make the detour. Besides, from the town of Chalus on the coast there was a road that would take me east towards Mashad.

'The air is thick and smells of flowers,' he continued. 'And the water is blue like an ocean. At night, all you can hear is the sound of the water breaking on the sand,' and he made a wonderfully drawn-out whooshing sound.

The Caspian had once been a playground for the rich international jet-setters from Iran and all round the world. I wondered now how it had fared, or whether it even still existed in Khomeini's Iran.

TWENTY

It was two hundred kilometres to Chalus. One hundred and fifty went slowly up, the remaining fifty plummeted straight down in a rapid, twisting nosedive to the sea. Tall fir trees clung to the cliff edges, their roots desperate for something to hold on to. Tunnels were blasted through the living rock and we passed a modern dam, one of the Shah's, which filled an entire valley. An obsolete road plunged straight into the still waters and reappeared on the other side, continuing on as if nothing had happened; curious sights indeed, although the man across the aisle from me in the bus rounded things off nicely when he produced an old copy of *The Catcher in the Rye* and started to read.

I reached over and tapped him on the shoulder, making him jump slightly as if by electric shock.

'I'm sorry,' I said.

His eyes went wide, his mouth hung open. It took a while for the words to come out.

'You're English?'

'More or less,' I said, my exact origins being rather complicated.

'I thought . . . well, I mean, when I saw you before, I thought you were Pasdaran.'

Now it was my turn to be shocked. 'Pasdaran! What made you think that?'

He broke into a smile and stroked his own clean-shaven chin. 'Our beloved leaders and their army try to grow beards like yours. It's very Islamic.'

There was a definite note of sarcasm in his voice and I had the feeling I'd just met another sceptic. I was beginning to wonder where all the true believers were, and whether it was my destiny not to encounter any.

His name was Hassan. He was from Teheran. He was twenty-seven years old, and as the journey continued I heard how six of those years had been spent studying engineering in Tunbridge Wells. His mother and father had lived there for two. Regretfully, in 1979 and like so many other Iranians driven by curiosity or concern over their property, the Islamic revolution forced them back to a new Iran and he had been unable to leave since. Speaking English was, for him, like stepping back in time.

His hair was thin, the colour of chestnut, and he wore a pair of John Lennon glasses that came from a store in London's Portobello Road. His accent, oddly enough, was typical to the part of south-eastern England where he had lived for so long. The more he talked, the more obvious it became, as if he were gradually recalling those pleasant years, pulling them back into focus.

'You know,' he said, 'I think I can remember the name of the elderly couple from next door. It was Simpson. Yes, Mr and Mrs Henry Simpson.' He looked at me to see if the name meant anything. It was a shame really. More than anything I would have liked for it to have been otherwise.

That day, Hassan was travelling to visit his parents in a coastal village near Chalus, and in the Iranian way he asked if I would like to stay.

'What about your parents?' I said, but he assured me it would be no trouble.

'They'd be very happy to meet you,' he said.

The descent to the coast continued slowly. With so many hair-pin turns we could only inch our way down. One minute the cliff edge was on the right, the next it was on the left. It was not until darkness had fallen that we reached Chalus and from there, another bus took us along a flat coastal road until Hassan signalled for the driver to drop us off.

Suddenly, gone was the Iran of the desert. The still night air was heavy with the warmth and humidity of a thriving jungle. A jasmine bush climbed up the wall of the village baker's store and its delicate fragrance awakened the senses to a new world. From every tree came a chorus of wildlife, so that the land seemed to breathe and sing at the same time. It was vibrant and alive, so much in contrast to what lay behind us over the mountains. And all of a sudden I was filled with a strong sense of *déjà vu*. Into this same climate I had been born in Papua New Guinea in March 1963, the only son in a family of travellers, and now it was as if that first breath was being drawn once more.

'This way,' Hassan said, pointing up a dark side road.

We walked for just a few minutes before turning left in single file down a narrow and overgrown track. Progress was slow and wet; it had only just stopped raining. Huge leafy branches weighed down with water would spring to life as we nudged past, threatening to drench us at every step. Finally lights appeared and the path widened to reveal a cluster of wooden houses. They were all single-storeyed with low picket fences, lush gardens and verandas, although one house in particular had a tarpaulin strung up across the front.

'Pasdaran,' Hassan whispered, and he walked a little faster towards the furthest building.

It stood directly opposite a rice field, no more than an acre but probably home to several million frogs. The noise they made was terrific. At the gate to his home, Hassan selected a stone from a tidy pile near the letter box and indicated that I should watch and listen. Then he lobbed it into the centre of the field. Almost instantly the croaking stopped dead, as if the surrounding jungle were listening.

'Our secret code – to tell them who's coming,' he said.

'Ingenious, but why?'

Hassan's grin widened. 'Because around about now they'll be getting the cards out for a spot of gambling and,' he glanced over to the Pasdar's house, 'you never know when neighbours will drop in uninvited.'

Reza and his wife Zara seemed not at all surprised to find me on their doorstep with their son. They talked to me for a while and invited me to stay for the night. He was taller than Hassan, a retired officer from the Shah's army, grey-haired and balding with long slender fingers. She was younger – a small, slim woman with a wonderful laughing face and a quick sense of humour. Time had been kind to her. She was still beautiful and her eyes were bright.

They had been sitting playing Gin Rummy for small change at the dining table, completely against the laws of the land which forbid gambling, but after a cool shower I was also happily surprised to be given a glass of vodka, as well as a pair of sandals to wear around the house. It was in fact a holiday home: two bedrooms and a bathroom off a short hallway, plus the large L-shaped living room where we sat. The kitchen was round a corner. It was the first time I had seen tables and chairs in an Iranian house and when I mentioned this Hassan laughed.

'Normal Iranian houses,' he said, 'don't have alcohol either.'

'You made this yourself?'

'My mother is an expert,' and he leaned over to kiss her on the cheek.

That evening I sat with them round the table, brushing aside the occasional mosquito that had crept in through the wire screen doors, while Hassan and his parents tried to give me some idea of the life of the people in this area.

Most of them were village folk who knew no more of that other Iran over the mountains than of what lay over the sea. No doubt they imagined it all to be a land of dense forest and heavy seasonal rainfall such as their own. And when the great natural disasters came they had to succumb, for disasters in this mostly tropical region were as regular as the seasons. Flooding and earthquakes took their toll, and because of this inescapable punishment, the victims had grown strong and robust. Fortunately there hadn't been a major earthquake for some years, but they were sure it would come.

Then there were the other few inhabitants like themselves; city folk who came for a holiday from Teheran. Once there had been many more coming each year to the blue Caspian waters and to the white sandy beaches, even in relatively recent times, but the government had begun to install a growing Pasdaran presence to scare them all away.

Reza was direct about the government's actions, but not

bitter. He did not strike me as a bitter man, but more of a stern fatalist. Zara also preferred to laugh than to cry. It was Hassan who was the resentful one. He despised the power which was used and abused by ignorant and uneducated louts in uniform.

As they played on into the night, Hassan and I joked and laughed and drank more vodka, taking apart Iran's clerical hierarchy with our increasingly drunken condemnation. A little unwise perhaps with such dangerous neighbours, but Hassan was in no mood for caution. It started raining again and we sat there listening to the downpour slapping against the broad tropical leaves outside. It still didn't feel like Iran at all. Maybe this was why Hassan's family came here on holiday: to escape to a more relaxed environment, to gamble and occasionally get drunk? Maybe the mountain ranges that soared silently above the house acted as a wall through which the waterless desert of Islamic fundamentalism could not hope to pass? Maybe . . .

TWENTY-ONE

The morning was overcast and muggy. A strong wind was coming in off the sea and bending the trees, while the sky was drab grey and wet-looking. The rain, fortunately, had eased to a drizzle.

'You know,' said Hassan, 'in Teheran right now, it will be bright and sunny. Always the same.'

After a breakfast of tea from a large silver samovar and fresh bread daubed with a local honey, Hassan and I took a walk into the village. It was a strange place with an almost haunted feel to it. At one end of the main road was a square, about fifty metres across with several toppled columns lying smashed and broken in the weeds. Carved steps, strikingly similar to the ones at Persepolis, were visible through the vines, although they proved to be cheap imitations in moulded concrete. The whole structure was badly defaced and heavily overgrown, but there was no mistaking the resemblance to the ancient Persian city near Shiraz.

'What on earth was that used for?' I asked.

'Nothing Islamic, that's for sure, which is why they tore it down.'

In reference to the 'they', Hassan pointed across the empty road to an ugly grey concrete wall, topped with barbed wire. It was about a hundred metres long and too high to see over. A steel door set in the wall bore a green spray-painted stencil picture of a clenched fist, holding aloft a Kalishnakov machine-gun. The Pasdaran.

We walked away towards the outdoor market where, in small huts and on long benches, vendors were selling fruits and nuts, meat, bread and fish, including caviar for the first time in a long while. Hassan explained angrily that for most of the year, caviar was non-Islamic, forbidden, impossible to buy. The government could make more money selling it overseas. But on rare occasions, when the international market price fell and created a glut, then the government changed its mind and allowed it to be sold on the domestic market.

I took a closer look.

'It's not even real caviar either,' I said.

'What!'

'Lumpfish eggs.'

'Shit! Those bastards.'

We bought a small bag of roe and some fresh unleavened bread from a tin-shed bakery next door. The bread was baked on a layer of hot gravel which stuck to the underside and had to be brushed off. The stones were then periodically scooped up from the concrete floor and thrown back into the oven. We also tried to buy half a kilo of small apples but the fruit seller wouldn't agree. They were a new batch, he said. It was bad luck to sell anything less than a kilo on his first sale.

Superstition and ignorance, I thought, hallmarks of the wayward places.

We talked politics, religion and more politics. In Iran the two are inseparable. Hassan said the government had taken the country back into the dark ages, replaced sanity with insanity and made it impossible for anyone to live a normal life. It hadn't been perfect under the Shah, but at least it wasn't self-destructive. Why did Islam have to be on such a collision course with the Western world?

He looked around at the drab grey concrete buildings of the main street.

'Have you ever been to New Zealand?' he asked.

'Yes, my mother lives there.'

'Really! That's a coincidence. Do you know only a few months ago I wrote to the New Zealand embassy for immigration details.'

'And?'

'Nothing. For three months no reply, then last week – a letter, which had already been opened, saying they would think about it.'

He said nothing more for a while as we wandered along, and I guessed he was thinking about the implications of having his mail intercepted. He suddenly perked up again and smiled, 'But what does it matter. Tell me about it anyway.'

'The country? Well, it's a bit like Kent with more beaches. Or Scotland with a lot more sheep.'

'Religion?'

'Christianity and Rugby Union.'

He laughed.

'I love it. Now, before you go tomorrow, let me show you something of my country.'

After a short walk we came to a beach that was a mixture of sand and pebbles, swept continually along the coast by huge waves that smashed against the rotting wooden breakwaters. The other side of the Caspian Sea lay below the horizon. With a little imagination, I pictured the hordes of Russian holidaymakers on the far shores, dipping their unhealthy white bodies into the warm water and looking this way, out across the steel-grey sea, wondering what lay at its end.

An octagonal wooden tower stood at the far end of the beach with the Iranian flag flying from its pointed roof. Beyond it, walls of black material stretched across the sands down to the waterline.

'That,' said Hassan, 'is a screen for women bathers.'

The beach was empty now, but he assured me that on calmer, sunnier days the screens would extend a hundred yards out to sea, to separate the sexes. It was the same on the ski slopes of the mountains behind us. The runs were divided and set well apart from each other so that not even by accident could the genders meet, although I had to doubt the likelihood of skiing down a slope with a black chador billowing out from behind like a parachute.

However, here on the coastline the towers, for there were many more, acted as look-outs for the Pasdaran, and around the base an inscription was written: *We are all the soldiers of God.*

Hassan looked at me and sighed. 'Not exactly Brighton, is it?'

We walked on, deeper into the strange past of Salman Shahr. Set amongst a dense thicket of palm trees was a high tower rising straight out of the sand. It was much higher than the first, and there was an adjoining wall that ran parallel with the beach. Barbed wire stretched along the upper edges. It was the Pasdaran's main barracks and Hassan's instruction was to walk quickly past, but quietly.

'Does that mean we're not supposed to be here?' I asked.

'You could say that. They're not overly fond of people poking around in what you might like to call the bad old days.'

Fifty metres past the end of the wall it looked like a scene from a futuristic movie, where the future doesn't turn out so well. Half-buried in sand and broken by the waves stood the remains of a luxury seaside resort. Since the revolution of 1979, the sea had risen to smash down the doors and work away at the foundations, leaving some of the beachfront apartments tilting precariously. Others had been gutted by fire and were being swallowed whole by the encroaching jungle.

Man-made destruction and the decay of neglect; here the two had combined to create a passable imitation of the after-effects of some terrible catastrophe, an atomic explosion or devastating storm. Ayatollah Khomeini himself had once compared the power and might of Islam to a rushing hurricane that would sweep all before it. Salman Shahr, I suppose, was his case in point.

I walked over to where Hassan was kicking the sand away from something buried.

'What is it?' I asked.

He got down on his hands and knees and started digging with a piece of driftwood.

'It's a statue of a white swan. The symbol of this place.'

He stopped digging to explain. The tourists had come here from all over the world: America, England, Europe. The parties had been legendary. Fires burning all through the night. Champagne and caviar. The swans had hollow backs filled with wood and he remembered them as a kid, lighting up the whole beach. There had always been a fire burning somewhere, even during the day. The man who had owned and built the resort was a Zoroastrian.

The religion of Persia before Islam, founded by the prophet Zarathustra in the sixth century BC, Zoroastrianism recognised two principles, good and evil, as personified by Ahura Mazda and Ahriman. The worship of a continuous flame was also a major precept for the follower to adhere to.

'No wonder they came down hard on the place,' I said. 'What happened to him?'

'Went to America,' he said. 'Disappeared.'

Wise man, I thought.

TWENTY-TWO

The next morning the bus raced east along a coastal road which was broken and potholed, and in places had been swept away altogether by that year's heavy rainfall. The great expanse of sea was on the left, fields of rice were on the right, and the wooded Elburz mountain range pulled away in a graceful curve, taking with it the foul weather of the past few days.

Somewhat reluctantly, I had passed up the offer of staying with Hassan and his family for a longer period, although curiously in the end I had accepted their invitation to visit them back in Teheran instead. I say curiously because at the time I had no intention whatsoever of going back to the capital. My sights were firmly fixed on reaching the holy city of Mashad, where I would decide upon my fate concerning Afghanistan. There were, I admit, some small anxieties growing in my mind as to what that fate might be, but as the bus rumbled along, passing the towns of Nur and Babol Sahr, heading towards the Turcoman steppe and the Soviet border, there was never any question of my immediate destination – not just then anyway.

The sun shone and the land slowly dried out, until the lush green was replaced almost entirely by the gold of swaying wheat fields. I dozed with my head against the window, mesmerised by the feeling of warm sunlight on my face and the passing of silent shadows across closed eyelids.

Some hours later we passed down onto the edge of the open steppe, turned left off the main road, bumped along a small side street, and drove into the little town of Gonbad-i-Qaboos.

Men in tall black fleece hats and long black boots were strutting down the streets like peacocks. Their women, a few steps to the rear, were wrapped in chadors of brightly coloured chintz, adorned with flowers.

Nearby, behind a screen of plane trees, there was an old, unpainted wooden building, grey timbers warped and rotting, with a pale yellow tower of weather-beaten brick standing on a high mound alongside. It was round and hollow, and strengthened by ten triangular buttresses that ended just below its pointed roof. At its base, a dozen men might have stretched round it, fingertip to fingertip. It had definite size, but not ponderous bulk as that great traveller Robert Byron once said. In fact, there was something quite delicate about it; an illusion created perhaps by the bands of flowing Kufic script, top and bottom. For here was the ancient tomb of the mighty King Qaboos.

The body of Qaboos who died in 1007, was said to have lain suspended within the tower in a glass coffin which, defying gravity, had apparently just floated there. The tower was empty now though, save for a chill wind that swirled about inside, catching at the dirt and dust. He was believed to have been a powerful ruler before the coming of the Mongols, a man whose energies had been charged with the craft of building. Unlike those that came after him, he had not sought to expand his empire beyond the steppe, and so the skills had not been exported. The grasslands were his sole domain.

Unfortunately for his kind the Mongols did come eventually, bringing with them their inimitable foreign policies, and everything apart from the tomb was laid to waste. History might argue why the tomb was spared, but perhaps even the rampaging hordes stopped long enough to grow in awe of its strength.

Back in the town centre I met an ancestor of this epoch, a young manager of an electrical appliance store whose name was Murat. He was thin and gangly limbed – no relation to the Mongols there so I guessed he was one of Qaboos' lot – and had memorised a string of American slang sayings that infiltrated his conversation at peculiar moments. I asked him what he sold.

'Many, many things,' he said. 'From Russia, holy cow, I have many things.'

I was amazed to find these 'things' were in fact electric toasters: big, cumbersome, old-style electric toasters stacked neatly on wooden shelves. Murat proudly showed me his demonstration model. He pressed the lever down and made sure that I saw and appreciated the glowing red bars within. The automatic timer ticked happily away with superior efficiency until it erupted with a bang and we watched two bits of imaginary toast fly through the air.

The Iranian breakfast, I thought, was in for a startling revolution.

'How many have you sold, Murat?'

He rested a hand on the edge of a shelf and looked upwards to the left, a sure sign of someone preparing to distort the truth.

'I believe,' he said slowly and with much consideration, 'that we did this month, ten or twenty.'

'That's a lot of toasters for Gonbad-i-Qaboos,' I said.

'Say again please, how do you call these?'

'Toasters,' I repeated.

'Cool!' he shouted. 'Totesters!'

'No, toasters,' I corrected.

'Toe-tes-ters!'

I gave up in the end.

'What the hell,' I said. 'Toetesters it is.'

Murat grinned. 'Yeah, what the hell.'

Unfortunately, by the time I had returned to the bus depot my bus was nowhere in sight. From someone selling tickets there I discovered my mistake. The bus driver had said we would be stopping for only fifteen minutes, not fifty. Worse still, there were no buses going to Mashad for another two days, not from Gonbad-i-Qaboos anyway. In fact the only bus at all on this day was leaving in one hour for Gorgon, a neighbouring town to the north-east. It was a railhead station apparently and perhaps, he suggested, the morning train might get me to where I was going.

I bought a ticket to Gorgon. The man selling the tickets was also the driver. He would be leaving soon, he said, and he pointed out his bus. It was an ancient Mercedes model, painted all over with red roses.

On my way to board it, more or less resigned to my fate and possibly thinking that a delay in reaching Mashad wasn't such a bad thing anyway, I passed two old men shuffling along up to the counter, real grey-beards with colourfully embroidered skull caps perched on their shaven heads. Both carried crooked walking sticks, and something big and shiny tucked under each arm.

I chuckled to myself and thought of a smiling, contented Murat back at the appliance store. 'Holy cow!' he'd have said. 'Those are my toetesters!'

TWENTY-THREE

In Gorgon that evening the scene outside the Pasdaran headquarters was a typical one. Glassed-in boxes contained photographs of those who were last to be martyred in the Iran/Iraq war. The pictures were yellowed with age, corners curled from the heat of day, many showing grisly details of mortal wounds.

No one stopped to look any more.

Further away stood another reminder of war. An armoured personnel carrier sat on the side of the road in a no-parking zone, its cannon swinging wildly with the antics of some children playing inside. Passing cars and pedestrians alike, on their way home, faced summary execution.

I went over to the iron railings outside the old conscription office. Set back from the road in the middle of a clump of trees, it was a wooden building partially damaged by fire. In the name of God, I wondered, how many thousands of men and boys had lined up here to sign on, flushed with pride at the honour of their task? Ayatollah Khomeini's brave Revolutionary Guards, delivered in droves to defend against, then attack, the heathen Saddam. How many were to return in an envelope to be stuck with a pin against the martyr's board?

I slept the night on the cool courtyard flagstones of a small mosque, thanks to the bearded old mullah who took me in. He was a fine, tough old man with a dried and salted look, dressed up in the loose brown raiments of his kind, with a string of brown prayer beads dangling from his wrist.

A few others were there, already asleep in the darkness, the down-and-outers of the area, and I lay down beside them at the base of a wall. Unfortunately, the price of this free accommodation was a sore back and a deafening wake-up call at five in the morning. The mullah's prelude to the call for prayer, magnified a hundred times through loudspeakers that hung down from the minarets, was like that of an amateur singer in a small-town variety show who makes sure the power is on by blowing hard into the microphone.

Still groggy with sleep, I left the mosque as others were arriving in the early light of dawn, and trudged slowly down to the railway station, stopping for a while to drink from a well and to wash my face with the cool spring water. The first rays of light fell upon my shoulders, surely the most soothing feeling there ever was. A few folk were about, mostly men on their way to the mosque, but they didn't take much notice of me, nor I of them. My mind was several hundred kilometres ahead of my body.

The station was empty. The solitary platform with its long grey stretch of tarmac and wooden seats looked abandoned and lonely. I sat down and rested my head in my hands, wondering when the train, any train, would be coming along. By midafternoon I mused, I could be in Mashad. And yet by the same token I could also be in Teheran. Gorgon was equidistant between the two, but I surprised myself by contemplating the capital as an alternative again. What was it about that place? What was drawing me back? Surely not just Hassan's invitation? It occurred to me that it wasn't just a case of being pulled back to Teheran, but of being pushed away from Mashad and all that it stood for: either the success of my plans and therefore subsequent peril to life and limb, or the fading of those same plans into nothing. Though I didn't fully realise it then, I was becoming increasingly torn between the two possibilities. Part of me wanted to get to Afghanistan desperately, the other parts were less sure and lived in fear of the consequences, whatever they might be.

It was not surprising then that my heart began to resign itself to a delay in the return to Mashad. And when after I'd been waiting most of the morning, a train for Teheran appeared at the platform, it seemed that here was a sign. I jumped aboard and found an empty compartment. Perhaps someone else 'up there' wanted me to go back, just for the time being. Perhaps 'they' knew something about the particular course that history was soon to take in Teheran, something which would shake the very foundations of the Islamic world. It wouldn't have surprised me if 'they' had contrived my detour, just so I would be there to witness the event: for the death of a leader is no trifling matter. Not when it is the glorious leader of the Revolution; the defender of the oppressed and the enemy of oppressors; the very nemesis of the Western world.

TWENTY-FOUR

The dream was vivid.

People were running, fear, anger, confusion on their faces. Some passed close by and unseen hands clutched at my clothes, pulling me down. I wanted to run too but someone gripped my arm. I saw his face, deeply lined, with eyes sad but penetrating. A long grey beard flowed down across his chest. He was speaking to me, but the words were a mumbled whisper. I tried to hear him over the shouting and crying – I watched his lips. One word was repeated, over and over. One word: *Engalep*. It means revolution. Suddenly the clamour increased, the visions swirled together into a blurred, roaring mass of confused outlines and colour, and above everything came the piercing scream of a woman in anguish.

I woke with a start, lost for a moment, until the familiar features of my room at the Demavand hotel came back into focus. In the corridor outside, a demented wail rose and fell like a siren. More voices joined in, low and comforting, while others were louder and issuing instructions. I dressed quickly, noticing that the sun had barely risen outside, before grabbing my old black camera bag and stepping out into the chaos.

The two men leaning against the wall eyed me intently, then

resumed their conversation in earnest. Towards the stairs a shadow of black chador had gathered round a hysterical woman whose screams were subsiding into a lowering moan. All hid their tear-stained faces as I passed.

Half way down the stairs I ran into the old cleaner who was up against the railing, open-mouthed and eyes wide, a radio clamped firmly to his ear.

'Ali, what's going on?'

He barely even noticed me. I touched him lightly on the arm.

'Ali! Tell me, is it something to do with Khomeini? Is he speaking?'

At the mention of his leader, sudden recognition flourished in his eyes and he lurched towards me.

'Khomeini! Ayatollah Khomeini! Mister Richard, this morning – one hour ago. They say we must remain in our homes. The Imam is dead.'

The news came like an explosion.

Caution politely suggested that I remain in my room, preferably under the bed, while curiosity sent me tearing off down the stairs. I wanted to find Mahmoud to hear the whole story but there was no one about; even the office was locked. Someone had already tied a thick black ribbon across a corner of the Ayatollah's portrait, and in such a hurry that the picture was left tilting to one side. It looked precarious, as if the slender string upon which it hung was symbolic of the government's present predicament. It wouldn't have taken much to send the whole thing crashing to the ground.

Out on the main street just up from the hotel it was obvious a great many people had refused to heed the radio broadcasts. The low sun was casting long shadows across the processions of Teherani who were solemnly passing by, taking up most of the street and footpath. Everyone wore black, from head to foot, except for the Pasdaran who wore black arm bands over their green military uniforms.

I found Mahmoud standing in the sunshine next to a parked car. He was smoking a cigarette and quietly watching. When he saw me his first words were full of scorn. 'You see how Teheran is full of sheep now, with no shepherd.'

He was right. The crowds were wandering about aimlessly,

not knowing what direction to take next. I noticed, however, that Mahmoud was wearing black like everyone else.

'It is wise,' he said, looking at my coloured shirt. 'Some of these people are already saying Khomeini was poisoned.'

'Who by?'

'The West of course: CIA, KGB or the English, it doesn't matter. Right now they need someone to blame. Iranian grief is hard to suppress.'

I asked him what he thought would happen and with his hands he described a large explosion. The word was being put around that certain moderates in parliament were already positioning themselves to take control, ridding the *majlis*, the elected assembly, once and for all of a central authority. If this were to happen the fundamentalists would be up in arms and it was hoped, by those like Mahmoud, that both sides would obliterate each other.

'And what about the body?' I asked.

'Maybe they take it to Qom. But if you're thinking of going there,' he said, no longer smiling, 'can I give you some advice?'

'Sure,' I said.

'Don't.'

And that was all he said. Qom was the undisputed heavyweight of fundamentalist thinking in Iran. It was Khomeini's city, and during the revolution a lot of blood had been spilt down there. Besides that, and the fact that the police had thrown me out of the city, someone had also once remarked to me that there were more mullahs in Qom than human beings.

'I think I'll just take a walk,' I said.

Mahmoud pulled out a strip of black cloth from his pocket and tied it round my upper arm. It was a poignant gesture, one which I was truly grateful for.

'Khorsh harlem,' I said.

'Good,' he said. 'Speak more Farci, especially now.'

And with that I stepped out onto the crowded footpath, one more mourner in a sea of turmoil.

A couple of hours later in another part of the city, the double-decker IranFord bus I was travelling in ground to a halt and a jostling horde surged through the open doors. The bus, like many, was segregated. Some of the men crammed into the front section while the majority went upstairs. The women had only the back half of the lower deck to squeeze into.

I was standing next to the metal bar which separated the sexes. A teenage girl sat near a window, pulling her black headscarf forward to try and conceal her face. Her eyes were red, and her cheeks glistening. Another woman, older and not as pretty, gazed sullenly at the floor as if she had just rowed with a husband. She was standing, and was loaded down with heavy luggage so that, on one occasion when the driver braked hard, her cases tumbled forward and caught an edge of her chador, pulling it free and rendering her naked in Islamic terms. With acute embarrassment she struggled to regain composure. Tears welled up in her eyes, and while a few women came to her aid, the men around me simultaneously ogled and 'tisk-tisked' their disapproval.

All these tears were very strange. For the past six weeks I had heard nothing but condemnation for Khomeini, sometimes expressed verbally, occasionally with a look of disdain and often with a resigned shrug of the shoulders. Their standard of living had certainly not improved under the Ayatollah's regime, although some might argue that it wasn't all that good under the Shah either. The Shah had built railway stations, post offices and airports, and brought cheap television into the Iranian home, all of which coincidentally served his purposes well; back then, so much of the money gleaned from the oil revenues had gone into the coffers of the military. The Ayatollah on the other hand had added little to this list of civic construction, but had 'saved the soul of the Iranian people' and put Islam and Iran on the map. Neither leader put any more bread on the table.

As I stood there taking all of this in, it came to my attention that enquiring eyes were pointed in my direction, flicking up from my old walking boots to my jeans and shirt. The black armband was clearly visible, but this seemed to draw their attention even more. It was time to get out, but before I could do so one young man suddenly stepped forward to block the way. Even worse, he started speaking to me in Farci. I understood, partially, something being said about the mountains. Perhaps my boots made him think I was a climber. So I smiled and nodded in a way the Teherani do when they least like to be talked to, a polite way of saying bugger off, because today of all days was the worst for being singled out as a foreigner on a crowded bus.

I had visions of being mugged by a gang of highly emotional, grief-stricken Iranians, but fortunately a bus-stop appeared and that particular scenario faded from view. With a suitably distraught look I made good my escape and walked away, safe from the pressure-cooker environment of the public transport, but not exactly alone. Behind me walked the one I had just sought to avoid. In the relative safety of the open I resigned myself to being found out.

'Salaam,' I said, turning round to face him and raising my right hand to the heart in the Muslim fashion. Instead of the expected tirade of accusations, however, he did the same and then stood there looking me as if he were trying to think of something to say next. He was young, tallish and darker than most of the folk from Teheran. He looked like a student and so I hoped he was an educated sort, not prone to mindless violence; nor was there any of the excitability and raw pride which came with fanatical student revolutionaries. In fact, I might have been mistaken, but he seemed to be actually smiling.

He broke the silence just then by asking in his own language where I was from. And when I told him England his face positively lit up with admiration.

'Hah!' he said, bursting with knowing conviction. 'BBC!'

The name of my new-found friend was Hussein. At nineteen he was having a crack at growing a beard and a few wispy hairs stuck out from his chin. He spoke no English whatsoever, although by this time my command of Farci was quite reasonable. In his eyes I was a BBC journalist – what other reason was there for a foreigner to be in Teheran on such a day of world importance – and he took it upon himself to act as my personal guide. The world would hear through my words and his, the truth about the death of the Imam, and his chest swelled with pride at the thought.

Our first port of call was to be his home, to meet his family and friends and to see how a real Iranian family were grieving. There was no possibility of refusing him; declining such an offer was not the behaviour of an ace reporter. Besides, he said it was only a short distance outside the city and so I went along.

What harm could come from a short visit to a local village, after all? In all probability it would be a fascinating experience. But a short while later, heading south at great speed in a taxi which Hussein had commandeered for the journey, I discovered the unfortunate truth. Our destination wasn't exactly a small provincial village at all. Nor was it located on the outskirts of Teheran. Home for Hussein was none other than the city of Qom.

The road south was full of cars, trucks, carts and people making their way slowly to the place where everyone expected the funeral to take place. Every bus was full as it trundled past; the travel companies were doing a roaring trade. Any conceivable mode of transport was being utilised in the great exodus to Qom.

We sped past the oil refinery on the right, puffing out orange plumes of fire from a tall chimney, followed by an enormous salt lake a short while later on our left; its furthest shores were lost in a blanket of heat haze. The road climbed and fell in almost a dead-straight line, so that at the crest of every low hill one could catch a glimpse of our unchanging path through the immense desert. We passed the odd oasis; roadside cafés where you could buy a glass of tea or a watermelon to eat in the shade of a palm tree. At one truck stop there was even a spouting fountain, bubbling over with wonderfully cool water which we collected by the gallon in plastic bottles. But it wasn't for drinking. Every fifteen minutes or so we had to stop and pour water over the engine to keep it from overheating. It was a long, hot, slow journey, to a place that was almost certainly better avoided.

Later that day, in the centre of Qom there was an almost deathly quiet. The noon heat had forced everyone indoors and a huge weight seemed to have settled over the city, squashing the life out of it. A single car came down a main street and passed us by before driving off in the direction of the shrine. In the front were two men, both wearing the white turbans and brown robes of the clergy.

From a radio somewhere above, a deep voice was reading a speech and I noticed Hussein was quietly listening.

I tapped him on the shoulder.

'Khomeini?' I said.

'Belli,' came the answer. It was a recording of a lecture from the previous year which celebrated the coming war against the forces of evil. I asked if Khomeini meant real war, with tanks, jets and soldiers, but Hussein looked surprised. 'What other kind of war was there,' he said.

The forces of evil, I hoped, did not include a simple traveller or a bogus BBC journalist.

We started walking.

'Would you fight in this war, Hussein?'

'Maybe,' he said. 'But now . . .' He looked perturbed, as if caught between what he should say, and what he felt.

I persisted. 'Now that Khomeini is gone, you mean?'

He stopped and looked up the street to where the mullahs' car was coming back our way. It turned at the corner where we stood, and as they swept past I could see the mullah in the front seat clearly. He was young and immaculately dressed, with a look of complete stoicism on his fresh face. But there was something else in the picture, something ominous. Down between the two front seats was the unmistakable shape of a Kalishnakov rifle.

Hussein's answer to my question was cutting.

'Do not be so sure he is gone.'

TWENTY-FIVE

That evening, with the coming of darkness, the forty-degree temperatures receded slightly and a breeze had sprung up to stir the branches over Hussein's house. It was a house like all the others, a two-storey concrete structure with a balcony at the front, all sliding glass doors and thin, billowing curtains, set behind a high brick wall. Earlier, Hussein's mother had greeted me through her veil, through a gap in the half-open front door. That was practically the last I saw of her. He had two younger brothers though, Ali and Sadeeq, and all four of us stood on the balcony in the freshening air. But the breeze also brought word of something else that was stirring in Qom. The sound was coming from Fatima's shrine. Over the rooftops, like the beating of a drum, came the steady chant of voices.

I asked Hussein if what I had read was true, that Shia Muslims believed the spirit of the Eighth Imam, Fatima's brother, journeyed here every Friday from his own shrine in Mashad to pay her a visit.

'When my father lived, he believed this. But he was a very good Muslim. He believed everything. Fatima-el-Masuma died on her way to see her brother, Imam Reza in Mashad. Now he comes to see her in return. This is what they believe,' and he gestured towards the shrine where the crowds were gathering. 'But I study at Teheran University and do not believe.'

He smiled at me in a sad sort of way. 'Therefore I am a bad Muslim.'

We decided to take a closer look at what was going on. Hussein lent me a black shirt and we walked the short distance to the shrine, through cobbled inner city streets illuminated by only the occasional streetlamp.

At the shrine a great mass of people were pouring in through the wide entrances. There was a lot of shouting and beating of heads, mixed with the shrill, ululating cries of the womenfolk. We joined the throng, nervously on my part, and were immediately sucked in past the great wooden doors leading on to the central courtyard. On the inside there was little or no room to move. The great body of mourners moved *en masse*, obeying a collective whim to be near the shrine.

We came to the pool at the centre, and there I lost Hussein. One minute he was by my side and the next he was gone. I looked around but was met only by a wall of unfamiliar bodies and faces that returned my furtive gazes with a look fast approaching suspicion. Finally I caught sight of Hussein about twenty metres away, standing by a wall. He had simply pushed his way out of the crowd, dealing with each human obstacle in turn, male or female, young or old, without looking back. Now he was gesturing for me to do the same. I attempted to follow his example, with some success, until all of a sudden a tremendous hue and cry erupted all around me. Arms were flailing, voices were upraised and a great company of men, of which I was an integral part, began to spin round with ever-increasing speed. Our momentum gained in force with every second and like a whirlwind our path weaved drunkenly about the courtyard, sucking onlookers into the fray. What had started out as a mini-whirlwind was now a full-blown tornado, whipping the crowd into a frenzy of emotion. Fearful of being exposed as a phoney, I danced about with the best of them until after several heart-thumping minutes, the circle broke up and the crowd dispersed. A few die-hards continued with the chest slapping and head beating, but they swirled off in another direction.

I found Hussein standing over where I had last seen him. 'What was that all about?' I said, still catching my breath.

He shrugged, apparently seeing nothing in the crowd's behaviour that was in any way strange.

Oh yeah, I thought. Just some of the guys having fun.

This self-flagellation, something which features strongly in the Shia Muslim faith, was no isolated incident. Later, back in Teheran, I would witness the rite being performed in the fullest heat of day by thousands of men, some of whom would die as a result of their actions.

By now it was becoming increasingly difficult to move, even as far from the shrine as we were. A constant stream of people was still pouring in through the doors. Hussein wasn't keen on staying longer either, especially after my brush with Shiadom, and so we escaped by the nearest available exit.

Outside, in the small garden that fronted onto the main entrances, we stopped to hear one aged mullah preach to his gathering congregation. He was typically sad and sombre, and there were few dry eyes in this quiet corner. Even the children were attentive, sitting amongst their parents beneath the trees, watching his every movement – the sway of his robes, the way he stroked his long grey beard. He looked to me like a rather forlorn Father Christmas. Out of curiosity I asked Hussein if he knew about the most famous man in Western civilisation.

'Who?' he replied.

'Doesn't matter,' I said, and we made our way back through the darkened streets to his home.

Dinner was already waiting on the floor when we strolled in at about nine. I was given a place against the wall with a cushion at my back, while a large oscillating fan in the middle of the room was switched on. It was a long, rectangular-shaped room which, apart from a kind of dresser at the far end and a few family photographs, was empty of furniture. There were pictures of Hussein, Ali and Sadeeq, but none of his mother, or his father who had recently passed away leaving Hussein in charge.

Ali, the youngest and only about eight years old, acted as a kind of go-between, carrying even more plates of rice, vegetables and meat in from the kitchen where his mother remained throughout. She did appear once to greet the guest again, but I managed to embarrass everyone including her by standing up. My showing of respect roughly translated into a desire to leave, and so I sat back down again quickly and tried, somewhat unsuccessfully, to explain the complexities of Western culture.

We finished eating and both Ali and Sadeeq dutifully began to clear up. In the kitchen a samovar was whistling, signalling the imminent arrival of tea. Hussein and I retired to a smaller room where a battered old black and white television set was sitting in the corner, pouring out pictures of agonised mourners from all over Iran. One minute we were in Tabriz, then we were in Mashad, and now we crossed over to Hamadan. Wherever the cameras pointed, there were people erupting into fits of hysteria. A huge number of Iranians were obviously in a state of genuine grief, but the authenticity of this sorrow was upset by the Oscar-winning performance given by the newsreader who appeared next on screen. With haunting music playing in the background, his words stuck in his throat, he failed to finish his sentences, tears streaming down his cheeks. On national television he cried out and slumped over his desk, weeping pitifully. It was laughable, even a little absurd – although seconds later the mood swung back to serious again when the first close-up pictures of a lifeless Khomeini were shown. Almost instantly these scenes were greeted with a sudden crash of glass and metal in the doorway behind us, and there was little Ali, who had just arrived carrying a tray, shaking uncontrollably; his eyes locked on what, for him, must have been the final reality of the Ayatollah's death. His mouth was open but no sound escaped; he just stood there, twitching.

Hussein acted quickly. He jumped to his feet, took his brother in his arms and carried him out, and at that moment the little figure erupted in a fit of screaming. For a quarter of an hour the house shook with the young boy's torment. Sitting in the room, I felt the rising heat and claustrophobia of someone caught in a domestic crisis. The television continued to spew forth pathetic scenes and weeping eulogies, but nothing on earth could have compared to that awful sound coming from next door.

I slept on the rooftop. The night was warm. Hussein had given me a thin mattress and a blanket, and I lay on my back gazing at the stars. Somewhere in the night a dog was barking and an angry voice floated across the rooftops. There was a sudden yelp and the barking stopped.

Against all previous reports, it had now been decided that

Khomeini would be buried in Teheran, in the cemetery devoted to the martyrs of the Iraq/Iran war. He would lie beside the bodies of those whose death he had precipitated. But for one day, tomorrow, his remains would be put on show in an open-air mosque called the Musallah, in the north of the city. Would I return there tomorrow, Hussein had asked. I'd told him yes. Sadly, he would not be able to join me. His duty to his family was greater than his duty to me, which of course was completely correct.

'It's a big event,' I had said, trying to make him feel better. 'The whole Western world will be watching.'

'Perhaps,' he'd said a little distantly. And then he had gone back downstairs, leaving me alone with my thoughts.

TWENTY-SIX

In Teheran the next morning, sombre black flags hung from almost every rooftop and from every window. The green of the city's parks was cast in shadow by the sheer number of these fluttering symbols of death. The morning papers were full of news of processions and displays of solidarity all over the country. The moderates in government were becoming edgy, although there was still no sign of the rumoured takeover.

Back in the hotel I was on the telephone immediately to Hassan. It took several attempts before I finally got through.

'Hassan, it's me, Richard.'

There was a slight pause that left me hanging mid-breath.

'You're back!' Hassan's crackly voice came down the line.

'Yes,' I replied. 'Can we meet some place?'

Another split-second pause that spoke volumes about what he was feeling and thinking. Had our friendship changed overnight with Khomeini's death? Was I now a liability to be kept at arm's length? I was relieved when he spoke again, sounding more like his old self. He proposed that we meet at the People's Park in an hour.

'I'll try,' I said, 'but the traffic is horrendous.'

'This is Iran,' he called back, and then the line went dead.

Hassan was waiting in his old 4WD jeep. The park was close to where he lived but it had taken me an hour and a half by bus. Many of the roads were blocked, diverting traffic along main thoroughfares. Nearly all the shops were shut; only essential services remained open. The numberless people still walked the streets, but now they had direction: the Musallah. Up there, the shrouded body of Ayatollah Khomeini was lying in state in a refrigerated glass box.

I climbed into the passenger seat.

'Nice day for it,' he said with a grin.

I was glad to see again that he showed no trace of fear or reticence about meeting me. In fact he was as eager to see the Musallah and the body as I was, and it was his suggestion that we tried to drive as close as possible, park the car somewhere safe and then walk the rest of the way in. He reached down under the seat and produced two miniature portraits of Khomeini, rather artfully drawn in black and brown pastel, which had come from a Pasdaran checkpoint up the road that morning, and he stuck both against the windscreen for effect.

We managed to get quite close before encountering a road block where a young but fully armed Pasdar stood on guard. Behind him, hundreds of people were making their way on foot to the gates of the Musallah. The Pasdar waved us on and down the next street, a smart residential lane with big trees and even bigger houses, where there was an empty block which had been turned into a carpark, I thought, just for the occasion. This turned out to be only partly true, for it was actually the spot where one of Saddam Hussein's missiles had landed, although instead of rebuilding, the ruins had simply been bulldozed over.

We parked. A few hundred metres further on were the main gates.

The Musallah had no structure as such, only a high wire fence, barbed at the top, forming the perimeter. Streaming through its wide entrances was an immense crowd, dressed all in black, filling the landscape, the streets, the footpaths, everything – a noisy, shuffling, vacant crowd.

Over their heads, roughly a stone's throw away, rose the platform that everyone had come to see, like an island in an ocean of black. At its edges stood the Pasdaran, Khomeini's protectors, apparently unarmed but looking down fiercely at the crush of mourners below. And in the middle, hoisted even higher, was the Imam, all in white, lying in a glass coffin within a much larger glass container.

Waves of people were pressing forward to get a better look. Many were passing out in the heat. Bodies were pulled out every few minutes and handed back overhead to the waiting ambulances. Nearly all were men who had lapsed into unconsciousness from the repeated slapping of heads and thumping of hearts. A few looked far worse. Apparently there had already been fatalities.

Water tankers were driving into the crowds, dispensing water from taps along the sides and spraying the people. Quite unexpectedly, we managed to hitch a ride on one, thanks to a number of journalists from the Islamic press. They had seen my camera and we were invited on.

The tanker edged into the crowd and took us up close.

I could see the unmistakable outline of his face, the grey beard, the white robes and the black turban on his chest, symbol of the Grand Ayatollah. Beneath the coffin, shrouded by a green curtain, a refrigeration unit pumped the glass box full of cold air. The curtain billowed and rippled in the breeze. Hassan nudged me.

'They will say a strange wind blew about inside, when there wasn't a breath of air outside. They will call it a miracle.'

'Who's they?'

'Peasants, villagers, nomads.'

Down below, the mass of people struggled forward to see their leader. Small groups closer to the platform exploded in frenzied bursts, while many individuals stood in a statuesque pose of silent grief: arms folded, heads bowed. Up until now the

Open-air mosque, Samarra, Iraq.

The Ayatollah Khomeini's funeral, Iran.

ما از مظلوم دفاع میکنیم و بر ظالم میتازیم

WE DEFEND THE OPPRESSED AND FIGHT THE OPPRESSOR

Revolution Square, Teheran, Iran.

Young girl, Panjumlang, Afghanistan.

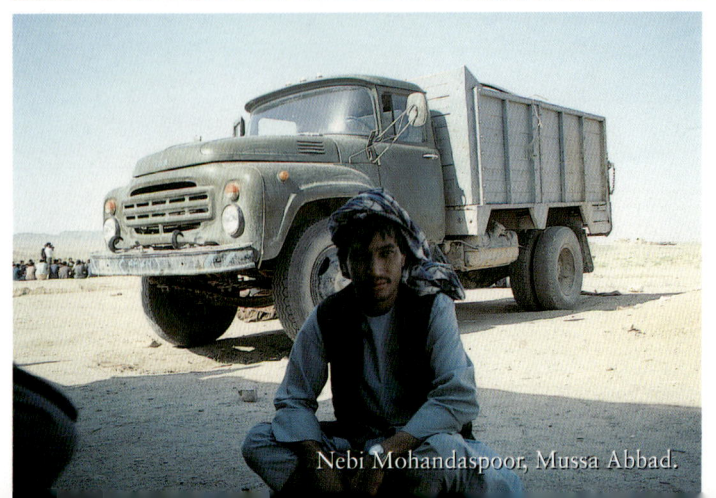

The author, Massoud Mohandaspoor.

Nebi Mohandaspoor, Mussa Abbad.

The long walk to Pakistan.

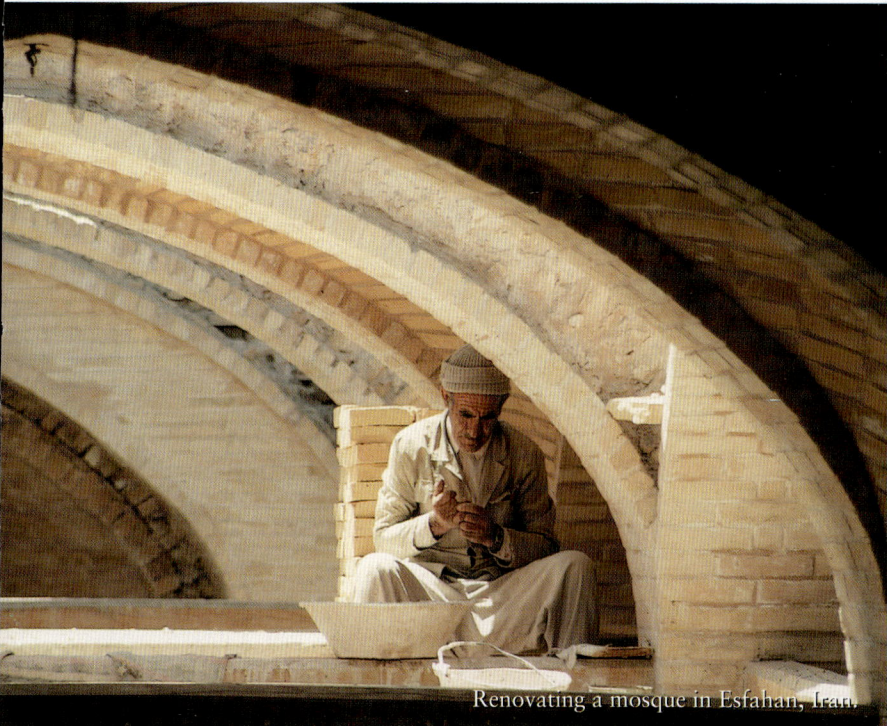

Renovating a mosque in Esfahan, Iran.

A make-shift mountain school, Afghanist

Herat, Afghanistan.

Members of Hezbollah, Mussa Abbad, Afghanistan.

Persepolis, Iran.

Herat, Afghanist[an]

Sangin, Afghanista[n]

On the way to Herat.

Mussa Abbad, Afghanistan.

Classroom in a rice field.

Herat, Afghanistan.

Anti-aircraft gun near Piesang, Afghanis[tan]

Gorgeh, Afghanistan.

My Himalayan home, Pasu, Northern Pakistan.

Tannoy system had played solemn music, but this was suddenly interrupted by a voice: deep, rumbling, familiar. Those who had so far managed to restrain themselves succumbed to the sound of Khomeini, and in a matter of moments there was hardly a dry eye in the house. The water tanker was pulling away, returning to the perimeter. The glass coffin grew smaller, and it struck me as a strange thing – almost mystical – to gaze upon a dead man's body, then hear his voice fill your ears.

The multi-storeyed Qods hotel where we went for an alcohol-free drink that afternoon was actually the old Hilton in Islamic disguise. Above the once-grand marble entrance it read: *God Oh God. Preserve Ayatollah Khomeini until the revolution of the 12th Messiah*.

The wish had always been bound to meet with disappointment, but at least it wasn't hostile. In Mashad, the sister hotel to this one welcomed its guests with a pleasant *Death to America*.

Hassan and I had gone there for a dose of Western life, partly because of the exhaustion that fundamentalism brings, but also because at the Musallah there had been a sudden invasion of helicopters, out of which had been hanging television cameras, and behind them fair hair, denim shirts, blue jeans and trainers. The newshounds had arrived, leaving me with a sort of shipwrecked feeling, like a marooned mariner who hopes the passing vessel will spy the smoke from his fire, but who then stamps the fire out for fear of being found and taken away from his tropical isle.

The hotel lounge probably hadn't changed since the fall of the Shah, though it was quiet now. The floors were covered in fine carpets, every table was set with damask napkins and the cutlery was highly polished. In fact, the only things that didn't gleam like new pins were the waiters. They were an untidy bunch who loitered about and seemed genuinely surprised to see us, as if customers in these parts were a great rarity. We sat near a window overlooking the empty pool outside and waited while one surly chap took our order. There was a kind of beer substitute on offer for those desperate enough to try it, as well as tea, coffee and an assortment of ice-cream flavours, although these we were told were 'off'. It was, according to the waiter, utterly disrespectful to the Imam to eat ice-cream on such a day. In the end we opted for tea, but his pen failed to work and he ambled off to find another. Ten minutes later there was still no sign of him.

We left the hotel and Hassan drove me back down to Revolution Street. I wanted to get some photographs of the processions but he was tired, so we arranged to meet back at his apartment that evening.

I also needed some more film and so I quickly ducked into the Demavand hotel. Mahmoud was looking bored behind the reception desk.

'Are you not marching today?' I asked jokingly on the way past.

He shook his head, smiled and turned over another page of his newspaper. It was one of the political dailies. I also noticed the portrait of Khomeini was once again straight and secure behind him. The fundamentalists in government may have been worried, but they were still holding on to power.

Upstairs, I collected the film and then hurried back outside.

The main roads were overflowing with men and women in black, carrying banners, flags and enormous portraits of the Imam. It was like standing beside a tremendous river, aware of the powerful flow but not really a part of it. I was content to walk along its banks.

At a crossroads nearby, a Christian church sat opposite an office of the Pasdaran. Both were surrounded by high brick walls and barbed wire, no doubt to prevent contamination from either party.

I left the crowds and took a shortcut through an alleyway to one of the bridges spanning Hafiz Street, where the view was good. The broad, four-laned avenue below me was taken up completely by the procession, and for a good mile or two in either direction there was nothing to see but a black ribbon of heads. Men on the left, women on the right, separated even in sorrow.

I watched the proceedings with a growing sense of confidence and security. The women passed below me in their ordered columns, voices raised in a sad but moving chorus, while small clusters of men occasionally burst out in full cry. Unwisely perhaps, I started taking pictures.

Minutes later and without warning, a strong hand wheeled me round to face a group of youths bristling with all the religious mania I had so far managed to avoid. People came rushing towards me. It seemed that they appeared from nowhere, out of the cracks in the pavement. The one who held me in his grip was much shorter than I, but thick-set. He wore a dirty brown cap and a black shirt buttoned up to the neck. His face was contorted with rage, and the veins stuck out from his temple.

'Passport!' he screamed.

I could see from their badges they were members of Teheran University's branch of Pasdaran. Not students, but young, stupid, militant types who make it their business to know everyone else's. The growing crowd around us shuffled its collective feet, sensing a fight.

'Passport!' he yelled again.

Feeling that the situation required all the tact and diplomacy at my disposal I simply told him, quietly and calmly, to bugger off. Naturally he didn't understand, which was probably just as well, but they seemed to think that I didn't understand them either. We glared at each other, not knowing what to do next. A few curses were uttered. I heard the word 'infidel' being spat out, but that was all. It was stalemate.

Then, quite surprisingly, the crowd began to side with me. One or two older men began to express their disapproval at the young Pasdar's actions. I was obviously a guest and had meant no harm; here was a day for peace! This was met with general approval by the majority of bystanders, and another man stepped forward and took me by the arm while the remonstrations continued. I could hear the young Pasdar arguing as I was led away to safety, his screeching voice rising above the others. He would have dearly liked to have seen me thrown over the bridge on the spot.

After that worrying incident, I decided that perhaps it was wiser to side with caution and retreat from the scene once and for all.

TWENTY-SEVEN

Tomorrow, said Hassan, as we sat in his apartment that night, Khomeini would be air-lifted to Behesht-i-Zahra, the Gateway to Heaven, which was the huge cemetery outside the city. He had made his first speech there after his return from exile in 1979. The cemetery had been a smaller place back then; now it sprawled.

Khomeini's dying wish was that all the next day, free buses would attempt to ferry the millions there for the burial. Then in time the site of his grave would be turned into a place of pilgrimage for Shia Muslims everywhere. A great shrine would be erected on the spot with a golden dome at its centre, visible for miles around. These were his plans and no doubt they would come to fruition, for even as we spoke, huge crowds were converging on the area.

But what happened next is history.

The crowds at the funeral could not be controlled. They broke through the barriers and tore the clothes from the body. What should have been a solemn burial turned into a disaster. And when, eventually, order was restored and the helicopter carrying the body managed to land, the government representative could say only a few words before a freight container was upturned and slammed over the grave, to stop the mourners from carrying away the earth.

When it was all over, it was hard to know whether to laugh or cry. Only then did I know why I had come back. Gone were the feelings of doubt and anxiety about the future; gone was the crippling indecision. The frantic activity of the past few days had left me feeling positively charged. I was ready for anything, all manner of trials, although perhaps not the morning of my departure.

I had said goodbye to Hassan at his apartment and was on the train to Mashad as it rolled out of the station, checking that my things were all in order, when a moment of sudden panic seized my heart. A rush of adrenalin coursed through my veins, my head pounded, and in that carriage there was heard a single cry of despair.

Horton!

I felt my pockets but they were empty. I searched through my bag. Nothing! I stood up and checked under the seat, along the aisle, under the feet of my fellow passengers, all to no avail. The privacy of the people didn't matter a damn; their discomfort was nothing compared to my grief. My elephant was missing.

There are few tragedies in life that can compare with the loss of a friend. Horton had been with me for years; he'd sat on my desk at work, drawing the admiring eye of many a passing secretary. We were a team. Masquerading as a marble paperweight in my office at JWT of Berkeley Square, he'd helped to write advertising copy for television, press and radio. He was no bigger than a ping pong ball, but he had travelled the wide world over and was an old soul – a trusted travelling companion. It hurt badly that he was gone.

TWENTY-EIGHT

The one or two days I had planned to be away from Mashad had by now stretched into a week. People were wondering what had happened to me. Some were even beginning to entertain the idea that somehow the Ayatollah's demise and my disappearance were connected. The word 'spy' was being whispered in shadowed corners. Luckily my return came just in time to call a halt to these suspicions.

Apart from this, life in the serai went on as it always did.

There were the usual processions of sellers bringing in their wares. The Afghan traders, still dirty from their recent desert crossings, stood around haggling over the price of their carpets.

'It is a quarter the age you say.'

'Fool!'

'Liar!'

'In the name of God, can you not tell a prayer rug that our grandfathers would have knelt upon?'

And so it went on and on, until some form of an agreement was reached.

My persistent search for an answer to the question of Afghanistan also continued – this time, however, with a much greater degree of success. On the same day that a detailed map of the country came into my hands, I received word of the location of a rebel group.

The source of the information was a big, grizzly man whose nefarious activities were said by many to include gun-running and drug dealing. He lived the life of a recluse up in the mountains near the border and rarely came into town. When he did, it was to see his brother who worked as a repairer in the serai, and it was through his brother that we met. The gun-runner told me where to find the headquarters of Hezbollah mujahedeen. I wasted no time.

Through the high-arched entrance way of the Hezbollah building there was an inner courtyard where men in flowing turbans and loose-fitting shalwar camise stood around with their hands clasped regally behind their backs. An old man interrupted his discourse with a youth to show me the way to the commander's office. Crowded corridors led off in several directions and a broad wooden staircase rose up on the left. Weary faces greeted me with curious stares but when I smiled in return, their immediate response was warm and friendly. All would place their right hand to their heart in the traditional Muslim greeting.

In a simple room at the top of the stairs the commander stood with his back to the open window, issuing instructions to an adjutant. Both men had long turbans that fell down their backs, and long black beards neatly groomed. The adjutant was dismissed. I kicked off my boots beside the door and entered.

Abdul Hashemi was head of the Mashad office. He had a long face with a shark's-fin nose, and was very busy. I explained briefly the reason for my visit and he listened politely, but with growing interest.

'You are alone?' he said in Farci.

'Yes.'

'Journalist?'

'No.'

He gestured for me to stay and then he left the room. I went over to the window and looked out at the railway station. Ironically, on my way to and from the station, I had passed the innocuous-looking building I was now in on several occasions without ever suspecting who dwelt within.

A few minutes had gone by before Abdul finally returned, followed by a man wearing glasses who was probably in his late forties. He was of slight build with greying hair. We shook hands and he surprised me by introducing himself in English, as Nasur Ahmad Najar, ex-schoolteacher from Herat, now helping to run Hezbollah affairs. He studied me curiously before asking why I wanted to enter his country.

He added, 'There are so many dangers.'

I repeated the reasons: the journey through Islam, my interest in Afghanistan, the mujahedeen, the book.

'Do you wish to become Muslim?' said Najar.

'No.'

'Then you are not coming to fight the Jihad?'

I told him no again and he shook his head gravely.

'You are a writer?'

'Of sorts,' I replied.

'And you realise that Hezbollah cannot guarantee your safety? What you are asking is a very difficult thing, difficult even for our people.'

'I understand completely.'

Again he tested my resolve, describing atrocious conditions and great risks, and just as calmly I reaffirmed my acceptance of those conditions. They were clearly impressed. The only person who was not, was me. My own coolness towards the threat of death was disturbing. It is one thing to be resolute while in a nice safe office, I said to myself, but quite another when looking adversity straight in the face.

My behaviour, however, seemed to meet with some approval. The conversation became increasingly positive. I could feel the balance tipping in my favour. It seemed that after all this time, after despairing on so many occasions of ever coming this far, my goals were about to be realised.

Abdul drew Najar to one side, speaking far too quickly for me to understand, although I soon learned that my request would be put to the Commander-in-Chief of all Hezbollah forces, Haji Qary Ahmad Ali. A decision would come quickly apparently, and so I went with Najar to his office and waited. For a time we talked about the years he had spent teaching at his small school in Afghanistan, before the fair-skinned, blue-eyed soldiers came and told everyone to go home. He recalled the lessons from over a decade ago and corrected the mistakes I made in Farci. But still, hours passed and nothing was heard. By the end of the afternoon I was beginning to lose hope of an early reply. Then, at about four o'clock, Abdul Hashemi reappeared suddenly at the doorway. He was clutching a pile of papers and seemed not to notice me sitting on the window-sill. He asked Najar to sign a hand-written document, then the two men engaged in a long and animated conversation which ended with Najar abruptly turning round to face me.

'So, do you still wish to go to Afghanistan?' he said.

I replied without hesitation.

'Good,' he said. 'You go in ten days' time.'

It was the beginning of the toughest and most rewarding experience of my life.

TWENTY-NINE

The final days in Iran went quickly. There was much to organise with Hezbollah, and the Afghan market near the shrine provided ample opportunity for buying a suitable disguise that would see me through Afghanistan: namely an olive green, long-sleeved, knee-length shirt and balloon-like trouser ensemble, the shalwar camise, plus a waistcoat and turban befitting an ordinary Afghani.

Many afternoons I spent with Najar, meeting for the first time those who would later become good friends – young mujahedeen with proud defiant faces and maturity beyond their years, and older men who chose to stay in the background, letting the curiosity of youth ask the questions.

Occasionally, however, one or two wise old veterans would stop me in the corridors and politely raise the subject of religion. A bony finger would stab at my chest.

'Christian?' they would ask.

I would nod and say, 'Farghat yek Khorda.' There is only one God.

Satisfied that the infidel wasn't a heathen believer in many gods, they would smile, roll their eyes to heaven and saunter off. I was impressed by their readiness to accept a non-Muslim. Infidel I was, but the word was not used in a derogatory fashion. It merely described someone of a different road. Far better that I should convert to Islam, they would say, but the most important thing was to have religion at all.

The Hezbollah commander-in-chief remained something of an enigma during this time. Word of his coming and going was never announced, which made it impossible for me to see him. I cornered Abdul Hashemi one day and asked him if he could arrange a meeting. He looked doubtful.

'Haji Qary is in Afghanistan. Perhaps, the day after tomorrow, he is in Mashad.'

Then he raised his hands in the habitual expression, God only knows.

The problem was that Hezbollah, although an important mujahedeen group, were small and their influence limited to the Herat area. From Herat city, where Hezbollah had their main base, I would have to walk the 600 miles to Pakistan. And to have a real chance of reaching Pakistan safely, I would have to contact a larger group – ideally, Jamiat-i-Islami.

Jamiat were liberal thinkers compared to some of the other groups. They weren't Islamic fundamentalists, they were Islamic moderates. An Iranian-style government installed in Afghanistan (as desired by Hezbollah), would not have suited them, nor their wealthy foreign backers. The royal families of Saudi Arabia and Kuwait feared another Iran in the neighbourhood. Consequently, Jamiat were well supplied with arms, equipment and money to keep them in the forefront of domestic affairs.

The difficulty, I perceived, would be in transferring between the two groups, when neither was especially fond of each other. The mujahedeen of Hezbollah were Shia Muslims. Those of Jamiat were Sunni. My hope was that once inside Afghanistan, the delicate negotiations could be achieved without alienating myself from either group.

Then, with just two days to spare, I came into contact with someone who would eventually have a great influence on my passage through Afghanistan.

Dr Seddiqi was a man who often mediated between the different factions. He had friends in high places. He was not an old man but his face was battered and impassive, like someone who had been through the wringer of life a few times. His office was a small white-washed room within a two-storey building, overlooking a mechanic's yard in a residential area near the shrine. Down below his window, the engine of an American Dream was being coaxed into life. The Great Satan wore dirty white-walled tyres, peeling red paint and ageing chrome. This strange brand of duplicity reminded me of the traffic police I had seen in Teheran, riding around on Harley-Davidsons.

Inside the office, an electric fan blew at the corners of Dr Seddiqi's paperwork and his elderly assistant quietly snoozed in a chair in one corner.

'The Jamiat commanders are in Teheran for another week,' he said. 'But the respected leader of the Harrakat group is a close friend of mine. He is in Afghanistan now.'

On a sheet of headed paper he began writing.

'His name is Hossein "Chok" Gharmani and you will find him in a village called Raydan.'

From the top of a filing cabinet he took out a framed photo of a sturdy-looking man with streaks of grey running through his flowing hair and beard. He pointed these features out for me to remember him by.

'Give him this letter and he will help. He is well known and liked in Herat, and has friends in many groups, including Jamiat-i-Islami.'

Dr Seddiqi raised a cautionary finger. He had one more important piece of advice. I should have nothing to do with any mujahedeen from Hesbe-i-Islami, he said. There were some there who would betray me to the government, because the government paid good money for Western writers and photographers found in Afghanistan. It was the only way they could substantiate their claims that foreign intelligence agencies and mercenaries were busy exploiting the war.

Dr Seddiqi's warning was a valuable reminder of the rebel group who were notorious for changing sides and turning their guns on their allies, usually in return for favours from the government. The incidents involving Hesbe-i-Islami were generally responsible for reports in the Western media of disunity amongst mujahedeen forces.

I slipped the letter into my shirt pocket and he got up from his desk to see me out.

THIRTY

Far from being quiet and restful, my last night in Iran was full of surprises. There were a great many friends at the serai to thank and sadly, say farewell to. But when this was finally done, Farid met me downstairs at the entrance and with a mischievous grin, announced that we were going to a special party.

'This night,' he said, 'we are going to be free men. We shall be *Darveesh*!'

With that curious statement, he grabbed my arm and we hurried through the dimly lit back streets, emerging several minutes later opposite a small park.

We waited inside the gates. Two men appeared suddenly and began walking towards us. They were both middle-aged, clean-shaven and tidily dressed in long-sleeved shirts and Western-style trousers. One had a jacket folded over his arm. I noticed it was roughly patched with odd coloured material in several places. Their shoes were also scuffed and worn. They reminded me of past wealth that has slid into poverty.

Behrouz and Davood were indeed two men down on their luck. With hardly two rials to rub together, they had long ago joined the ranks of the Dead-eaters, feeding off an age-old Iranian custom. A family remembered their dead with a feast, given on the same day each year, for the friends and relatives of the deceased. The announcement of a *Surr*, as it was called, was occasionally printed in the papers, but like other Dead-eaters these men relied upon their own lists, compiled over the years. They had been dining out on the dead for so long, an evening meal could be found any day of the year.

'And tonight?' I said to Farid. 'Is this the big party?'

He nodded.

'But what if they find out I'm not even Iranian?'

The thought of walking into someone's home and sitting down to dinner seemed crazy, even dangerous.

Farid remained confident. The *Surr* would be very big and full of people. We would walk in, eat and leave. He told me to think of it as an opportunity to see a unique side of Iranian life. '*These people are Darveesh!*' he exclaimed.

Behrouz and Davood were looking at me impatiently so with Farid in the lead and following his nose, we made our way to a nearby house protected by an ivy-covered wall. A flickering tube of neon hung over the arched entrance. Inside, there was an inner courtyard ablaze with electric light. It was crowded, but what people! There were men in brilliant white, ankle-length robes with black and white chimney-pot hats on their heads. Their hair was long and plaited, while the older ones had beards to rival any Ayatollah's. In the bright lights of the courtyard, it appeared we were entering into the company of celestial beings.

Behrouz and Davood showed no signs of hesitation and walked straight inside. Only Farid stopped to whisper last-minute instructions.

'*Darveesh* are followers of Ali. They say, "Ya'Ali!" Don't say anything else, OK.'

Upon entering, we were greeted by a member of the family and escorted to a low, carpeted platform at the back of the courtyard. Amongst the seated bodies of men, the familiar figures of Behrouz and Davood were already huddled round a large wooden bowl, hungrily scooping up a thick stew with pieces of unleavened bread.

Comfortably seated on the rugs and with our shoes nearby, a full and steaming bowl was also placed between Farid and I. It was a delicious *Khoresht* stew which, like the others, we ate quickly and without a word being said. Afterwards, tea was brought and we moved aside to make way for other guests. When it was possible to talk privately and not be overheard, I asked Farid if he knew who the feast was for.

'That man over there,' he whispered, pointing to a black and white photograph. The face was old and strong, a patriarch's, with long, seemingly unkempt hair. Beside the picture, several more of the robed *Darveesh* were gathered in a group, listening respectfully to the words of a very old and fragile-looking man who bore a slight family resemblance to the one in the frame. He was, apparently, a brother.

The group broke up and after a short while, he began to make his unsteady way into the crowd. Immediately the noise in the courtyard ceased, bread was put down and people got to their feet. He went slowly, carefully, and shook the hand of each guest in turn. He came to me, took mine and held it for several seconds.

'Ya'Ali,' I said respectfully.

He nodded, with eyes downcast, then spoke a few words in a low, murmuring voice. I didn't understand, but there was no need to reply. I stayed silent and he released my hand.

Shortly afterwards, Farid signalled it was time to go.

Walking back along the dark street, he explained that those few words had been a blessing, the bestowment of good fortune and God's favour. What puzzled me most was why he had picked me out.

'You're going to a war zone, my friend,' he said. 'You will need it.'

True words. I needed all the heavenly favours possible, and certainly a few more lives than are usually available for the average mortal. But there was something else, a niggling premonition that caused me to feel they would be needed sooner than expected.

I waved goodbye to Farid and continued the rest of the way to my hotel alone, deep in thought over the future. I started to cross the road. There was the hotel in front; they were about to lock the doors. I ran. There was a screech of tyres, and in that same moment a giant battering ram hit me hard in the side.

The shock was so great, so unexpected, that I lay on the road for a full minute, watching two red lights and a licence plate accelerate away. I thought they might have stopped, but they didn't. Perhaps they were scared of trouble. Perhaps they were drunk. It seemed to take a long time before the tail lights disappeared into the night.

I had been more than just a little lucky that night. I had escaped with only a few scratches and a bruise on the back of my leg the size of a football, but there was no doubting that my injuries should have been much worse. But for my legs having folded beneath me, absorbing the impact of a glancing blow, it would have been a different story. The blessing had come just in time.

Back in my room, I discovered that one of my lucky shells had been crushed in the fall. Three shells tied together, three pieces of good fortune. Now there were only two.

THIRTY-ONE

A fortnight before leaving England, I had rung my mother in New Zealand. She had wanted to send over a gift, something useful, she had said. A Saint Christopher medal perhaps?

On the spur of the moment I asked her to go down to the beach and to select three shells.

She laughed.

'You're sure?' she said.

'I'm sure.'

'Just three?'

'Three will do.'

The three cockle shells arrived a week later. Each one had been drilled through with a pin, and a slim piece of yellow wire tied them neatly together. Attached was a note which read: *Magic shells. Three. Keep safe. Use sparingly. Guaranteed to last a lifetime.*

As a joke of sorts, they came to represent three pieces of luck. A life for each. When she found out she was mortified.

'You never told me. Three lives! Only three!'

I left England soon after this.

Two weeks later in Istanbul, a letter was waiting from my girlfriend. Apparently my departure had been closely followed by the arrival of a whole shoebox full of cockle shells.

THIRTY-TWO

The early morning was clear and cool but certain to heat up before long. I had washed in the *Hamam* across the street and was standing by the open window of my hotel room, wearing the shalwar camise and turban of an Afghan.

Spread out on the bed were my possessions. An old khaki bag – patched and dirty but light and easy to carry, my journal, a knife, the map, my camera and my lightweight poncho. Of my own clothes I kept only the T-shirt and a pair of underpants. The inside pockets of my waistcoat held the few remaining effects: toothbrush, soap, passport and money. I had six thousand Afghan rupees. More than enough, I had been told, for several months in Afghanistan. At the current rate on the black market, it was less than twenty US dollars.

In the courtyard at Hezbollah, there were at least a dozen heavily bearded mujaheds standing around looking extremely tired and drawn. Their clothes, hair and skin were covered in a fine, chalk-coloured dust from the desert. In one corner, a few had washed and were kneeling in prayer, their *patou* spread out beneath them as a prayer mat. Others had wrapped themselves in these light, all-purpose blankets to ward off the morning chill and stood with their hands clasped behind their backs, prayer beads dangling from fingers, looking for all the world like sombre clergy. Nejah was nearby and I asked him what was going on.

'These men came from Afghanistan last night. They are brave mujahedeen who have fought for many months in Herat and will now rest in Mashad. Soon you will be going with others to take their place.'

'How soon will that be?' I asked.

He looked vaguely at his watch. Either he didn't know or he wasn't telling. After a moment he said, 'In a few hours.'

It was such a harmless statement, but my time in Iran had taught me not to trust it. Words like these sharply illuminated the gap between our respective cultures. In the West, time is a constant thing. Here, it was only a notion. Accept 'in a few hours' and you may find yourself waiting for days. Conversely, you may also be called upon to move like the wind only minutes later.

'Come,' said Nejah. 'There is someone you should meet.'

We went upstairs to where the sunlight was streaming in. Sitting on the floor in Najar's office was a mujahed who had evidently been waiting for us. He was not a large man but he had about him an aura of great fortitude. His hair was longer than usual, black as coal. He had eyes dark like a hawk's, the kind that are most difficult to read but seem to observe everything.

Nejah spoke first with a string of Afghan greetings.

'Salaam Aleikum Nebi. Chitouri? Monda nabashi. Zenda bashi. Jon jorasti?'

The mujahed rose to his feet, hand on heart, replying with equal graciousness, before turning and exchanging a similar salutation with me. In the native Afghan language of Dari, there were many such expressions reserved for various meetings, either between friends or strangers, and a simple greeting could sometimes be longer than the actual conversation at times. A passerby might enquire as to your health and that of your family, wishing you long life, a tireless journey and many children in the process, before asking for the simplest directions.

'Nebi is one of the group leaving with you today,' said Nejah. 'He will be there to help you in Herat.'

I thanked Nejah and then repeated my appreciation to Nebi in Farci. He nodded and smiled, showing a set of very white, straight teeth. His face bore traces of Mongol ancestry: the high cheekbones and up-tilted eyes. His skin was smooth and darker than most and at a guess, I reckoned he was about twenty-four.

At that moment precisely, there was a loud clamouring in the stairwell outside, running feet and chattering voices.

Somewhere down below the window an engine was being revved. The smile on Nebi's face vanished and he sprung towards the door, sweeping my bag up from the floor in the same fluid motion.

'Bia!' he cried. 'Come!'

There was no time. I slapped on my boots at the doorway and managed only a hurried farewell to Nejah before charging down the stairs. A white pick-up truck was fast moving out of the courtyard and both Nebi and I threw ourselves at the vehicle, much to the delight and encouragement of the handful of mujahedeen already huddled in the back. Some of them I knew by name, a few by face only. They were a mixture of all ages. The youngest was no more than sixteen; the oldest a grey-haired man with laughing blue eyes set into a wrinkled smiling face. As we raced through the streets heading for the open road, he repeatedly jabbed his finger at me and then in the direction we were travelling, heartily shouting against the roar of wind and machine.

'Jang! Jang! To war! To war!'

Now there was no turning back.

For several hours we hung on in the back as the countryside flashed by. The road climbed, then dipped into narrow valleys. Hills and mounds were smooth and covered in tufts of brown grass. Watercourses here and there flowed down away from the road and dwindled to rivulets a couple of inches wide.

Just before the border town of Tayebad, we forked right off the tarmac and headed south-east along a dirt track that ran parallel to a rocky escarpment. The ground was dry and open with hardly a tree in sight, and there were hawks riding the thermals overhead.

Not far to the right, we passed a few small houses and a sad-looking mule tied to a stake outside, but no sign of the owners. The windows gaped dark and empty. A mini-whirlwind of dust swept on by. The owners, if they were at home, preferred not to see or be seen: 'Them that asks no questions isn't told a lie. Watch the wall, my darling, while the Gentlemen go by.'

Sight of the buildings was lost when the road dipped down onto a rocky river bed. It was deeply rutted in places with the tyre marks of heavy vehicles, no doubt belonging to Hezbollah.

The high river banks could safely conceal the passage of their illicit border crossings, by day or night. However, around noon when a sufficient distance lay between ourselves and the main road, we left the protection of the river bed and took to the higher, faster ground of the open desert. Turbans were wound round faces, leaving only the eyes visible, as protection against the immense clouds of dust that consumed us whenever we slowed. Everyone kept quiet. Talking was a sure way of collecting an unpleasant mouthful of grit.

More hours passed and our journey seemed to be endless. We veered right then left, then right again, occasionally swerving wildly to avoid the deeper ruts. A mountain range loomed ahead in the distance, coming ever closer, and it grew apparent that we were aiming for a saddle between the two highest peaks. It had to be our destination; there was no other gap in the range for us to pass through. I nudged Nebi in the ribs.

'What's that?' I asked.

'Mussa Abbad,' he stretched out his arm towards the pass, then flopped his wrist to indicate a valley on the other side.

'Iran?'

He shook his head.

'Afghanistan?'

This time he smiled broadly and, nudging me back, said, 'Yes!'

It was early evening when, at last, we stopped before the foothills, although any thought of rest was dismissed when the others jumped down and set off at a cracking pace. Only Nebi walked slowly, unperturbed that we weren't keeping up. I glanced back to see the rear lights of our pick-up speeding away across the desert and was just about to say something when, only fifty yards away, a large vehicle gradually began to appear, piece by piece, from its netting of desert camouflage. Where only desert had been before, there was now a Russian troop carrier, army green and open-topped except for the driver's compartment.

It felt like an initiation into the clandestine operations of war: the art of concealment and subterfuge. But it also brought home the fact that other, more chilling initiations waited over the border.

The Soviet troops had withdrawn long ago, yet the war continued unabated over those hills. Afghan versus Afghan, with the rebel mujahedeen united in their hatred of the communist government forces and their former Soviet backers. But whereas before there had been real enemies and real targets, now the sides were less well defined – the ultimate consequence of any civil war.

Only the ambitions of these mujahedeen remained clear. Their conviction was set in stone. The goals for their country – the eviction of all communism and a return to an Islamic state – were unchanged. If they hid their vehicles, their supplies and ammunition, it was out of necessity, but an unwavering strength of purpose was etched into their faces.

Our journey for the rest of that evening and through the night was taken at a punishing speed over difficult terrain. We couldn't see in the dark, but the impact of hitting the hidden ruts and ridges that criss-crossed our path was certainly felt. The further we went, the higher we climbed, the more it seemed likely that bone as well as metal would not survive. Within half an hour my hands were cut and bleeding from gripping the rough iron sides of the troop carrier.

With some difficulty I noted the position of stars and watched the spiral of the heavens. Orion rose up, then the Pleiades, and both began their long march across the shimmering void. All the while not a murmur of complaint was heard from anyone. Even the engine never missed a beat, though it was subject to such abuse that it was impossible not to admire the Russian engineering that could make such a machine.

In time, the wide saddle between the twin peaks was reached and the way became a little easier. Behind us the land dropped away onto the broken flats somewhere below, while up ahead it lifted towards a dark ridge silhouetted against the night sky. Afghanistan beckoned, but it was Nebi who pointed to a group of flickering lights half a mile in front that signified the presence of a new threat.

He rapped hard upon the cab roof and our speed reduced to a crawl. We had no headlights and a stiff wind was blowing in our faces. Whoever it was, they wouldn't have seen or heard us yet.

'Pasdaran!'

Someone behind spat the word out with disgust. Evidently no one had expected to see any border patrols.

Our path was altered to detour round the camp, and many anxious moments were spent waiting for a flare or some sign of activity. The lights grew closer and it was possible to make out the faint outlines of a small building and a few tents. There was no movement. Either they were asleep or not at home; either way we did not intend to call in for a visit. Gradually the camp drew level. We crawled ahead obscured by the darkness, inching our way to safety; the engine hissed as if in contempt of those who would have tried to stop us, and before long the lights were left behind.

Now everyone could relax again. Now we were close. Conversation became refreshingly euphoric as we drove through the remaining hills and descended down into a wide, flat valley. The air was cooler and suddenly sweeter, away from the claustrophobic atmosphere of the pass. High above, the sky was brilliantly clear and full of stars, and a three-quarter moon, newly risen, hung low above the distant mountains. An occasional firefly shot past leaving a streak of red in its wake.

In front of me, Nebi spread his arms out wide.

'This,' he said proudly, 'is Afghanistan!'

Somehow, by some trick of moonlight, the land had transformed. I studied the resolute faces that eyed me intently and recognised that, in a way, they also had changed. Having crossed the border they had finally come home. This was their land and theirs alone. The change was not without, but within.

I drifted back again, and focused upon the figure of my smiling friend.

'Massoud Mohandaspoor!' said Nebi. 'This is now your Afghan name. Mohandaspoor is the name of my family and Massoud, my brother.'

High overhead, the fireflies became brighter and bolder. And suddenly they weren't fireflies at all, but tracer bullets cutting a lethal arc across the vast Afghan sky.

It was true. Nothing would ever be the same again.

THIRTY-THREE

The Hezbollah fort sat on top of a barren hill just a short distance inside the Afghan border. It was a low, flat-topped, single-storey building made of dried mud mixed with straw. It had two bare rooms, the largest of which we had collapsed in to sleep that night on the floor. Unfortunately, dawn came quickly and with it the morning prayer. I awoke with a start to the sound of someone bellowing in my ear.

'Massoud. Bia! Namoz, namoz.'

Without knowing it, I had fallen asleep across the mihrab, the arched recess set into the wall that points to Mecca and the direction in which all Muslims must turn to pray. The mujahed's alarm was because I was not only preventing the first prayer of the day, but my slumber was a slap in the face to the faithful.

I got up immediately, muttered my apologies and stumbled outside in time to witness a magnificent sunrise. We were enclosed in a long, bowl-shaped valley about five miles wide and running east to west. There were no trees, just desert rock and mountains coloured red with the rising sun. From the same direction, as if all good things come from the east, a strong, cool wind whipped the material of my shalwar and blew away the last remnants of sleep. I stood transfixed, feeling the incredible space spreading away from me, sensing the absence of boundaries, a land unlimited.

Kneeling on the open ground on my right, a small group of men were bowed in concentrated prayer, ironically with their backs towards the sunrise, facing west to a distant Mecca. They were suddenly armed now as well, their Kalishnakov rifles close to hand, safety catches on but with a bullet ready in the breech.

The guns Hezbollah possessed had nearly all been captured from the enemy at some point in time. Even the ammunition had been seized from raids on government posts. Over the years they had built up a sizeable cache of weapons that were hidden in various places, mostly in the mountains nearby. Later it was hinted that we might be collecting them on our way out to Herat, but when I asked if this might be soon, no one could tell. Only Nebi seemed to have an inkling and his advice was to stay close. This fort was obviously a staging post and a hasty departure could come at any time.

Nevertheless, I decided to go for a short walk that morning to better acquaint myself with my surroundings. I set off over a short plateau of hard earth before dropping down onto a path that wound its way up and over a series of low hills. The land was dotted with a grey-green tufty grass, but no other vegetation. At one stage I passed the twisted and rusted remains of an old truck, which looked as though it had been turned inside out with the force of some subterranean explosion. The chassis was bent upwards through the roof, the front axle was where the front seat should have been, and the engine was half buried in the sand twenty paces off to the side. Later, I would discover that this was what a land mine could do to strengthened steel.

Another track led down further onto the valley floor, then forked right towards the western edge of the mountains and the Iranian border. In the distance there were two tall structures barely visible, which might have been Pasdaran watch-towers, but as the sun rose higher, the coolness of early morning disappeared and the beauty of the valley at that early hour was gradually hidden behind a shimmering heat haze. The wind too became hot and dry, bringing with it the unmistakable dusty smell of the desert. I retraced my steps and eventually returned to the fort, leaving my boots on the pile outside the weather-beaten wooden door.

In the large room where I had slept the night they were nearly all there: the young, the middle-aged, the old, sitting cross-legged against the walls, drinking tea and talking, or peering into pocket-size mirrors and taking a comb to their sizeable beards. The rest manned look-out stations on the roof, and further afield were anti-aircraft guns pointing towards the mountains and Herat. Our small band of new recruits had brought the fort's contingent to about thirty men, though there were some who would soon be going back to Iran for a rest. They were the quiet ones, immediately noticeable for their familiarity with the weaponry. Their often sober manner spoke volumes about the hardship of life in Herat.

At the far end of the room, sitting with a group of older men who wore turbans of a bright white silk-like material, was Nebi. He stood up, smiling as I approached and asked politely where I had been. I pointed out the place.

'By the truck,' I said.

He made a chopping movement against his shin, just below the knee. The message was crystal clear. Some of the paths were also mined.

I bent down to each man in the group, shaking their hands warmly and uttering the traditional salaam of greeting. They were all smiles and graciousness, but the last man even paid me the honour of standing up. It was Nasur Ahmad Nejah.

'So,' he said in English. 'You're called Massoud now.'

He was grinning from ear to ear and shaking my hand furiously. He had come via a different, but no less difficult route in the night with the Hezbollah Commandant, Haji Qari Ahmad Ali, the man I had yet to meet. I mentioned this to Nejah and he laughed. Apparently I just had.

Our group had appeared as an informal gathering up until then. Now it slowly dawned on me that this wasn't entirely the case. We were positioned in a rough semi-circle around the man on my right who was leaning forward slightly, resting an elbow on his knee, thoughtfully stroking his thick black beard with large, meaty fingers and listening to one of his commanders. Some years ago his left arm had been completely blown off, but he was still a big man, with a full, fleshy face. His shalwar camise was dark blue; his waistcoat a pale fawn. When he spoke, it was with the quiet, confident air of leadership.

Presently he got to his feet and we all stood up as he left the room, followed immediately by an entourage of heavily armed men who had been sitting by the door. Unfortunately, because there was much that I wished to discuss with him, it was the last

I would see of him for some time. Just then, Nebi signalled for us to depart too, but Nejah interrupted and took my arm.

'Dr Seddiqi asked me to give you this,' he said, opening his hand to show a small vial of scented liquid. 'It is Muhammadan – very agreeable to Muslims. Use it when you meet with senior commanders to ask their help in reaching Pakistan.'

'When did you see him?' I asked.

'Yesterday, just after you left. He was very sorry he missed you.'

'I am sorry also.'

'He also said to tell you, do not forget the Harrakat leader, Houssein Gharmani.'

I put a hand to one of the inside pockets of my waistcoat. Dr Seddiqi's letter was still there.

'Don't worry,' I said. 'I won't.'

We wandered about for most of that first day, keeping to well-worn paths and avoiding those which were smooth and unmarked. Nebi showed me where the toilets were: a narrow ravine with plenty of stones to keep clean with, and the location of the target range, where the empty rounds from the anti-aircraft guns were lined up on the crest of a ridge. The two were uncomfortably close to each other. Obviously there was nothing like a stray bullet to get the bowels moving. But in the late afternoon everyone gathered to watch the test-firing of a home-made rocket launcher. The device – which was half Russian design, half Afghan – consisted of a single metal tube welded onto a bulky tripod. It looked highly unstable, if not downright dangerous.

Here, a veteran mujahed named Haiden Seiah came fully into his own. Whereas most of the Afghans were of average height, this fellow stood well over six foot tall and could carry the weapon easily upon his shoulders. He set it down outside and began adjusting the sights and carefully taking aim, concentrated, competent, attentive to every detail. Once in a while his voice would rise above the hubbub of other voices, yelling for this or that. Someone would run off and return with a tool, only to be severely chastised for taking too long or bringing the wrong one. Finally he announced with a heavy sigh and a shake of his head that he had done all that could be done.

The three-foot long missile was gingerly carried over by two men and then slowly inserted into the tube. Two wires attached to the firing mechanism were unwound to a distance of no more than twenty feet. Quite incredibly, torches were emptied of their power source and the batteries – six in all, with Russian labels – were lined up, end to end on the ground. A final 'all clear' was given. In the hushed silence, Haiden Seiah touched the wires to the connected batteries.

Nothing happened.

He rearranged them, checked that the points of contact were good and touched the wires again. There was an embarrassing silence, after which the only explosion was his voice.

'Bring more batteries!'

After some frantic searching they were duly delivered, but several more unsuccessful attempts were made and the crowd began to lose interest and drift away. The occasional mocking laugh was heard but Haiden Seiah took no notice. Engrossed in his task he carried on looking for the cause of the failure, connecting and reconnecting the wires and arranging the batteries. In due course I also retired to a safe distance, looking for rest in the shade of a long, low wall. But it wasn't to be. A split second later, a sudden deafening explosion sent a rushing wall of desert rocks and dirt hurtling down upon me. I saw little else, momentarily blinded by the dust, but in my mind was the ugly thought that Haidan Seiah was no more. We located the rocket launcher first, upside down in a hole – a little dented but in one piece. Then as the clouds of dust blew away we found him also: very much alive, still holding a wire in each hand and looking very pleased with himself. It had finally worked. The blast had only been from the force of the backfire. Ten or fifteen seconds later, several miles away on the other side of the valley, a single billowing cloud rose silently into the air. According to the jubilant Haidan Seiah, it was bang on target.

Afterwards the group scattered and the rocket launcher was dragged out of the hole to be put back on its feet. Having passed the test it would be taken to Herat city to join the ranks of single and multiple launchers Hezbollah professed to own. In this comparatively quiet corner of Afghanistan, within just two or three miles of the Iranian border, it was difficult to imagine what Herat would really be like. Here the demonstrations of firepower were entertaining, the streak of tracer fire across the night sky almost beautiful, and I deluded myself into thinking the threat of war was a long way off. Only when night eventually came again was the reality of our situation brought sharply home by the not-so-distant thump of helicopters across the valley.

The evening meal of bread and stew had been eaten, and the last dregs of the tea poured out and drunk, when the lamps were extinguished and waistcoats were taken off and folded into pillows. I did the same and stretched out on the hard floor, this time clear of the mihrab in the wall. But within half an hour any thought of sleep was forgotten when the helicopter gunships arrived in the area. There was nowhere to hide, nothing to do except lie there, listening as the wind brought the deathly sound of their presence in waves. It came close and then faded away, close and away. Putting away my fears I tried telling myself that the time was still early, and that the pilots had not the moon's help. The earth of our hiding place was that of the surrounding desert, difficult to see even in daylight. But as the night drew on, the heavy chattering of rotor-blades became the howl of an animal. Alive and sinister, they were beasts without shape, prowling for a kill in the darkness.

THIRTY-FOUR

Over breakfast next morning the talk was subdued from so little sleep. The enemy had passed us no more than half a mile away at one stage, although after that they luckily had not returned. We ate the bread and drank the sugary tea with only the occasional word to one another. Afterwards, many retreated to a quiet place to try and snatch a few hours' rest, but it was already hot and the flies had arrived to do their worst.

A young mujahed dressed all in white came in with a bandolier slung over his shoulder. He carried a heavy machine-gun in one hand and a grizzly old ginger tom in the other. Both he set down in a corner. The cat limped because its left front paw was missing.

I asked him if the cat was his.

He nodded, and began dismantling the gun for oiling while the cat looked on. The incessant buzzing of flies was joined only by the sound of his movements.

'What happened to its leg?' I said.

Without looking up he said, 'Kartoos.' This was probably a well-worn conversation.

'Someone shot your cat!'

He shrugged. The flies buzzed. The cat licked its remaining paw. I tried to attract its attention and it looked at me, as if to say, take a hike pal. The animal was in no need of sympathy.

'Hey cat!' I said.

It was fun to speak English again, to hold a conversation which no one else could understand. And besides, it helped to pass the time, as well as to relieve some of the tension from the night before.

'We had a family cat once, she was called Snookums.'

'Is that right,' the cat seemed to reply, pausing mid-lick. 'Sounds like a damn silly name to me. Handle herself in a fight, could she?'

'Not really.'

'Caught her own meals?'

'Never,' I replied.

'Slept on a nice cosy blanket too, I suppose?'

'All day and every day.'

'Yup,' said the cat derisively, 'I knows the type.'

No one seemed to mind or even notice this slight show of insanity. The fact that the *feringhi* spoke to animals was treated with casual indifference. Such oddities were undoubtedly par for the course in Afghanistan. Although the old ginger tom did come and sit quietly next to me.

'You better stick with me kid,' he purred. 'Things can get tough round here.'

A few hours later around midday, there was a vastly different scene to behold. A single shout from outside had everyone rushing to and fro. Guns magically appeared at hand, extra ammunition was pocketed and they were away out of the door, pausing only briefly to slip on a pair of shoes before racing headlong towards the truck. It was as if a sleeping hive had been suddenly attacked, sending the swarm into action.

Suddenly I was the only one left in the building. What on earth was I supposed to do? Damn this indecision, the truck was about to leave!

The sight of Nebi unlocked the paralysis and I charged after him, barefoot with boots and bag in hand.

'Into the front, Massoud!' he cried, and I leapt at the open door, throwing myself in.

Minutes later we were thundering across the open valley towards the mountains, with the driver keeping one eye on the road and one on the sky overhead.

'Are we going to Herat?' I shouted.

He yelled back. 'No!'

'Then where?'

He didn't answer, but his eyes flicked from the ground to the air with ominous regularity.

A dry and narrow gorge provided quick access into the mountains and before long we were deep within the range. High banks of scree, interspersed with walls of stone, flashed past only inches from the window. We disturbed a family of falcons nesting in a ledge overhead, their cries lost in the roar of our engine. Out in front, small rodents scurried here and there into holes and crevices. Part of me was wishing I could do the same when suddenly a fist thumped the roof twice which brought our journey to an abrupt halt. Urgent voices issued commands, followed immediately by Nebi's familiar cry for me to follow him and the others. Our intent was still unknown, but even so, I shoved my boots on, jumped down and set off up a steep slope after everyone else, more wary of being left behind than caught in the fray. Although it was just about then that I felt something crawling around inside my left boot.

Our desert valley was plagued with beetles and grasshoppers of all shapes and sizes, harmless creatures that flew in on the wind and arrived *en masse* each day. This one had apparently flown into my footwear and decided to set up camp, oblivious to the danger it would soon face from five thrashing toes. Unfortunately, at that precise moment my own existence was also seemingly at risk and so, quite selfishly, I kept running and left the hapless insect to fend for itself.

When we did finally come to a breathless stop, having reached the top and the shelter of a large rocky outcrop, and while binoculars were trained on the land below us, I did manage to do the honourable thing. I whipped my boot off and with a thump on the sole, attempted to expel what I thought must surely be only the squashed remains of a once poor and innocent creature. Incredibly, however, it landed perfectly on its feet in one piece and moved. It was still alive! But it wasn't exactly what I was expecting. Glaring back at me with several pairs of eyes was a very mad, very lethal-looking spider.

I knew it was dangerous when it started shaping up for a fight instead of running away. When you're a bad mother of an arachnid, you don't have to run from anything. When your species is written into the annals of nature under the heading *Don't Touch!* you are quite aware of who's boss. Unhappily for the spider it had never encountered the likes of the company I now kept, and so for a split second more it looked every inch a threat to mankind before being pulverised unceremoniously by the butt of a Kalishnakov.

Unfortunately that was not quite the end.

I had been bitten on the top of my little toe. No more than a tiny red mark. The toe, however, was already numb and a tingling sensation was beginning to spread through my foot. At first I could only sit there and wonder at the irony of dying from a spider bite in a war zone. No one had ever said to me, if the bullets don't get you, the wildlife will. I calmed down and thought rationally.

The spider's remains were excavated for identification. It was not, I trusted, a relative of the Black Widow or any other highly venomous spider. In its original shape, it probably matched a twenty cent coin for size, while the colouring was a mottled, leopard-skin tan. It looked nasty, but perhaps that was a good sign. Appearances can sometimes be everything in the animal world, and so I felt better after this observation and tried to ignore the numbness creeping up my leg.

Meanwhile the suspected enemy activity turned out to be no more than a ragged convoy of refugees on their way to Iran. It was a false alarm. We were going back. I got to my feet and hobbled after them as fast as possible, cursing my luck and the apparent indifference of the others to my condition. The truck had turned round and was pointing in the opposite direction. I climbed up into the back. Nebi, at least, seemed concerned.

'What is wrong with your leg?' he asked.

Lacking a suitable word in Farci to describe 'numb', I told him the leg was dead and difficult to walk on.

'Why?' he asked.

'Because of the spider!' I replied tersely.

He looked confused. Then it dawned on me. Their lack of interest was not from a flimsy regard for potential life and death situations, but from the sheer ignorance of one. I stuck out my foot and showed him and everyone else the reddening bite.

'Allah!' they cried.

A murmur swept through the truck as the news was passed from man to man. I overheard some of their whispered conversation.

'Massoud has been hurt.'

'How?'

'A spider!'

'Is he sickening?'

'Already his leg is dead from the poison.'

'Oh God.'

In all truth, there was some inflammation and irritation, but it was going down. I tried explaining this but they wouldn't listen. Our camp was deemed too distant for this emergency and so we made off towards another, which surprised me slightly. Up until that moment I had thought we were alone in the valley, although soon enough, out of the desert as if from nowhere, there appeared a small community of huts.

They were a friendly rebel group, guarding an outpost such

as ours. About twenty men with the same array of weaponry as we had at our disposal. We were offered every courtesy, as well as the contents of their medical kit. Even their leader came to give his personal attention to the wound, yet it never occurred to me to ask who they were. It was therefore some time later that I discovered these men were Harrakat mujahedeen, and their leader none other than the Houssein Gharmani of my letter, better known to his friends simply as 'Chok'.

The man who would prove invaluable to my plans to talk with Jamiat-i-Islami was built like a barrel, as his nickname implied. He looked a little older than the photograph I'd seen of him in Dr Seddiqi's Mashad office, and the streaks of grey running through his hair and beard appeared wider than I remembered. His face was also more deeply lined and weather-beaten, but it was definitely the same man. He was probably still in his early forties.

Without surprise Houssein read the letter carefully, then slipped it into a pocket of his waistcoat without a word. I watched and waited, hoping to hear some kind of acknowledgement, but his only remark was to hurry his people up with a bandage. I remained quiet, knowing that it would not help my cause to look as though I expected heaven and earth to be moved. After all, the Afghan way was to speak once and then let matters rest in the hands of providence. *Inshallah*, as they say – God willing.

We left the Harrakat camp soon after and returned to our own. I couldn't help but feel disappointed, but at least some solace could be gained from the fact that the letter had been delivered. I asked Nebi on the way back if he knew himself anything about the Harrakat leader.

'Brave mujahed,' he replied. 'Killed many Russians.'

'A good leader?'

'Very good, Massoud.'

Silence.

'He is friendly with Jamiat, yes?' I asked.

'Jamiat, Harrakat, Hezbollah – all brothers, Massoud. Al Hamdulillah, Praise be to God.'

Another silence.

'What of the letter? Do you think he will help?'

A wide grin spread over his face.

'Of course,' he said.

Evidently Commander Gharmani had been impressed with my patience, sitting there while a spider's poison lay in my veins, then delivering a letter. Not even one of his own men would have done that, he had said.

THIRTY-FIVE

Our movements were never announced in advance. Secrecy was a weapon the mujahedeen kept razor sharp. Stories and rumours were hatched to keep everyone on guard, though it might also have been a natural wariness brought on by past experiences of treachery. There were newcomers, myself included, who could not yet be completely trusted. But when I awoke late one night to the sound of whispered voices and hurried footsteps, it was clearly apparent that something was going on.

Outside, the truck was being hurriedly loaded with guns, ammunition, rockets and wooden crates packed with other explosives. Alongside the main hut, a deep trench had appeared which the men now worked swiftly to hide again with wooden boards and a covering of earth. Others came to help in the task and before long the entire fort was awake and buzzing with activity. Our departure came soon afterwards.

Around midnight we passed through the mountains via the gorge and entered a barren, stony plain on the other side. There were twenty-five of us squashed in the back with enough firepower to take on an army, or conversely, to blow us all to pieces if we ran over a mine. It was another exceedingly rough ride with mortar shells rattling in their cases and clinking noisily against each other. I sat on a rocket to stop it rolling round, and watched another mountain range loom in the darkness ahead, black against the grey eastern sky.

Like the time before, the hours passed slowly with only the bright stars overhead and in the west to gaze upon. The mountains came closer and curved round on our right, steadily growing more apparent as dawn approached. But the growing light, normally so welcome, now brought the risk of being spotted from the air. The landscape offered little protection and Shindand airbase was somewhere to the south-east. At daybreak, the peaks shimmered in a halo of sun rays, and my tired eyes began to turn early morning shadows into Soviet gunships and fighter aircraft.

Fortunately a village soon did come into view, much to the delight of us all. The high walls appeared first, and then the latticed pigeon towers that collected the copious droppings for fertiliser. From a distance it looked like an oasis, with a few tall poplar trees rising above the flat-topped buildings. It might have been a large village: a working, farming community thriving on the riverbank of the Hari Rud, too far out west maybe to be disturbed by the fighting. For some time this was how it seemed and the chattering, laughing voices of the younger men rang out, until one by one, they fell silent in the sudden way that birds are frozen by the passing shadow of a hawk. It was extraordinary, until my eyes saw what they had seen. Closer to the village, the gaps in the walls that might have been gates became blast holes, and all serenity vanished.

Quite suddenly hundreds of graves littered the desert around us, and from each rocky pile rose the tall and slender poplar branches to which the coloured flags of martyrdom were tied. There were so many it was like passing through a forest of saplings in early winter, when the leaves have all blown away. Fluttering in the rising wind instead were ragged pieces of coloured cloth, many of which had been sewn into small triangles with passages from the Koran inside. They were identical to the ones the men of Hezbollah wore round their necks or tied to their machine-guns. The delicate stitching and embroidery was the mark of a loving wife or mother.

Within the village walls, here and there amongst the rubble, were the remains of houses – a broken staircase perhaps, poking up into the air, leading nowhere. In other places, huge holes in the ground were testament to the power of aerial bombing. The streets were almost deserted. Two small boys in tattered clothes ran out from behind a burnt-out bus and sprinted across the road. A woman in a tartan chador darted through a doorway. There was no one else to be seen. The vast majority had undoubtedly fled to Iran long ago, with only a skeleton population deciding to remain behind. The others were the silent inhabitants we had already passed on the way in.

We went to ground for the rest of the day in the shady but airless courtyard of an abandoned *Medreseh* or religious school. A wild garden of mulberry trees grew in the centre, and the branches were hanging low with the weight of the sweet white fruit. A deep well provided buckets full of sparkling fresh water and so we washed, drank, and tried to sleep away the hours. But the flies and heat made relaxation almost impossible. The day was spent waiting, each man to his own.

Night came and we ate the usual meal of rice and bread, washed down with tea, before making the most of the cooler temperatures to grab some sleep. Amongst the others, Nebi and Nasur Ahmad Nejah were doing the same, although any notions of sleeping the whole night through were short-lived. In a repeat performance of the previous day, our journey recommenced a few hours before daybreak.

We roared out of the village onto a dirt road running parallel to the blue-green Hari Rud. The river lay three-quarters of a mile away on our left, while a little further away on the right yet another mountain range stretched out in front. We were hemmed into a natural corridor between the river and the rock.

For the most part our journey was smooth and straight. Dawn arrived and the mountain peaks shimmered in a halo of sunlight. We praised our driver, Ahmad, for his ability in handling such a difficult vehicle. Stories of his skill and bravery were recounted for the benefit of those who did not know him well. There was nothing apparently that we could not achieve with Ahmad at the wheel. His reputation rose to the heights of invulnerability. Morale was at an absolute high. We were close to Herat. Soon the journey would be over.

THIRTY-SIX

The first shell landed well behind us and sent a harmless mushroom cloud billowing into the sky. As the smoke and dust rolled upwards, it looked almost wonderful. The roar of the engine had drowned out the explosion – there were no teeth to the bite.

The false sense of security this generated was immediately extinguished when the desert around us erupted with a thunderous boom. The second, third and fourth shells arrived almost simultaneously and I felt, rather than saw, the explosions. Shock waves know no barriers to their path. They pass right through flesh, blood and bone as if it were air, and shake the very breath from the soul.

'Massoud!'

It was Nebi's cry, but my eyes, my whole body, had shut tight from the shock.

'Paieen!' he yelled.

Eyes open again, I ducked as another fierce salvo obliterated the section of earth we had just travelled across. Something large and deadly zipped past overhead: a razor-sharp lump of hot lead. Fear was the thought of what it could do to a body.

The accuracy and severity of the attack was frightening. We'd had two narrow escapes in less than twenty seconds. I searched the sky, but there was no sign of any aircraft. The attack must have been coming from the river.

Someone shouted. A hand thrust out. Barely noticeable against the desert backdrop stood a cluster of low buildings.

Ahmad's reaction was instant. He pulled the wheel over hard right and sent the truck bucking and groaning into the desert, quickly putting distance between us and the road. They had its range, and ours too if we stayed anywhere near it.

A lone shell burst well off target. Then another even further away. For a moment it seemed we had got clear, but before long the battery corrected their mistakes and the threat returned anew. Once more Ahmad veered away and again we bought ourselves valuable seconds. The shells exploded harmlessly. Each time we changed position the range-finders sought us out and the ground in front or to the side would burst upwards, spraying a mixture of earth and metal. I gritted my teeth whenever the truck lurched over the rutted ground, fearing the blown tyre or broken axle that would leave us stranded. But we were fortunate this particular fate was avoided and with every moment the stretch of desert that lay between us and them increased.

Time passed with agonising slowness as the chance game of cat and mouse continued. There was nothing to do but stay down and hope like hell for deliverance, listening as each salvo screamed in. There would come a dull thud and a blinding roar, followed by Ahmad's violent evasive action throwing us and our cargo against the sides. But after every explosion I would open my eyes and thankfully see daylight.

The thoughts which raced through my mind at this moment were many and varied. I even found time to wonder about our attackers; whether they were firing at us out of grim determination to reduce our party to ashes, or simply out of boredom. Where we nothing more than a fairground shooting attraction, like plastic ducks running the gauntlet of sideshow contestants? If so, what was the prize – a fluffy animal? It seemed unfair to die from someone else's boredom.

The words of an old Eagles song appeared out of nowhere, something about a peaceful easy feeling. Nebi, I noticed, was reciting something else – something more pertinent to our situation – and his lips moved quickly to reach the end of his prayer.

And then as suddenly as it had all started, the shelling stopped. As the seconds ticked by in which there were no further mortar blasts, the feeling that this threat had passed grew stronger. The seemingly innocuous buildings which housed the enemy were now lost in the dust kicked up by our truck. The danger lay behind us. Already the men were standing up and gazing back the way we had come, back at what might have been. Then a single voice rose up over the engine noise.

'Praise be to Allah!'

The reply was heartfelt. Having survived the shooting gallery, it was the chorus of a thankful humanity.

We carried on at the same breakneck pace, crossing a bridge over the Hari Rud, where the torrent of water swung from the north bank to the south, digging ever deeper into the earth to form its narrow channel, before we finally came to rest that afternoon in the village of Shekiban.

The local mujahedeen commander was an old, grey-haired man, venerated for his knowledge of the *Koran* and for his bravery. In a room of his home, the story was told by his men of how he had refused to leave the house when the bombers came. He had waited out the storm and survived unscathed while the buildings around him fell. The hand of destruction had been stayed by his belief in God. However, the rest of the village was not so fortunate.

Three-quarters of Shekiban was little more than eroded rubble, melting away with the seasons. Like the previous village it was partly ringed by mighty defensive walls that stood fifty feet high in places, guarded by equally lofty gates of stone. It was an ancient place that had survived for centuries against the elements, only to crumble and fall in a single day to the forces of man. With nowhere to live and the ever-present threat of renewed attacks from the local government fort, most of the inhabitants had vanished.

Before we departed, they took us to see the fort in question. We crept up through a series of narrow lanes before coming to the edge of an empty wasteland, created by the soldiers as a first line of defence. Nothing or no one would have been able to approach without being seen well in advance.

Like a castle, the building was tall, square and blockish with towers at each corner, a single gate and a flag flying from a pole within. Other than that, any indication that the place was lived in was missing, although we ourselves paid special attention to remaining hidden. There was an ugly brooding quality about it; it was dark and sinister, and I was not sorry to leave the area, nor the village. Misery and sorrow lay deep in the ruins of Shekiban, and it was like a chill wind blowing through the soul.

Onwards our journey continued and in the middle of a blazing sunset we came to our next port of call, the lakeside village of Sangbast – the point from which we would continue on to Herat by foot. Here, the mountains had swung away and the land opened out into a wide plain through which the Hari Rud continued to flow. There was a small reservoir fed by the river, or one of its tributaries, and the village itself appeared to have survived the ravages of war quite well.

Later, while we were given succour by the local village leader on the roof of his house, it was heard that the Russians had agreed to something of a truce with the mujahedeen of Sangbast. The village would be spared if the large Soviet garrison nearby was left alone. It was situated on the side of a hill about two miles further up the road, and at some stage during the night we would have to pass directly beneath it.

That time came soon after dark.

It was Nasur Ahmad Najar, the ex-teacher responsible for my rapid advances in Farci, who arrived out of the deepening gloom with news of our impending departure. But there was a note of sadness in his voice that sounded like a farewell. Everyone knew the responsibilities of his job back in Mashad were considerable. Many times I had sat in his office and witnessed the steady stream of people bring their problems to his desk. He was both accountant and manager, counsellor and priest. He was fighting a war of paperwork when he longed for the field of battle, though now he was turning back with the truck. Nothing was said of it. He merely embraced each one of us in turn, touching cheeks in the Afghan way, and then was gone.

Down below, there were twenty donkeys to carry the cargo of explosives we had brought with us. Twenty donkeys that would have to be kept very, very quiet. We left before the moon was up and the black night cloaked us like a second skin. Once past the village lights we followed a track down into a darkened copse of trees and bushes, where visibility was severely restricted and the ground underfoot was alarmingly uneven. There was no discernible difference between earth and sky. The only way of keeping track of the others was by hearing alone. Up ahead, whispered voices reached me through the darkness, urging the donkeys onward.

Luckily, after an hour of stumbling and cursing, the track did turn up onto a lighter, smoother pathway and our speed increased. But for the first time since leaving the village I could see up ahead a blaze of floodlighting coming from the government stronghold. The sleepless eyes gazing out from its shadowed ramparts would be searching for just such a passing convoy as ours, though our path lay beyond the range of their illuminations.

Eventually a halt was called to let the stragglers catch us up and to make any last-minute adjustments to the heavy packs the animals carried. Each donkey was weighed down with up to six missiles, three to each side, and as many guns, grenades and bullets as possible. The missiles were identical to the one Haidan Seiah had successfully launched over a week ago. Big and heavy, and as dangerous as sin, their capacity for destruction was tremendous.

Soon enough, however, the stragglers did appear out of the gloom and we moved on in single file. I walked in the middle, sandwiched between the butt of one donkey and the plodding head of another, evidently to prevent any noisy amorous advances that might lead to our discovery. But we had covered only a short distance when a desperate voice from behind me cried out a shrill, 'Look out!', and I whirled round in time to watch in horror as a hundred pounds of high explosives began to slip from the beast's back and fall. There was no possibility of stopping the avalanche. The missiles landed on top of each other, ringing out like hammers upon a blacksmith's anvil.

In the still night that sound must have carried for miles, let alone the stone's throw distance to the fortress. They were torturous moments, in which all eyes were trained upon that brightly lit building of concrete and steel on the hill, half expecting it to spring to life and disgorge an army of men. We waited, but by some miracle nothing happened. Every nerve was tingling, every heart pounding furiously, but the only movement that followed was our own. Wary of tempting fate, we quickly shouldered the missiles and carried them until we were safely out of immediate danger. Only then was it possible to stop and burden once more the luckless beast.

For the rest of the night our journey continued, passing silently through two or three sleeping villages where it seemed only the resident dogs knew of our presence. There were further problems with ammunition boxes slipping through the ropes and netting the donkeys carried, but none was as ill-timed as the first. The loads were soon tied again and on we would go. After the first ten miles, distance and destination became unimportant statistics. The necessary thing was simply to keep putting one foot in front of the other, and not get lost in the darkness.

Happily, as the sky began to lighten, the way did become clearer and for the first time I was able to gain an idea of the flat, open countryside that surrounded us. The dirt road, although overgrown with weeds and desert brush, suddenly widened to give an impression of its former glory as an ancient route to Herat. Quite possibly it had seen the passing of all manner of beasts and men, some having brought their wares from afar to sell and barter, while others carried swords and bows and came riding on horseback. Herat had begun as a camp for the armies of Alexander the Great hundreds of years before Christ, but from there it developed into an important trading centre upon the Silk Road. Its beauty achieved great renown, with travellers calling it the City of Gardens after a time. Even now, here and there the road was closely bordered by tall pines that sighed as the desert wind dragged through the upper branches. I was saddened that I would never see Herat in a time of peace or, as Byron did long ago, observe the seven sky-blue pillars against the delicate heather-coloured mountains. And in the midst, a 'blue melon-dome with the top bitten off'. For this was the ancient Musallah of Herat, a wondrous product of the golden age of Islamic architecture.

He wrote of it: 'The beauty is more than scenic, depending on light or landscape. On closer view, every file, every flower, every petal of mosaic contributes its genius to the whole.'

It was different now, of course. The seven minarets I would later discover had been reduced in number. The blue melon-dome was surrounded by ruins. Closer to the city tracer fire lit the sky, the bomb craters began to appear more numerous, and the crumpled remains of an old Soviet fighter aircraft were strewn across our path.

THIRTY-SEVEN

Hours later, lack of sleep and the length of the journey had left me disorientated. What had this man said, something about Kuwait or Paris? I must be dreaming. Where were the others? We had become spread out, but when I had last looked they were still in front. Where had they now disappeared to? And surely this Afghan must also be one of us?

'Salaam Aleikum Massoud. Chitouri? Injah Kuwait, unjah Paris. Koojah mireed?'

He was chuckling to himself and leading me forward by the arm, off the road and down a narrow alleyway. The wall had fallen in many places and we were forced to pick our way over the rubble. The houses on either side were broken shells blackened by fire.

Exhausted, my hope was that here was our destination.

'Is this Herat?'

'Herat?' he said. 'Yes, here is Herat. But here is Kuwait.' He laughed out loud again. 'And Paris! Of course there is Paris, but Kuwait is better. Better food, better water – much cooler in Kuwait too. Come, Nebi is looking for you.'

I felt relief to know my friend was nearby. It might have been my own fatigue or maybe I'd simply not understood his Farci correctly, but I was starting to believe this guy was a nutter.

Nebi was waiting in the small enclosed courtyard of a house that appeared relatively intact. The courtyard itself had a wall and some trees for shade. On one side of the arched entrance-way, a small garden contained a single rose bush which someone was trying to grow. It formed an impressive scene, considering that everything else in the square mile was a picture of devastation.

'Welcome to Kuwait,' he said with a wry grin. The man behind me giggled hysterically once more and rushed off towards a blast hole in the opposite wall.

Kuwait was the name Hezbollah jokingly used to describe this half of their base or *komiteh*. The other half – Paris – was through the hole in the wall. Between them they formed the only two habitable buildings in the whole of the village known as Golawar. The rest of the area was the scene of a major disaster. Eleven years of war had turned the western part of the city into rubble and that was exactly how the Russians planned it. Intact, the houses would have provided ample cover for the mujahedeen forces. Demolished, there would be nowhere for the resistance to gain a foothold and stage their attacks. A similar tactic was used by the United States in the Vietnam war. The defoliant sprayed over huge areas of jungle was designed to deprive the enemy of a place to hide and fight in.

The *komiteh* was concealed amongst the ruins only a short distance from the main road. We were close to the city centre, right on the edge of the no-man's-land surrounding it, and even at this early hour the crack of sporadic gunfire could be heard. Over a hurried breakfast of tea and stale bread, Nebi briefly outlined the situation.

Hezbollah controlled this part of Golawar. Other groups such as Jamiat-i-Islami had other sections and other villages to look after – the borders were loosely defined. Unaccompanied in these zones I might be mistaken for the enemy and shot. It wasn't a good idea to venture up onto the roof in daylight, either. Snipers were about and they seldom missed. There were minefields as well, further up the road.

'How far?' I said.

'Not far, Massoud. I will show you later.'

As before, when the giggling guide had stopped me falling asleep out on the road, the effects of the long journey had begun to take their toll.

'That man,' I said, yawning.

'Abdul Ali?'

'Diwana?'

Nebi looked surprised. 'Abdul Ali, mad? No, he's the cook in Paris.'

He suddenly grinned, showing off a set of clean white teeth, and asked me if I had ever been to the real Paris. I told him several times, and he looked at me then in the sort of way that people generally reserve for observing eighth wonders of the world and aliens landing in the back garden. Finally he said, 'Is it big or small?'

'Big,' I replied.

'As big as Kabul?'

'I think bigger. Much, much bigger.'

'I would like to see the real Paris,' he said.

'What about Mecca?'

'Of course I will make the Haj to Mecca first. But afterwards, I should like to see Paris. I have a friend there.'

'Afghan?'

Nebi shook his head. 'French. A doctor. Three years ago he helped many mujahedeen here.'

Now I could understand the reason for his interest. I asked if he had a name and address but he didn't.

'It is enough that I can remember his face,' he said. 'So I will go to the hospital in Paris and thank him for coming so far from his home.'

'Very difficult,' I said. 'There are many hospitals in Paris.'

He paused with quiet resolve before answering.

'Then I will look inside every one.'

After sleeping through the heat of the day in a cool cellar beneath Kuwait, I went with Nebi as promised to see a minefield. He carried his Kalishnakov and we half walked, half jogged across the open spaces between houses. His back was hunched over as if a low ceiling hung above our heads.

Presently we came to a halt behind a small thicket of bushes and trees, a few yards short of the road.

'There,' he said, nodding his head forwards.

The flat stretch of fine dust and hard rock before us had once carried a stream of traffic to and from the city. Now there were no footprints, no donkey trails, no marks of any kind. It was a completely even surface, as smooth as a beach after high tide, brushed flat by the wind.

'Mined?' I said.

He nodded again. No expression, calm as you please. Hezbollah had watched the mines being laid the previous year, and so they knew where to find some if they needed any. Government mines clearly worked just as well when used against the government.

'How much of the road is mined?' I asked.

He leaned forward slightly and pointed out a green flag alongside a single storey building, about a hundred and fifty yards up the road. It was an average Herati house of sun-baked mud. The only difference was that everything around it had been bulldozed flat.

'To there,' he said. 'There is Herat city.'

From the top of a badly damaged watchtower, built by the Russians in the first years of the war, we could survey the lay of the land undetected. In the near distance was the ribbed dome Robert Byron saw on his first journey to Herat, although the 'seven sky-blue pillars' he described now appeared to number only five. It was saddening to think that these monumental examples of ancient Islamic architecture had survived five glorious centuries only to become the central arena for a vicious war. Two minarets had been hit by artillery fire so far. Of the other historic buildings said to have been part of the Musallah, I could see nothing. Somewhere over in the distance, perhaps beyond those trees or behind that wall, lay the remains of what might have become one of the world's great architectural treasures. The rest of the countryside looked more or less as it did from lower down, there was just more of it visible: scorched earth where swaying fields of rice and wheat should have been. Chaos reigned where once there was order. Unfortunately the city centre, where many people still eked out a living, was below my line of sight. Only the medieval fortress was visible to the north, raised up above the land on a mound of earth. The government forces could see far and wide from that position. Only the mountains behind them were higher.

Nebi made no comment, but after a while he started down from the tower and climbed out through a hole at the base. I went also and found him at prayer, kneeling on the bare earth and facing towards Mecca. About five minutes went by, after which he got up and walked over to where I was sitting beneath the tower.

'Can you hear them?' he said calmly.

'Who?'

'Listen!'

Then I heard it as well. The faint but unmistakable sound of automobile engines.

Past the minefield, past the army post at the end of the road, past the waving green flag, some of Herat's civilian population had finished work for another day and were heading home by bus.

The strange life led by the people of Herat, as I came to understand it, never ceased to amaze me. The city was under siege, yet it functioned quite normally. A bazaar existed, and many open-fronted shops. There was also a bank, a hotel and even a cinema, although no one was certain if this still operated. A few older mujahedeen were able to go in regularly to the city, unarmed but effectively behind enemy lines. The soldiers never bothered them, for they looked to be ordinary old Herati men after all. On the other hand, the younger men had no such freedom. If caught within the city two alternatives were usually put to them. They could admit their allegiance to the mujahedeen and face imprisonment or a possible firing squad. Or they could be drafted into the army and find themselves transported to the furthest end of their country, unable to return home.

That evening in Kuwait was a real treat. We were seated on a low platform outside one of the rooms. A cool breeze had sprung up and for a while the sound of gunfire had ceased. An air of calm descended upon the city. It was dinner time.

Each man was handed a portion of cooked goat's meat to go with his usual ration of rice and bread. Such was the rarity of the occasion that the delicacy was left until the end to be savoured. Then Abdul Ali arrived from Paris clutching several bowls of rice, one between five or six men, and all hands dived in. For ten minutes we happily chomped away. Unfortunately, the tea which followed was interrupted by war.

It began with a single burst of tracer from a heavy machine-gun, fired from a government position. Out of boredom again perhaps, the hapless soldier had foolishly let off a few rounds, only to suddenly find himself the object of every mujahedeen gun within range. In seconds the sky was filled with the luminous spray of tracer bullets: red beads of light that, given the right angle, floated in slow motion through the air before vanishing. The angle which wasn't so attractive was the one that pointed in our direction. When the return fire came, it flashed by and exploded with terrifying force upon the ruins around us. Beauty was soon replaced by ugliness.

Several flares were launched into the sky, who by we couldn't tell, but they were immediately turned upon and extinguished in a few short bursts. Then the mortars started up, followed by the heavier bang of bigger artillery. Incendiary shells whistled high over our heads and landed with a horrific crunch in the neighbourhood. Fires leapt up and before long, patches of the skyline were lit with an orange glow.

It was a simple case of tit for tat. Whenever a shell went over in one direction the return fire would follow soon after, usually ten times as fierce if it came from the government side. It was clear who had the greater firepower, and the entire shooting match was designed to show which side that was. Still supplied by their erstwhile cousins from across the border, the government forces could afford to throw their weight around. When the battle relented and peace and quiet resumed, I asked someone if they knew the reason for it all. But the answer came with a shrug of the shoulders. The pointlessness of war, it seemed, was pointless even to talk about.

Having said that, it was fairly crowded in the deep, protected cellar that night, and almost empty on the rooftop.

At dawn next morning, under a pink sky, I went for a better look round the *komiteh* while the others were at prayer. It was still cool so I kept myself wrapped in the blanket I had slept in.

The cooking area was the tunnel between the two courtyards. A small dark room off to the side, with traditional oven holes dug into the earthen floor, was the bakery. Next to it, a padlocked wooden door no more than waist high led into the storehouse where sackfuls of rice, flour, tea and sugar were kept. On the Paris side the courtyard was also surrounded by high walls, although it was bigger than Kuwait and completely bare of plant life. In one corner a flight of stairs led up to a second storey where there were several rooms used for eating and sleeping. Like those in Kuwait, they were empty save for a flat-woven rug on the floor and niches in the walls for guns and ammunition. On the roof was an ugly pile of wood and rubbish for the cooking fires. Abdul Ali had been right. Paris was a dump.

But from the rooftop was a view which belonged on the canvas for its beauty. The sun was climbing over the trees which lined the road travelling east, casting a soft and eerie light upon the surrounding land. Long shadows fell across the ruins. And it all seemed somehow familiar. Memories of past experiences usually carry with them a code, so that we can know the time and place. But here there was nothing but the faintest twinge of recollections that were gone before they could be grasped. As a child, Herat had featured greatly in my imagination as the homeland of the Afghan. Was I now looking upon a scene pictured way back then? It seemed highly implausible, even preposterous, but I still couldn't shake the sensation of having been here before.

In a sharp return to earth I found Nebi back in Kuwait, shoving a fresh magazine into his Russian-made Kalishnakov and putting a couple of extras into his inside waistcoat pockets. The old sandshoes he used to own, always worn with the laces undone and the backs turned down like sandals if there was nothing much happening, had been replaced by a new pair, brand name Adios. A blatant but clever Pakistani rip-off. These ones he wore properly however, with the laces firmly tied.

'Come on,' he said.

'Where are we going?'

'To visit another *komiteh*,' he replied. 'Do you want one of these?' and he tapped the butt of the gun.

I thought about the offer and decided against it. The only shots I intended taking were with a camera, not a Kalishnakov.

Still, the problem that faces the supposedly neutral observer is the one concerning involvement. How far away do you stand from the events happening around you? How close do you allow yourself to get? There is only a fine line between observer and participant.

We were joined on this occasion by two other mujaheds, Karim, who had been with us since Mashad, and Sadiq, a fun-loving but distinguished war veteran at the age of nineteen. He had been in Herat for several months and wore a chest pouch that carried four spare magazines and several hand grenades. One of these he insisted on taking out for a demonstration. Our conversation translated into something like this.

'See this, Massoud? This is the pin. Pull the pin out and throw. Two seconds – Boom. Small fuse, you understand.'

I sensed a trick. 'Yes, very interesting Sadiq. The pin stays in.'

'Pin in. No danger to my good friend, Massoud. Pin out, still no danger.'

'But safer in, true Sadiq?'

'Pin in or pin out – no difference. See this?' He was pointing at a lever which he held down firmly with all four fingers. 'This means we are safe.'

The grenade was thrust into my hand and I held it as Sadiq instructed. It was heavier than expected and a reasonably strong grip was needed to keep the lever down. If the pin were pulled and the grenade thrown, the lever would fly off thus activating the timer. I knew this not from Sadiq, but from reading war comics as a kid. To be on the safe side I checked to see that the pin was still secure. It was not even there.

'Sadiq!'

I got no further. The missing pin was in his hand. I yelled at him. The knuckles of my fingers were turning white as my grip instinctively tightened. But instead of rushing to install the pin, Sadiq insisted I return the grenade to him. There was some truth in his words. My experience of explosives was limited.

With great care I let him take the grenade, and with equal carelessness he allowed it to slip through his fingers. With a heavy thud it hit the ground, a small puff of dust rose up, the lever released and landed a few yards away.

Two seconds is not very much time. You might get five or six paces from a standing start, and then an extra few feet with a dive at the end, but not enough to escape the full blast. Consequently, what you do is root yourself to the spot like an idiot and shut your eyes tight, waiting to be plastered all over the neighbourhood. Alternatively, if you happen to be two smart-arses called Karim and Sadiq, you stand there unmoving, quietly chuckling away to yourselves. An unsmiling Nebi picked up the grenade from where it lay, unscrewed the top and showed me where the detonator should have been. Then he tossed it back to the giggling Sadiq with a few words of disapproval. Sadiq, as I came to understand, was something of a practical joker.

We visited the humble abodes of several mujahedeen groups that morning, all within a radius of two or three miles. The buildings they inhabited were similar to those at Hezbollah. Sun-baked mud walls, open windows without shutters and a roof to keep out the weather. One had suffered badly from a recent mortar attack and outside the building, row upon row of freshly made mud bricks were drying in the sun. They would be used to patch up the holes before the summer ended.

In every place we were welcomed and made to sit down while tea was brewed. Curious faces, both young and old, watched my every move and I became conscious of how I sat, spoke and drank my tea. In every case, however, I was always made to feel at home. The cleanest glass was allocated to me, the best sugar lumps were put within my reach. I was a guest. But more than that, my presence was like a boost of morale for them. I was the living embodiment of the outside world listening to their story.

Hafizullah Khatabie was a man who had been in the army in Kabul when the Russian troops arrived in 1979/80. Confused as to why such an army was necessary, he had asked one soldier what his purpose was in Afghanistan, and the answer had been startling. It was because of the American and Chinese invasion, the soldier had said. His duty, as ordered by his commanding officers, was to drive these armies from the country. When it was explained that no such invasion had taken place the soldier had refused to listen.

Another man had seen his neighbour taken outside his home

and shot at point-blank range through the ear. The neighbour had been a highly respected musician who had defied a command to perform before an important delegation of Russian officials.

There was also a teenager, Daoud, with several fingers missing on his right hand – the tragic result of picking up a butterfly bomb when he was a young boy. These small and attractive toy-like mines where dropped in their thousands across the countryside. Children especially were the target.

By late morning I had listened to many more such stories, when two helicopters suddenly began to patrol the area we were in, a possible sign that an attack was imminent. We had to go back via a short cut, reducing the chance of being caught out in the open. The new route took us away from the helicopters, but close to where the minarets stood in no-man's-land – an area of constant observation. Sufficient cover could be found, however, by threading a way through the derelict houses and gardens.

In someone's living room we found an unexploded bomb lying half buried on the floor like a beached whale. Had it gone off, the entire three-bedroom house would have ceased to exist, leaving only an enormous crater to mark the spot. A hand lightly touched my elbow; it was Sadiq.

'The grenade was dead Massoud, this is not. Go carefully please.'

We rounded the exposed tail on tip-toe, more than a little wary of the sleeping giant.

From time to time, through a window or doorway, I caught sight of the famous minarets and blue-domed mausoleum. In a sense my position was an extremely privileged one. There were historians and scholars of ancient architecture who would have given everything to be in my shoes, if only for a moment, to glimpse what had remained off-limits for so long. To pass by so quickly verged on the blasphemous.

'Nebi, is it possible for me to get closer to the minarets?'

We were walking through the remains of an old walled garden that had become choked with vines. The grapes were nearly ripe.

'It is possible,' he said without slowing.

'I'll be gone no more than five minutes.'

He stopped where the wall finished and peered round it cautiously.

'You cannot go alone. I will take you.'

Sadiq puffed out his chest.

'We will all take you!'

One by one we darted across the road and into a house on the other side. The back had been blown out and there were other houses beyond it. We passed through the remains of three and then came to a halt. A narrow, steep staircase led up to what once had been the second floor. Just the one wall remained, with a window at its centre.

Four minarets were grouped together to the left of the mausoleum, while the solitary fifth, different from the others in that it possessed two balconies as opposed to one, stood to the right. These blue columns once formed part of the grand mosque (of which there was said to be no equal) and *Medressa* of Gohar Shad, wife to Shah Rukh, son of the Mongol conqueror Tamerlane. The buildings were over 550 years old. Veterans of numerous wars, they were still standing – but only just. Half way up one of the furthest minarets something had bitten out a large chunk. In all probability it was the work of a stray missile.

Fortunately much of the beauty and craftsmanship was still intact. The delicate mosaic had survived and seemed to radiate a lustre that belied its age, helped partly by the soft afternoon sunlight from behind me.

Nebi called from down below and I turned to leave, but in doing so something caught my eye, a flash of light from a building not two hundred metres away – the type of flash that comes from reflected light. Off a car windscreen? In Herat? More likely binoculars, surely. Nebi had few doubts.

Our path was retraced at lightning speed, yet we reached only the first house when the mortar shell exploded nearby. The second struck the building we had just evacuated. I caught a glimpse of tumbling masonry and of dust billowing out in grey clouds. We hurled ourselves headlong through empty rooms, through doorways and windows, anxious to get as far away from the scene as possible. There were other explosions, but not nearly as close as the first few, and after several minutes the terrifying sound began to seem further and further away, eventually dying altogether. Only then did we stop to catch our breath, before warily making our way back to base.

That brief attack however, played havoc upon my nerves for several days afterwards. If a jet passed close by, my hands would involuntarily clench. At night, the sporadic hammering of heavy machine-guns kept me awake. The shallow craters of mortar bursts which littered the hard ground were a constant reminder that we were always within range. Shrapnel lay about the place: a form of static terror, solid hunks of lead covered in razor edges. There was too much of it near our *komiteh* for my liking.

A large defused shell was shown to be packed with thousands of needle-sharp inch-long nails, designed like arrows so they would fly straight, and I began to take it personally. Someone out there was trying to get me. The predictable response was to learn how to use a gun.

There were three types which Hezbollah owned: Russian, Chinese and for some strange reason, Egyptian AK47s. No doubt the Soviets sold them the franchise. Perhaps we would soon be seeing feluccas on the Volga. In any case it was the same machine-gun, except the Chinese versions had lighter triggers.

Target practice was an abandoned yellow Mercedes taxi near the road, or the empty shell casings of anti-aircraft bullets on top of a wall. I could hit the door of the Merc from a hundred yards – no problem. If a bright yellow taxi ever tried to jump me from behind, it would have been dead meat. But hitting anything smaller was a little different. While Nebi knocked off the empty shells with a machine-like regularity, I simply knocked bits off the wall.

'You're good!' I said.

He shrugged. 'Haji Qary can do the same with only one arm.'

The one man who had been conspicuous by his absence all this time was the commander-in-chief, Haji Qary Ahmad Ali.

Because of the risk of assassination by the government, his visits were rarely announced and he was never without at least one bodyguard. I hardly knew the man, having met him only a few times, but apparently he knew all about me.

One morning, several weeks after my arrival in Herat, it was hinted that if I wanted to speak with the commander I should stick around. It was my big chance. There were matters of my future which I urgently needed to discuss with him.

Using the privileges which came with living in Kuwait, I took a shower and washed my clothes. The lightweight material dried in minutes.

To pass the time I sat and talked about the commander with Abdul Ali, the exuberant if not slightly crazy cook.

'So you think it will be difficult to speak with Haji Qary?' I said.

His brow furrowed and he inhaled sharply through pursed lips. He looked concerned.

'Difficult, very difficult.'

'But he will be here soon, yes?'

'Who knows, who knows.'

I tried a different tack.

'Do you know what he did before the war?'

'Yes, yes, he was a mullah.'

The news was a little disquieting but I let Abdul continue.

'Very good mullah. Twenty years of study and there is nothing in the *Koran* he doesn't know. You must hear him lead us in prayer. Do you pray, Massoud?'

'Of course, but different from you.'

'Today. How many times?'

'I, er . . . today you say . . . once maybe, but it depends.'

'Only once! Ah, but you must pray a very long time.'

'Yes, well . . .'

'Many hours, I think.'

Change of subject.

'But I'm learning about Islam.'

Abdul Ali's eyes brightened.

'Listen,' I said. 'Bismilla'hir Rahmani Rahim. La illa'heh illa'illah Muhammadu rasulu'llah.'

'You know the *kalimeh*! I am sure Haji Qary will speak with you once he knows this. Wait here.'

Suddenly he was off and running through to the next courtyard. Two minutes went by and he reappeared, smiling broadly.

'It is done. He is here now, come with me.'

I was admitted into a long rectangular upstairs room in Paris. At one end there were large open windows that reached down as far as the floor. At the other, where a few mujahedeen had congregated round their leader, two small windows were blocked with dry brush. As I greeted them and made my way to a space on the floor between two men, the brush was doused with water and a cool breeze flowed through the room.

Haji Qary sat absorbed in a letter of his own writing. He wore a grey-blue shalwar camise but no waistcoat. The loose end of his turban fell down his shoulder and gathered in his lap. He put the paper aside and bid me sit closer. He waved a young mujahed to bring some tea and then consulted his watch. It was of Russian origin, with a tiny oval portrait of the astronaut Yuri Gagarin on the strap.

'I understand you wanted to see me.'

'About Pakistan, yes.'

'The journey to Pakistan is very long, Massoud. I advise you to return to Iran. We can take you.'

I thought of what the Iranian police would do to me if I was caught in their country again without a visa – prison, surely. Besides, it had never been my intention to go back.

'Thank you Haji Qary, but what you suggest is impossible.'

He scratched the stump of his missing arm.

'It will take a month at least for you to walk there.'

'I realise that.'

'I have no horse to give you.'

'Walking is fine.'

'I cannot guarantee your safety.'

'I'll take my chances.'

He gave a grunt and began to twirl his prayer beads round his forefinger. After a while he said, 'Then I will do what I can.'

THIRTY-EIGHT

Days passed. I waited patiently with the men, went on patrols and saw more of the same blackened villages and sadly, the graves of past inhabitants. Then one afternoon in the alleyway outside the *komiteh*, where a group of us were sitting in the shade, a stranger arrived with a bullet wound to his upper chest. He had lost a lot of blood and his face was ashen. Before collapsing he muttered something about *dushman* – the enemy.

The man was in his late twenties with a bushy black moustache and three days of stubble on his chin. His clothes were patched and dirty and on his feet he wore a pair of shoes made from old tyre rubber. While the wound was cleaned and bandaged, a curious mob gathered round the unconscious figure.

'Does anyone know him?' someone asked.

Heads shook in unison.

'Did anyone see which direction he came from?'

Similarly, no one was sure.

'Then look for identification.'

His pockets were checked but nothing useful was found. He had stumbled in from nowhere, unarmed and in obvious need of help. We carried him to one of the cool cellar rooms below Kuwait and he was laid on the floor, with someone's folded *patou* for a pillow.

We waited.

One of the commandant's deputies was informed.

Ten minutes later the man died.

The anonymity of the death, as well as the abrupt way in which it happened, was greatly saddening. There was no way of informing his family or even his friends. Whoever they were, they would possibly never know his fate, nor ever find out the location of his grave. He was given a simple burial in a grove of mulberry trees, in the garden of a nearby house.

The incident caused me to wonder over my own future. The figure underneath this innocuous pile of stones could have been me, on another day, in another part of the country. Was the risk of trouble with the Iranians less than the risk of death in Afghanistan, I began to ask myself – an anonymous death at that, in an unknown land? It took a while for these feelings to subside but when they did, the stark reality of my position returned. I was in too deep to go back now. I had to start out towards the Pakistan border and day by day reduce the distance in between. I needed to move on. There is no problem that cannot be solved by walking.

As it happened, I had not long to wait.

As I was standing over the grave, my meditations were suddenly interrupted by a heavy hand that slapped the middle of my back.

'Salaam, Massoud!'

The booming voice belonged to Ali, a huge man with size thirteen feet and a propensity for hitting the people he liked.

'What are you doing?' he said.

'Trying to think,' I replied.

'Ah, good. Massoud thinks, Ali fights,' and he punched me hard in an affectionate kind of way.

'Massoud also takes photographs, eh! Photographs of many brave Hezbollah mujahedeen in Herat city. The people in your country will not forget this place. Is that true?'

'That's probably true,' I said.

'And the pictures you have taken of Ali, it is the same?'

'Yes, the very same I hope.'

'Good! Very good!' He breathed a sigh. 'I thank you for this because I do not wish to be remembered only by my enemies. Now I have some news for you. You are leaving for Pakistan today. I pray that God goes with you.'

We were away just before sunset, Nebi, Karim and a

commander called Algia Abdul Wahab. He had a long black beard that was trimmed to perfection and his skin was a deep nut-brown colour. When he took his turban off, it revealed a shaven head at least three shades lighter than the exposed areas of his face. He had a wife, four children and eight cows.

'You are from Inglestan?' he asked en route.

'Yes.'

'Ah!' he said knowingly. 'So you like milk.'

Our departure had come, as usual, without much warning. I had shaken the hands of those mujahedeen nearby and taken off after Nebi, who had my light bag already slung over his shoulder and was striding off up a track, under and over the remains of some buildings. I was sorry to go without saying a proper farewell, but that might have taken hours. I left that afternoon, in a sense, as quietly as I had come.

For an hour we skirted round the southern edges of the city, the track following the course of a stream then veering off across some barren fields. Another hour and we came to a village. I was instructed not to speak, lest my imperfect Farci roused suspicion, and so we passed unobserved through narrow lanes, with houses that looked in better condition than those we had left behind. These obviously provided homes for a small population of both men and women, and at one stage our pace slowed noticeably when a woman's soothing song came from somewhere nearby. Minds and hearts immediately softened to that peaceful sound.

Then, in the early evening in another village further on, we came to the home of Algia Abdul Wahab and a decision was made to stay until morning. It was a farmhouse with many of the more prized stock kept in shadowed straw-filled rooms below the living quarters. Outside was a small orchard, as well as several fields for wheat and barley, though none grew there now. Algia Abdul Wahab had sons but they were too young as yet to tend to the land, and he himself was often called away from home.

In a large, well-ventilated room his youngest son waited upon us with great care and attention, bringing plates of food the like of which we hadn't seen in many weeks, and laying them on the floor where we sat. Amongst other things, there were cooked aubergines, tomatoes and rice as well as fresh melons and yoghurt. A pitcher of water was also brought so we could wash our hands, before and after eating. Perhaps contrary to popular belief, the Muslim faith is certainly not dirty. Like Christianity, it believes cleanliness is right up there next to godliness, though the style of living in Afghanistan could at first be seen to be contradictory to this creed. At an Afghan meal, for example, the right hand is used to feed oneself – but never the left. Such an act would be highly impolite and distasteful to any Afghan, since all food is shared and the left hand is strictly reserved for personal hygiene. 'What do you think of my home?' said Algia Abdul as we tucked in.

'Very nice,' I replied, manipulating a ball of rice into my mouth with a deft flick of the thumb. 'And very big.'

'This house once belonged to my grandfather's father's father who fought against your Inglestani army many, many years ago. My grandfather's father also fought against the Inglestani and my grandfather after him. But my father did not. He is very old now and listens to the Farci edition of the BBC World Service.'

The obvious irony passed unnoticed, and so I asked if he too listened to the BBC.

'Of course,' he replied. 'Two nights ago there was a report on the fighting in Kandahar. You must be careful near this city, Massoud, the Kandahari are not to be trusted.'

Kandahar was the only other city on my way to Pakistan. It lay near the border, about twenty days walk from here. According to those who should know, in between I could expect aerial bombardment, formidable mountains and if Allah was willing, safe haven in the villages along the way.

'Do you know these villages?' I asked.

Algia Abdul just shook his head. Nebi and Karim weren't sure either as no one they knew had ever made the trip. Their homes were in Iran after all, although I had thought they might be a little more forthcoming with ideas and information on the journey ahead. It was a prime example of how confusing life could sometimes be with the mujahedeen. Information was rarely volunteered; it had to be extracted with numerous questions. I began with the simplest.

'Where are we going tomorrow?'

'Gorazan,' came the reply.
'To a Hezbollah *komiteh*?'
'Yes.'
'And after Gorazan, where?'
'Seoshan.'
'Hezbollah also?'
'No.'
'Who?'
'Jamiat Free Fronts.'
'Not Jamiat-i-Islami?'
'No. Not the same, but similar people, Massoud.'

It was all a little confusing, but the mention of Jamiat-i-Islami proved encouraging. Whereas Hezbollah's influence remained strong in and around the Herat region, the Jamiat group were much larger and had connections all the way to Pakistan. I needed their help. The exact nature of Jamiat Free Fronts could be worked out later.

THIRTY-NINE

Early next morning, after a short walk through Algia Abdul's village, we came to a main road and boarded a very battered-looking bus. The old man standing beside me decided to strike up a conversation about the inefficiency of Herat city's public transport system. He was on his way to work in the city, like the other twenty-odd people standing around us, and was thoroughly annoyed about the absence of seats. It wasn't that they were all full. There weren't any seats full stop – or even windows for that matter, front, back or side.

On the other hand we were on our way to Gorazan, situated at the far end of this two-mile stretch of government-held dirt road, a ring-road that encircled part of the city. The bus provided a quick way of getting to the village, but hardly the safest: our three Kalishnakovs against four tanks and two armoured vehicles parked by the side of the road, and the armed soldiers outnumbering us ten to one. The old fellow poured scorn upon them as well.

'Dogs,' he said as we bumped and lurched along. 'They will answer to God one day.'

We left the bus at a T-junction, near a heavily guarded bridge spanning the Hari Rud. Two tanks, one at either end, sat looking like fat bouncers at a nightclub door. With guns concealed, the four of us made our way nonchalantly across the road and down a track to the next village. Our destination was on the far side at the local *komiteh*, which was found to be enclosed by a high wall and set back from some trees. In the distance, wheat was being threshed in the old-fashioned way, with yoked oxen trudging wearily round and round, trampling the wheat with their hooves. A tenth-century traveller might have met with the exact same scene. Nearby, a stream poured into a large pond and overflowed at the opposite end, the water carrying on to help irrigate the village rice fields. Outside it was a pleasant pastoral scene. But inside, within the high walls of the *komiteh*, it was sheer hell.

As we entered through a low wooden doorway the heat became tremendous, and not a breath of air was felt. A young mujahed, perhaps eighteen or nineteen, with wild unkempt hair and an equally wild look in his eyes, took us into a messy room, plagued with flies. Two men lying on the floor got up lazily to shake our hands. They were older but looked no better. For some reason I took an immediate dislike to one of them. His name was Daoud.

We sat down and drank tea from dirty glasses. Talk centred on a friend of Algia Abdul, who should have been here waiting for us. His absence was obviously not part of the plan; he was supposed to have helped us on the next stage of our journey, and I could tell by the expression on Nebi's face that this was a matter for grave concern. Then there was mention of another village, back towards the Hezbollah base we had just come from, but exactly what was being said about it was difficult to determine. It sounded as if there had been some fighting.

A short while later Algia Abdul got up suddenly and promised he would be back, without saying when. Minutes later, Nebi also did the same, leaving Karim and I on our own to sweat it out in the heat. My hopes of an early departure were dashed.

The rest of that first day we spent in the company of Daoud and his men, but they were far from friendly and worse still, they insisted we stay within the *komiteh* walls. Much of the time we sat silently in the room, for the sun shone directly onto the tiny courtyard outside and it was without shade; there was little wind where we were either, though the branches of the trees outside could be heard to rustle occasionally. A second day came, and then another, and still there was no sign of Nebi or Algia Abdul. Flies crawled over everything during the day and mosquitoes reigned in the night. Each morning my forehead was covered in bites and I grew anxious about malaria. Scorpions were also in abundance in the rooftop woodpile, near to where we slept. Once I caught a large amber-coloured specimen climbing down the wall above my head, and with a heavy stick, smashed it with all my strength. Incredibly, it shook off this attack and carried on as if nothing had happened.

The wildlife proved to be the least of my problems. The greatest threat was soon to come from a completely different quarter.

In the late afternoon of the fourth day of waiting, with Karim asleep on the floor, I caught the three men rifling through my bag.

The wild-eyed youth sprung back with fright and scuttled away. From the remaining two there was little response, except for Daoud who sat there and sneered. I was furious. All the pent-up frustration of the past few days began to boil over. I snatched at the bag and saw the few remaining rolls of film I had were missing.

Daoud shrugged his shoulders when I demanded to know where they were, and made a snide comment to his friend that angered me even further.

'Film? What film?' he said silkily.

Karim stirred, but all I could see through my rage was Daoud's mocking sneer. I hit him hard in the chest with an open hand, knocking him flat. Five rolls of film spilt out of his pockets onto the floor. He jumped to his feet, red-faced and angry. We were on the point of launching into each other when Karim woke up and stepped in, still groggy and half asleep. The instant he saw the open bag he guessed what had happened.

Daoud stormed out and Karim looked suddenly worried.

Still steaming, I threw the film into my bag and found some more under the mat Daoud had been sitting on. The other man sat unmoved with his back against the wall.

'Let's go,' I said to Karim.

'Where?' he replied.

He wiped a hand over his eyes. I was putting him in a difficult situation. Algia Abdul's orders had no doubt been to stay with me, and possibly to remain near the *komiteh*.

'Away from this place,' I said.

He looked at the ground, searching, but I didn't wait for an answer. Half way out the door leading into the courtyard, I caught sight of him hurriedly collecting his things and assumed he was coming.

The gate to the outside world was set in a wall only ten yards away. I had to get out. But anger and frustration at being cooped up all this time made me reckless. When a threatening Daoud appeared with a Kalishnakov across his chest, I tried to force my way past him. He caught my shoulder, his face working with rage, and shoved me back against the wall, screaming, 'Moushkel!'

He then indicated that I was a Soviet spy who took photographs.

'I am a friend of Haji Qary Ahmad Ali!' I bellowed.

He relaxed his grip and in that brief instant, I pushed with all my weight and sent him sprawling awkwardly in the dust. As I opened the gate and looked behind, Karim was still nowhere in sight.

My tunnel vision was by now absolute. I remember striding off across a small field of harvested wheat, and then, seeing someone run out in front, yelling hysterically. It was not Daoud, but the young wild-eyed mujahed waving a gun. He fired erratically and the ground exploded at my feet. I stopped dead. His voice was high-pitched and strained, barely intelligible.

Tiny bubbles of saliva appeared at the corners of his mouth. The acrid smell of cordite was very strong. I should have been scared; fear would have been a wise emotion to show at that moment, but the feeling that drove me to take another few steps towards this crazy youth was anger, complete and unmitigated fury. In this brazen and quite dangerous mood, I had somehow got it into my head that he wouldn't shoot.

What saved me then from losing a foot or two was the Islamic cavalry's timely arrival. Karim appeared close by with a Kalishnakov levelled at my assailant. He spoke rapidly and in measured terms, the nature of which was all too clear. The young man blinked, dropped the gun and took a step backwards. He looked surprised, like someone who is roused from a daydream. A sweat had broken out on his forehead. Beads of perspiration were running down the side of his face. Tears rolled down his cheeks. We watched him wander off with his face buried deep in his hands.

'Crazy man,' said Karim, sadly. 'Allah protect him.'

FORTY

We escaped to the *komiteh* of a certain Commander Azim, barely a mile's walk outside the village, but far enough away from Daoud. Beyond these walls, an orchard of apple and mulberry trees stretched for roughly ten or fifteen acres, and row upon row of untended grape vines surrounded a large, deserted white house at the centre. The owners had long ago traded land for the safety of Iran.

Commander Azim was a strong and experienced leader, with a tally of kills that included the single-handed destruction of three Soviet tanks and the capture of a fourth. It was parked outside.

'Tomorrow!' he said that night with a roguish grin. 'Tomorrow we will drive into the city to the markets.'

But in the morning when we awoke, he had gone – on a mission, one of the men said, and it was left at that.

The *komiteh* was an ancient fortified caravanserai, built in the days when traders travelling the Silk Road were simple prey for marauding tribes. Caravanserai like this one were used for protection at night and were strong and easily defended. The high walls measured four feet thick and at each corner watchtowers provided an unobstructed view of the surrounding countryside.

Later on, Karim and I wandered into the orchard grounds, sampling fruit from the overhanging branches as we went. The white house was enormous by Afghan standards. It possessed two floors, both in a dishevelled state. The first contained a number of small rooms – possibly for servants – and an entrance hall with wide stairs in two flights. The second floor was undoubtedly the main living area. Two large semi-circular rooms, one on each side of the house, were apparently for morning and evening use. The bay windows were tall and wide, and a cool wind whipped the ragged curtains.

'What do you think?' I asked Karim.

But Karim was busy going from room to room, gazing out the windows at the extent of the property below, a look of awe upon his face. It was still a beautiful home, even after years of neglect. Whoever had left it must have done so with a broken heart.

We had started back along a track through the mulberry trees when, from behind a wall, two men appeared walking swiftly towards us. Karim stiffened, instinctively reaching for the safety catch on his gun, but only for a second. It was Nebi and Algia Abdul Wahab.

There followed a lot of head shaking and clicking of tongues as Karim explained what had happened, and Nebi was very apologetic.

'Please, don't be,' I replied. 'I was also at fault.'

But he was adamant. 'You are a guest!' he said, and the matter was not spoken of again. To accept any blame on my part would bring dishonour upon him.

Instead, he squatted down and drew some lines in the dust. For the past two days, he told us, they had been involved with a major attack force, combining several mujahedeen groups in an attempt to capture a local village to the north-west. The man who was supposed to have been waiting for us a few days ago, having received news of the attack, had opted to go and join Hezbollah. This much was gleaned, with difficulty apparently, from Daoud's men.

'But with God's help,' boasted Algia, 'we were victorious!'

Nebi, however, was more subdued. There had been casualties, I could tell.

'How many shayeed?' I asked.

'Ten,' he replied. 'Two from Hezbollah – Adbul Guffarr and Behshir Heydari. They were caught in the open when the tanks came.'

I listened to the story with a heavy heart. Both men I knew well. Behshir was always wanting his photograph taken, loaded up with every weapon he could get his hands on. He was only eighteen and it had been his first trip into Afghanistan. Abdul was older by six years and spoke only when he had something important to say. He and Nebi were alike and equally respected amongst the others. It was Abdul who always wore white and who had befriended the fierce old ginger tomcat back at the border fort.

Nebi pointed at the short distance between us and a nearby mulberry tree.

'Massoud, I came this close to the enemy, this close!'

Laid across his lap was a new and better machine-gun. There was no point in asking what happened next: to the victor the spoils.

He got slowly to his feet and adjusted his turban.

'Harrakat?' he asked.

'Harrakat,' I nodded. 'Let's go.'

We walked for three or four hours along the stony banks of the Hari Rud to Seoshan, and arrived just as the sun was touching the pine tree tops. Wide canals flowing with crystal-clear water from the Hari Rud followed the main pathways through the village. A group of young girls were scouring pots and pans with sand and water but when Abdul Algia greeted them, they giggled and hid their faces.

Past the closely built houses a stone bridge spanned the main canal. Next to it was a peculiar hut of mud brick, built slightly over the canal on stilts. It had no windows as such and looked like it might be an outhouse. Beyond this was the home of a Jamiat Free Front Commander, Sufi Seqi, a two-storey building like a terraced house in any London street. On either side were ten or twenty houses almost exactly the same, some with small businesses opening out into the street. I recognised a tailor's shop and a general foods store selling amongst other things sugar from Pakistan and soap from the Soviet Union.

'Salaam,' Nebi raised his voice through the open doorway.

We waited outside until a small boy appeared round a corner and bid us to follow him upstairs. In a side room to the right of the entrance, the floor was covered with straw and a cow was scratching itself contentedly against the handlebars of a motorbike.

Sufi Seqi gripped my hand and smiled with great warmth. He was broad-shouldered and tall, and this he accentuated even further by wearing a dark shalwar camise and a black turban. Everything else about him was also black: his hair and beard, his eyes – only they were laughing eyes. He had a cavernous bass voice that welcomed us and then roared at the boy for being slow with some tea.

'Sit and rest my friends,' he rumbled. 'What brings you to Seoshan? Whatever it is, I am very glad of it. How are you, Nebi? And Abdul, you are looking well, God give you long life.'

As Nebi explained why we had come to him, he listened with great interest and cocked his head slightly at the mention of where we had come from. When Nebi had finished, he smiled at me.

'You are Massoud?'

'That's right,' I replied.

'You gave a letter to my friend, Commander Houssein Gharmani?'

'Yes.'

'Then it is done,' he said.

I noticed that even Nebi appeared surprised.

'I also have a letter from him,' he continued, 'which already explains who you are and what you are doing. Because of this, I will do whatever is necessary to help.'

If it was coincidence, then it was uncanny. If it was luck, it was outrageous. If it was my plucky little guardian angel, then it was completely believable; bless his little cotton socks.

Later it is almost dark when several mujahedeen clump up the stairs, bringing the kerosene lamps. Shortly afterwards, plates of rice, fried aubergine, tomato and a prickly green vegetable called *Kado* are brought in. Sufi Seqi does a lot of the talking. His deep voice reverberates round the room. He tells me that he would one day like to learn English, and advances the idea that I should stay to become his teacher. It is a suggestion which I politely turn down.

When everyone has eaten their fill, the plates are cleared up and the last of the tea is poured out. Finally, one by one, the men stand up and thank their host before wandering back to their homes. Those of us that remain fold our waistcoats into pillows and stretch out under our *patou* to sleep. The lamps are extinguished. The noise abates, though I can hear the cow shuffling about in the straw below us, and the unpleasant whine of mosquitoes. A dog barks somewhere in the middle distance and then stops.

'Tomorrow,' I whisper to Nebi, 'you are going back?'

He lowers his eyelids and hesitates before answering. There is a sadness in his voice.

'After morning prayer, Massoud. God willing.'

Then he too folds his waistcoat and lies back with his eyes closed. The respect I have for this man is great. He can't read or write, but that is just the product of the fighting. He is a man educated in the ways of war, and his inner strength has been forged through a lifetime of hardship. We lie side by side as the night slowly passes, and I marvel at the way our two worlds have come together for this brief time. The experiences we have shared shall never be forgotten. For my own part at least, I have been moved from where I used to be, and can never go back.

In the morning with the coming of dawn, it is time for them to go to prayer. I wait outside the mosque by the stone bridge for my friends to return. From out of the mosque's wooden doors comes Karim first, then Abdul Algia, and I thank them both for their kindness and friendship. They shake my hand and we embrace. Nebi is the last to appear.

'God go with you my friend,' he says. 'You will return to us?'

'One day, I hope.'

'Good,' he says, 'I will be waiting.'

He takes my hands and asks one final favour. 'The world is great, but you are free to travel and see many sides. God has given you this honour. I ask you, go to the house of my enemy, the *Shurevi* capital Moscow and ask, why did they attack us? I would very much like to know. You will do this?'

I say, 'Yes.'

The other two men shoulder their weapons.

'Yes,' I repeat. 'Of course I will.'

Nebi is smiling as he hugs me to both cheeks. Then he reaches inside his waistcoat and withdraws a Russian Kalishnakov bayonet. The sheath is metal and blunt at the end from digging fox-holes. Such a knife is a rare and highly prized thing amongst the mujahedeen.

He hands it to me.

'Come back soon, Massoud,' he says.

Then he turns on his heels and walks away.

My name is his family's name. We have shared everything together and have seldom been apart. It is hardly surprising then that I feel I have just said goodbye to a brother.

FORTY-ONE

'We,' said the old man snootily later that same morning, 'are Sunni Muslims, not Shia. We are not like your Shia friends. Here, water is sacred.'

He was talking about the small hut on the river which, far from being an outhouse, was in fact a place for washing for prayer, its sanctity almost that of a mosque. He then showed me to a narrow recess in a wall, overhanging someone's garden, with a round hole in the floor and clumps of earth nearby. It was my first lesson of the day. Having learned the ways of Shiadom with Hezbollah, especially in matters of daily ablution where water was used for cleaning the nether regions, I was now confronted with a whole new set of rules. Water was out. It was back to using the bare earth.

The second lesson came shortly afterwards, near the bridge opposite the mosque. It was an old lesson but an entirely sensible one. Think twice before accepting lifts from strange men.

The powerful motorbike tore along the river bank and skidded to a halt beside me. The rider told me to get on and gunned the engine impatiently. His turban partly hid his face. I assumed he was one of Sufi Seqi's men and climbed on. The speed at which he negotiated the narrow paths was frightening.

On the other side of the village, where the bombed-out buildings outnumbered the 'whole' ones, was an old, ramshackle farmhouse with a long tree-lined drive and a corral for camels. There were ten of the beasts, all sitting facing the same direction, munching on bread and watermelon.

A grey-bearded man, with patches of bright cloth sewn round the worn edges of his waistcoat, came out and escorted me into an empty room.

'Wait here,' and he pointed to some cushions in the corner. I sat down. I had my camera bag and the knife. Whatever was happening, at least I was ready.

A few minutes went by.

'Have you seen Commander Ghollum Yeyah?'

I looked round to see a red-bearded mujahed staring at me through the window. His Farci was guttural – more Arabic sounding, and quite different from the accent I was used to.

'No,' I said. 'Have you seen Commander Sufi Seqi?'

He crinkled up his eyes and looked puzzled.

'Who?'

'Sufi Seqi,' I repeated.

He shrugged indifferently and disappeared for a few seconds, until I caught sight of him running across a courtyard into another building. I was beginning to feel that my previous assumptions regarding my readiness were incorrect, and I reminded myself that one should never assume anything in Afghanistan.

Presently the door opened and a gaunt, wiry man in his thirties entered. I stood up and we shook hands and exchanged a few polite words. He seated himself against the opposite wall. I was about to strike up a conversation when Redbeard came in, followed by a very stern-faced fellow who bore the instantly recognisable qualities of authority: the majestic air, the immaculate clothes, the proud and defiant expression. Here, it seemed, was Ghollum Yeyah.

'Salaam Aleikum,' I said.

He acknowledged my greeting with a slow nod of his head. He was the perfect noble Afghan, of middle height, with a close-clipped moustache and neatly trimmed beard. A bandolier was across his chest and a pistol at his hip. His clothes, I could see, were of superior quality and came from Pakistan. The shirt pocket was lightly embroidered. He had the hard-bitten, tired look of a seasoned fighter and his presence was daunting.

'You are a writer?' he said, scowling.

'That's right,' I replied.

'And what good will your writing do us?'

'Perhaps a lot, perhaps nothing. I can't make any promises.'

He nodded thoughtfully and stroked his beard.

'Good!' he said. 'It is wrong to make promises you cannot be certain to keep. You are alone I see.'

'Yes.'

'Then you have risked a great deal in coming here.'

'No more than you,' I said.

'But this is my country and these are my friends.'

'I don't see any enemies of mine in this room.'

A faint smile flashed across his face and I took this to be a tacit sign of approval. But there our interview ended. Redbeard leaned forward and whispered something urgently to Yeyah.

'We must leave you,' said Ghollum Yeyah with his usual abruptness.

I followed them out. A sand-coloured Nissan jeep, its engine smoothly ticking over, was already waiting outside.

'Tomorrow morning,' he added, 'we will speak again.'

Redbeard gunned the engine, Yeyah and the other man climbed in, and then they raced out through the gates at top speed. Whatever was going on, it was something important. But once they were out of sight, an uneasy silence came down upon the old farmhouse. It was almost too still, like the quiet that comes before a storm.

The rest of the day was spent at the farmhouse updating my journal, seeking refuge from the afternoon heat and trying to make sense of my situation. More than anything, I needed friends in high places, but it wasn't easy to know who these people were. Was Sufi Seqi, for instance, more or less powerful than Ghollum Yeyah? Had he sent me here as a test, or was this the first staging post in the journey to Pakistan? If so, where was the next? Not knowing meant not being in control, and not being in control was thoroughly unnerving.

One other disturbing factor that had recently come to my attention was that according to Sufi Seqi, the government had placed a reward on the head of any foreigner found illegally in the country. The money was ludicrous; one million dollars, he had said. Anyone with a few scruples missing would undoubtedly hand me in for less than twenty. But by the evening I had failed to come up with any solutions. I could only prescribe patience, a policy of wait and see. I ate and slept up on the roof, accompanied by the elderly mujahed with the colourful waistcoat. He snored heartily for most of the night, a noise like the growl of artillery that pervaded my dreams and filled them with scenes of death and destruction.

FORTY-TWO

When I woke before dawn, I was lying dangerously close to the edge of the roof, and the air indeed was trembling with the thunder of big guns. Urgent voices and the bellowing of camels sounded in the courtyard below. In the half-light, the commanding figure of Ghollum Yeyah was only just visible. A hand clasped my shoulder and I looked round to find the old man beckoning me downstairs.

On the way down a mujahed was sitting on the bottom steps with a bloodied bandage round his head. He was quietly rocking back and forth, shaking with delayed shock. I passed him by, lamenting the lack of modern medicines I did not possess, and went out into the courtyard. Ghollum Yeyah saw me coming. His feet were apart, his hands on his hips.

'You wish to go to war?' he said bluntly as I came up to him.

It was obvious that they were. Activity was frantic; extra boxes of ammunition were being tied onto the jeep. It was also clear that he wasn't asking me a question, but stating the alternatives. If my answer was no, my *raison d'être* in Afghanistan was a lie, and a cowardly one at that. If I said yes, then I was worthy of their help. I chose the latter and feigned enthusiasm.

Redbeard was already in the driver's seat, waiting. Between the supplies and ammunition there was just enough room for me in the passenger seat, and I had to rest my feet gingerly upon half a dozen rocket-propelled grenades. We raced off and drove to the edge of the village, past an open stall selling watermelon, and stopped beside a group of people gathered near a bridge. For the next five minutes the young children swarmed around the jeep and stared. I took their photograph. They laughed, happy smiling faces. Then we were away again, out over the bare, scrubby desert which lies to the south of Herat.

The dirt road took us through two seemingly deserted villages before reaching the Hari Rud, and we crossed over where the river was wide and shallow. On the far side the road turned into a narrow track, and I was transferred onto the back of a waiting motorbike. The rider kicked the engine over and it started first time. Redbeard disappeared up river. All the time, the sound of gunfire and the dull thud of explosions came ever closer.

At one point, on the outskirts of another village, we encountered a funeral procession heading for the river. They were all mujahedeen. Sad, tired men carrying the body upon a stretcher at shoulder height. We pulled over to let them pass and as they did, the bloody figure came into view, stiffened with *rigor mortis* and robbed of dignity, the face locked in a mask of pain, the clothes blackened and in rags.

Every few minutes we passed other processions, but not all were the same. There were also villagers carrying their belongings away from the scene of the battle, children clinging to their mother's chador. They would no doubt return once the fighting was over.

A quarter of an hour later we left the motorbike behind and walked quickly along the banks of an irrigation canal, through someone's bomb-damaged garden, and into Korskack, the government-held village under attack by mujahedeen forces. Nearby, in a two-storeyed house, was the main command post. We approached several mujahedeen who were on guard outside.

'Who do you want?' one of them asked.

'Commander Afzali.'

The same mujahed nodded for us to enter. 'Inside,' he said.

We went upstairs into a long room where about twenty mujahedeen were seated round the walls on the floor. My companion introduced me to the commander, Jagtoran (Colonel) Azizullah Afzali, a short and stocky bulldoggish man who looked as though he hadn't slept in days.

We sat down and while the tea was poured, he told us that the battle was almost won. This was the first opportunity since the early hours of the morning for any of them to rest. The enemy had been forced to retreat to positions outside the village, although the threat of counterattack was still present.

'This night,' the commander said, 'they will come.'

The hunter, having cornered his prey, was in turn to become the hunted.

Shortly afterwards, a young man called Sayid offered to take me to the areas they had captured, places which, only a few hours before, had been inhabited by government troops and militiamen. Sayid was a twenty-year-old nurse whose medical training had come from the Red Cross in Pakistan. Because of this, the others referred to him as *Doktor*, a title he was quick to shrug off. He was intelligent, mature and could even speak a few words of English, but his deep blue eyes were set in a face that was scarred with having seen the true horrors of war from an operating table.

The sides of the road leading towards the village centre were lined with the walls of abandoned houses, each with a faded wooden door in blue or green. The road itself was concave from countless years of traffic, and the middle was soft sand. We kept to the higher and firmer sides for fear of mines, and eventually stopped beside the entrance to a narrow alleyway. Inches beyond the gate was a shallow blast hole where an anti-personnel mine had exploded.

'You see what the government do,' Sayid murmured. 'As they retreat, they mine everything. Even the doorways of homes.'

Of the three amputations he had assisted in last night, two of the victims were civilian women. All had been trying to flee. Advance warning of the attack had been given to those villagers who could be trusted.

Later, a passing mujahedeen patrol took us to what had previously been the government forces' main headquarters. It was in the village centre, which was an open area with few houses. In front of the building was a pond filled with cloudy water. A stray mortar shell had landed in the middle during the fight, and the silt had yet to settle.

Inside, they showed me a collection of empty vodka bottles, imported from Moscow, and boxes of Russian matches scattered about the floor, discarded in their haste by the guards on duty. A half-eaten meal was also left on the floor. The building had been abandoned soon after the first shots were fired, and the troops had sought refuge in the better defended posts spread throughout the village.

One of these mini-forts I was taken to see later in the day. It stood above a crossroads with tiny slits for windows, though on one side there was a neat round hole that marked the entry point of a mujahedeen rocket. Inside, the roof had caved in and there were dark stains on the floor and walls. This short visit, however, turned out to be extremely fortuitous for our group, since the government headquarters back in the village centre was ripped apart by a huge explosion, soon after we had left it. Miraculously no one was killed and there were only a few injuries, but the whole building was wired like a trap – a time bomb, just waiting to go off.

The men I was with began to get twitchy after news of this reached us. No doubt they feared similar devices lurked within the walls around us. So, led by Sayid, we took up residence in a house round the corner. It was cool and spacious, but best of all there were no bullet holes in the walls and bloodstains on the floor.

'Tell me, Sayid,' I asked. 'Is Azizullah Afzali together with Ghollum Yeyah and Sufi Seqi?'

'That's right.' Sayid smiled. 'You know everyone.'

'But not Ismail Khan.'

The smile all but vanished.

'Ismail Khan is the leader of Jamiat-i-Islami. We are Jamiat Free Front. Our mujahedeen fight many times more than Ismail Khan's men. They have all the money and weapons, but we do all the fighting. Sometimes we must steal ammunition from him, other times we buy from the militia.'

'They sell to you?' I asked incredulously.

He threw his head back and laughed. 'They sell to one of our spies, who they think is working for the government. But it is expensive. For this battle we had to spend 280,000 rupees. It was about seven hundred dollars.

'All the time, Commander Afzali asks him to join us. He says, "Together we can take Herat in a month." But Ismail Khan wants to be chief commander of all mujahedeen in Herat, not just an equal you see, and this is unacceptable to the other commanders. There is unity amongst the mujahedeen in Herat, but not yet with Jamiat-i-Islami.'

He went on to describe the increasing popularity of Commander Azizullah Afzali who, like Ismail Khan, had attained some rank in the Afghan army before the Soviet invasion. Added to this was the high status of the Afzali family in Herat. Azizullah's two older brothers, Hafizullah and Sefiola, were revolutionary leaders in the early 1970s until their assassination, reputedly at the hands of the KGB. They had been resisting Soviet interference in Afghan politics long before the actual invasion in December 1979.

Jamiat Free Front, he said, also attracted Muslims from other countries who came to fight in the Jihad.

I thought immediately of Redbeard, who certainly wasn't Afghan. The truth was they came from places like Saudi Arabia, Tunisia, Iraq, Turkey, Egypt, Morocco, even England.

'Do you know Yusef Islam?' he asked excitedly.

The name rang a bell. I remembered the husband of a famous English actress who turned Buddhist once, but that wasn't it.

Then it hit me.

'Cat Stevens,' I cried, 'is Yusef Islam! He was here, in Herat?'

'No. Jalalabad, near Kabul. Long way from here.'

Mention of the name brought back a host of memories. I even sang a few bars of *Where do the children play* and the tune stayed with me for hours. It was all the more striking for where the song was being sung; in such a land children shouldered rifles and learned about warfare.

Sayid and the others slept through most of the afternoon, covered from head to toe with their all-purpose *patou*, resembling cocooned insects wrapped in silken thread. When they finally stirred it was about four o'clock. I went out and collected some wood for a fire, and while the tea was prepared, a pot and some glasses were retrieved from the empty enemy fort. There was water in a well out the back.

Afterwards, with the shadows lengthening across the ground, it was decided that we should leave the house and find a stronger building, one which could better withstand the expected counterattack. The standard enemy practice after losing ground was invariably withdrawal, only to indiscriminately blast whatever they could from afar. While the mujahedeen tried to limit the destruction of civilian property in their attacks, the government forces couldn't give a damn. Often they were not from the region anyway. Soldiers enlisted from the far north had no qualms about wanton destruction in the south.

I asked Sayid what he thought would happen.

'If they attack,' he said, 'it will come just after dark. I doubt that they will use their tanks because they know we have the weapons to stop them. The militia, I think, will not fight. Only the soldiers will try perhaps, after the shelling.'

He looked about the house we were in with an expression of open disapproval.

'We had better go soon,' he said.

By the time darkness had fallen we had joined together with another band of mujahedeen in a fortified building, close to the damaged command centre. Small groups like ours were apparently spread across the village, backing up the main forces which occupied the forward positions. A meal of rice and bread was prepared and we ate in an upstairs room. If the building was hit indirectly, there was a better chance of survival up here rather than downstairs for the simple reason that if the structure collapsed, it wouldn't be on our heads. Faith was put more in God than the strength of ageing mud brick construction. As the last handfuls of rice were scooped up, the attack began.

Dust fell from the ceiling in a shower when the first shell landed. Heads ducked instinctively as the immense power and shock of the explosion was felt. I inhaled deeply and slowly, filling my lungs to the bottom as if it were my last breath. I thought of tomorrow, and the next day, and the one after that – envisioned walking through the mountains and gazing down upon the open deserts, saw myself crossing into Pakistan. Everything that was my future I concentrated upon, for the future is a wonderful thing to behold when the present is so threatened.

During the night, in the dreadful silence that followed each blast, when the distant firing of artillery or rockets was heard, all movement, all talking ceased. In those few seconds every ear was trained upon the heavens above, waiting to hear the telltale scream of incoming shells. Many times they did come, ripping open the night sky with such violence only to obliterate a neighbouring house or the small rice field behind us. Our own shelter was spared. But for a very long hour the blackness overhead was filled with the high-pitched scream of death, and that noise stretched every nerve to breaking point. Night was illuminated like the brightest day.

At first light, it was discovered that not everyone had been as fortunate as us. A torn and bloodied waistcoat was brought into the room for identification; the body had been unrecognisable. One of the older men rose slowly to his feet when he saw the garment. A stiffening came over his whole body. Little by little his face emptied of expression and his eyes began to redden and weep. I was later told he had lost his only son.

There seemed little reason for me to stay any longer in Korskack. The government soldiers, thankfully, had not come and were not expected to. Either they hadn't the stomach for a fight, or they hadn't the strength in numbers. As could be expected, my friends intimated it was the former of the two, but I wasn't convinced. When Sayid appeared riding a motorbike and suggested that we visit a local village called Nobadam, I gladly accepted. If the government troops were massing on the outskirts for the counterattack, I wanted to be well clear.

But Nobadam, only a mile or so from Korskack, turned out to be the same. It too had recently been liberated and the threat of artillery bombardment and attack was ever-present. Many of the smaller pathways were still mined, one of which I made the grave mistake of walking down. To my horror half a dozen round, pudding-sized anti-personnel mines were retrieved from the sand and put away for later use. Each one was eminently capable of blowing a leg off. And indeed, in another part of the village we found evidence to prove it: the remnants of a bloodstained shoe, with part of someone's foot still attached.

'One of theirs,' Sayid said, nudging the mess with a stick. The flies buzzed upwards in a dark cloud. For the life of me I couldn't see how he could tell.

We left Nobadam soon afterwards, stopping only to see its thousand-year-old *Medreseh*, or religious college, where the giant tree standing outside was said to be the same age. Then I returned with Sayid, back the way I had come across the river, back along the edge of the desert aboard a borrowed motorbike, back to the village of Seoshan. Always going back. I was beginning to wonder when I would ever be going forwards.

FORTY-THREE

The *komiteh* of Commander Jagtoran Azizullah Afzali was a strong fort surrounded by the usual defensive wall, and also by fields of harvested wheat. The ground was hard and cracked, and covered with the stubble of broken wheat stalks. In the far corner, peasant farmers in dirty white turbans were separating the chaff from the grain by pitching it up into the wind with a rake of forked sticks.

We rode into the courtyard through a wooden gate and left the bike propped up against a stable wall. Inside was a fine-looking chestnut mare which, Sayid explained, belonged to the Commander.

'One hundred and forty thousand rupees,' he said. 'This animal can outrun a tank!'

In the largest of the *komiteh*'s two main rooms we found Commander Afzali together with a small group of mujahedeen, some of whom I recognised from Korskack. I was greeted warmly, as a friend, and seated at the furthest end of the room from the door, a gesture of respect that was similar to being offered the most comfortable chair in the house. The

Commander spoke briefly to Sayid and learned of our visit to Nobadam. He nodded approvingly and then, taking an empty glass of tea, placed it firmly down in front of him.

'Are you BBC?' he asked.

'No,' I replied.

'Voice of America?'

'I'm not with anyone,' I said. 'I'm here alone.'

There was a short pause.

'The BBC,' he announced vociferously, 'I do not like. They speak only of Kabul and Jalalabad, but never Herat. They say a military victory is impossible for the mujahedeen. But here, you saw! We captured two large villages – important villages! A military victory is certain in Herat, God willing, and once the city is ours the other cities will begin to fall after it. The revolution began here and it will finish here. Tell this to the people of the BBC!'

I nodded.

'Thank you,' he replied, and then added, 'it is not easy for us, you understand.'

'War is never easy,' I said.

He sighed, 'That is God's truth!'

Our conversation was suddenly interrupted by the afternoon prayer. A man wearing a white *dishdasha*, the ankle-length Arab shirt, was hounding the men outside to hurry up and join him. He was a doctor from the Sudan apparently and a bit of a religious fanatic.

'Avoid him if possible,' advised Sayid with a grin on his way out to prayer. 'He is not like us.'

While waiting, I sifted through some Iranian books and pamphlets that were piled in a corner. Amongst them was an American instruction manual on how to use the RPG rocket launcher. The terminology was baffling, the facts and figures exhaustive, but it was written entirely in English and a joy to read. By the time I had finished, Azizullah and his men were filing back in and taking their places on the floor around the edge of the room. The floor covering was made up of overlapping kilim carpets known as *Dawhom*, for their colour, size and quality. On one of these I spread out my map of Afghanistan.

'Which is the best way to Pakistan?' I asked.

The commander pulled the sheet towards him and took out a pen. He started ticking off a number of villages and then stopped just short of Kandahar and the border.

'Here is Piesang,' he said indifferently. 'From there you can go by truck to Pakistan.'

He tossed the pen down onto the map and sat back. The way he spoke made it seem incredibly easy, as if the five-hundred-mile walk to Piesang, let alone the rest of the journey, was no more than a jaunt in the country.

'How many days?' I asked.

'Walking every day,' he said, pushing his turban back and wiping his brow, 'I think twenty. But that is every day, very fast, with very little sleep.'

I tried to appear undaunted, but my next question was broken off by the sudden and somewhat surprising arrival of Redbeard who strode in, shook the hand of Azizullah, greeted everyone else with his nominal style of courtesy, then looked me straight in the eye as if to say, well aren't you coming? No one could describe him as a man of many words.

'I am coming with you?' I asked him.

He grunted in the affirmative and I noticed Sayid give a nod as well. My plans of enlisting the help of Commander Azizullah Afzali were, it appeared, no more. I put away the map and stood up. The others got to their feet and at the door Sayid came forward with a *patou*. It was a gift, he said, from the Commander.

'You will need it in the mountains.'

'I probably will,' I said. 'Thank you.'

At the back of the room, Azizullah Afzali was absent-mindedly flicking through the pages of the RPG manual. Admittedly he was a man with a lot to think about. I slung the grey-green rug over my shoulder and followed Redbeard out through the gate.

That night was to be my last in Herat. Ghollum Yeyah had been the one to decide my future after all, and he was sending me on.

But as last nights go, it was one that would long be remembered.

On the roof of Yeyah's *komiteh*, the empty bowls of rice had been collected and the bread was being wrapped up in a cloth for the next day when a messenger arrived, bearing a special invitation. A war video, of all things, was about to be shown at a neighbouring house. My incredulity, I thought, was not unreasonable. However, when we arrived the rooftop cinema was already packed with about sixty villagers and mujahedeen, gathered in a semi-circle round a battered television set and similarly antiquated video recorder.

Somewhere in the darkness below us a generator was cranked into life and we hurried to find a seat. Lights were dimmed to increase the power, the screen flickered into life and a jubilant audience cried out with glee. As for myself, I simply could not believe what I was seeing. When the picture stopped rolling, the face on the screen was that of Sandy Gall, a well-known British broadcaster, introducing a documentary on the war in Afghanistan. It was called *Agony of a Nation*.

Because the narration included only a few subtitles in Farci, I spent the next hour or so translating as best I could to the captivated crowd. Their questions came thick and fast.

'Is it Kabul, Massoud?' someone would shout.

It was indeed Kabul, and a group of mujahedeen came into view.

'What are they talking about?' said another.

'The Russians and the government,' I replied. 'They are planning an attack on a Russian fort.'

'Ay Khorda! God give them strength. What else? What else?'

And so it went on. When a well-known Jamiat commander from the North was interviewed, roars of delight rose up into the air. When pictures of multiple rocket launchers were shown firing off round after round, the audience was practically on their feet and dancing. A tremendous feeling of optimism was in the air. Here was their Holy War captured on film and brought to them in an almost magical way. How could they lose!

Ironically, however, the truth was brought home unexpectedly while we watched these scenes of war. The local government fort opened up their artillery on a village hardly a mile away from where we sat. The trajectory was directly overhead and missiles were exploding with devastating force beyond the television set, lighting up the sky in brilliant flashes. When the shockwaves reached us, nothing could be done to stop the picture from rolling.

FORTY-FOUR

Next morning, Commander Ghollum Yeyah's last words to me were highly portentous.

'No one can know what will happen to you,' he said.

Earlier he had explained that I would travel to Pashtun Zorgan, a village about two days' walk away, where I could expect to find a major Jamiat-i-Islami group and either Ismail Khan himself or his right-hand man, Hariff Khan. There was only one catch. Part of the village was controlled by the mujahedeen group known as Hesbe-i-Islami and they were presently at war with Jamiat. I would have to be careful whom I trusted, for the Hesbe would gladly sell me to the government.

Half an hour later, I was in the desert between Herat city and the mountains to the south, ploughing through a very startled herd of wild camels at fifty miles an hour on the back of a motorbike. A young daredevil mujahed called Ali had offered to take me part of the way despite the risks involved in being out in the open. I had one eye glued on the way in front watching for potholes, while the other scanned the sky for helicopters.

We made it to the relative safety of the mountains without incident and left the bike to walk towards a camp of black nomad tents, scattered about the bare and rocky hillside. Like the hulls of upturned boats they were dug down into the hard earth and pointed into the wind. A party of bare-footed children, boys and girls, steered us in the direction of the largest tent and then ran off. The womenfolk also disappeared swiftly and peered out from behind the black cloth of their homes. It was the first time I had seen so many women in one place.

The headman came out to greet us. His name was Adam Khan, a tall, elderly man with a long grey beard and a turban the colour of sand. He would, he said, help the *feringhi* reach Pastun Zorgan, if it be the wish of Commander Yeyah. At this, Ali returned to his motorbike, taking with him my last contact with the known world.

Adam Khan showed me into his tent where his wife, a ragged, toothless woman with a broad smile, had lit a fire on the bare earth to make some tea.

'Sia yor Sabze?' she asked politely.

'Sabze,' I said, requesting green tea instead of black.

Meanwhile, the tent slowly filled with inquisitive neighbours who squatted on the ground and stared. I felt like an alien from Mars, come to Earth in the middle ages. In order to try and clarify matters I gave Adam Khan the letter in Farci from the Geographical Institute, and watched anxiously as he studied the piece of paper upside down. It was finally returned to me with a dignified nod and nothing more was said. Clearly he couldn't read, but then neither could anyone else.

Despite this, I was on the road again to Pashtun Zorgan a short while later, escorted by two armed men who looked to be better farmers or herdsmen than fighters. Their guns were in a general state of disrepair, but were gaily decorated with bits of coloured cloth and beading. They seemed to know where they were going however, and that was all that mattered.

The land was deeply furrowed with dry gulches made by the rivers and streams that would pour down from the mountains when the rains came. We followed an undulating trail that rose and fell all day long. At the peak a view was afforded of the surrounding area, though it remained unchanged. Not a tree or bush could be seen anywhere. There was just the mountainside on our right, and the shimmering desert to the left. I kept my head down and walked quickly alongside the two men. When a lone eagle flew up in front of us, they both fired and fortunately missed.

'The last time I saw such a bird was in the south of Iran,' I said, 'and it brought good luck afterwards.'

Around midday we stopped near a village where a stream flowed out from under a rock, and where, at last, there were trees for shade. We ate bread and rested for half an hour. Above the houses, lovely green rows of elegant beeches stood swaying in the freshening wind.

'This,' said one of the men, 'is Chishmarak. Next is Qa'leh.'
'And Pashtun Zorgan?' I asked.
'Tomorrow.'

Then the journey continued, through the hot afternoon and on into the evening. When we eventually reached Qa'leh it was almost nine, and exhaustion read on all our faces.

But Qa'leh was hardly more than a large fort held by just a few mujahedeen. Recent aerial attacks had forced them to abandon any ideas of a stronger contingent, but nevertheless they welcomed us in, provided food and water and a place to sleep. When they discovered that I wasn't Afghan, someone rushed off into another room and returned with a radio, explaining that it was almost time for the Farci edition of the BBC World Service.

'There was much fighting in Herat yesterday,' he said. 'Perhaps they will have news?'

My ears pricked up. Did they know exactly where in Herat? Unfortunately the answer was no. We listened carefully for an hour but there was no report. Only talk of further unrest in China after the student democracy riots, and mention of a coup attempt in South America. I couldn't shake the feeling, however, that the fighting in Herat was centred on Korskack.

The following day we set out again and by mid-morning we had passed the worst. Eight or ten miles away on the far side of the desert, straddling the Hari Rud, was a long line of plane trees and what looked to be houses. This, they said, was Pashtun Zorgan. To the left was Hesbe country. To the right, Jamiat. I made sure our path went to the right.

We reached the village hours later, and walked along the edge past a line of poplar trees towards a main gate. There was a hobbled camel standing outside and a dog sleeping in the shade near an irrigation canal. Neither was in any way bothered by our presence. The place seemed almost empty.

The Jamiat *komiteh* was found a few hundred yards away,

however, tucked in behind thick walls and a doorway plated with the flattened metal from old ghee cans; the labels were still attached. My two nomad friends, who clearly knew their way around, introduced me to the mujahed on guard and I was duly admitted. They, however, had other business to attend to in the local market and so I was left alone.

Inside, a stream meandered through the centre of the courtyard. Trees and shrubs had sprouted from its banks. Stables to the immediate right were open and empty. A few mujahedeen were scattered about and one was tinkering with the engine of a motorbike. The machine was upside down, its innards spread about in obvious disarray.

'This way,' said the guard.

I followed him towards two large rooms connected by a raised patio. The sun was high and even in the shade it was hot and airless. A cloth banner hung across the front of the building with Ismail Khan's portrait at its centre.

'He is here?' I asked hopefully, looking at the banner.

The man shook his head.

'The Commandant is visiting a Jamiat hospital in Zendajan.'

He counted out four of his fingers and held them up.

'Four days from here.'

Downhearted, I drew solace from that fact that such information might not be imparted so readily if it were completely true. There was also a chance that if Ismail Khan wasn't around, his right-hand man Hariff Khan would be.

This, to my relief, was just so.

But Hariff Khan was a suspicious man. His beady eyes were set close together, seemingly magnifying their effectiveness as tools of perception. He stared without speaking for minutes on end. I explained what I had been doing in Herat, who I had been with and why, and he stroked his pointed black beard with long bony fingers. When he did speak it was to ask why I had not come to Afghanistan with Jamiat-i-Islami in the first place. I told him my allegiance was not with any one particular group, but with all.

His eyes suddenly widened.

'Even Hesbe-i-Islami?' he demanded.

'No!' I replied vehemently. 'Not Hesbe. They are worse than

dogs!' and I spat on the ground for good effect. He accepted this contentedly.

'And now you wish to go with Jamiat to Pakistan?'

'God willing,' I said.

For the rest of the afternoon and most of the following day, I helped fix the motorbike, which was a Japanese model with serious but not unsolvable electrical problems. For this gesture of goodwill I was allowed to wander more or less where I liked. When the confines of the *komiteh* became oppressive, and the anxiety of waiting became too much, I had only to seek solitude in the wide-open desert, or to sit in peace by the shady banks of the nearby stream.

Then, on the morning of the third day, Hariff Khan returned with an answer. He had written a letter, he said, that would help provide safe passage to the border. It was the best he could do. But that letter was everything I needed.

FORTY-FIVE

It was late afternoon. The old woman lay on her back in the wooden wheelbarrow like a pile of black and crumpled rags. Her mouth was open and she was moaning – partly in prayer, partly in pain. A thin, quivering, calloused hand covered her eyes. Her young grandson was rushing her into Pashtun Zorgan. She had been working in a field and had stepped on a mine.

'How far is it?' he asked, breathing hard.

Abdul Muhammad answered. 'Two days,' he said. 'Through the pass.'

'There is a doctor?'

'Yes.'

The boy nodded and we watched him head off up the trail

until he disappeared from view. Abdul Muhammad could only shake his head with despair and then look to the sky, pleadingly.

'Afghanistan!' he whispered.

I had met him back in Pashtun Zorgan. At that time, he had been preparing to return home to his village in the mountains and had offered to show me the way. He was a slightly built man in his fifties, but with taut, sinewy muscles in his arms and legs. His leathery skin was a rich brown colour, from a lifetime of exposure to the harsh wind and sun, and when he smiled his face crinkled up and his blue eyes shone brightly. Only he wasn't smiling now.

We walked on in silence for another hour or two, picking our way down a steep ravine. The last two days, I reflected, had been long and hard, what with the infernal heat, the steepness of the ascent and Abdul Muhammad's unwavering quickness of foot. We had left Hariff Khan and walked east for half a day along the Hari Rud, then waded several hours up through a narrow river gorge into the Qasa Murg Mountains. At any other place, the cliff was sheer and impenetrable.

For many years, Abdul Muhammad had said, the Russians paid little attention to the gorge, until two hundred mujahedeen used it to ambush and capture an entire ammunitions convoy.

The water had been swift and cold, but not deep. At the other end we dried ourselves and climbed steadily up through a series of gradually narrowing valleys. There were few trees at two thousand feet, and even fewer at four thousand. At every half mile or so was a sharp bend, hinting that here at last the top lay hidden. But there had always been just another rocky valley, rising up to another bend.

We finally reached the mountain pass at sunset and lit a fire amongst the boulders, huddling round it with some bread and dried apricots. It had grown cold quickly and we took it in turns to search for wood in the darkness.

That had been yesterday.

At dawn, before the heat got up, we had carried on down the other side of the mountain, zigzagging our way across the steeper sections until, some time after noon, the badly injured old woman and her grandson appeared along the trail. The difficult ground we had seen they had yet to tread. The chances of her survival once out of shock would have been close to zero.

I came to from these sad thoughts when my boot caught on a rock and I went for a tumble down the slope. Dragging myself up, I brushed off the dirt and was suddenly looking down upon a wide, fertile valley of bright green grass. Tiny black dots at the far end were nomad tents, and curls of inviting wood smoke could be seen rising up from the cooking fires within. It was a beautiful pastoral scene which promised rest and food, but when we reached the bottom our path took us in another direction.

The hours passed and still we travelled on. I became more and more used to Abdul Muhammad's fast-swinging yet relaxed step. Fatigue drifted away and like the long-distance runner, a rhythm was struck which made our pace seem effortless. It was a welcome return to the old way of travelling, before modern modes of transport taught us that distance is subject to speed. Here speed was a constant, something beyond our power to control given the various physical constraints, and rather than being measured, any journey was simply undertaken.

I took to singing any old song that came to mind, running through the Beatles, Crosby, Stills and Nash, and was just about to start on another old classic when late in the afternoon we came across a farmstead standing alone in the middle of the valley.

'Is it yours?' I asked Abdul. But he shook his head and walked on towards the building. It was made of the usual dried mud and straw, and in one of the windows I noticed a single pane of glass. A stream flowed past near the front door. Abdul Muhammad shooed away some chickens and thumped the wooden door.

'Aziz?' he hailed.

Shuffled footsteps sounded from inside and the door was opened by a tall, elegant man in his late sixties, wearing a white turban and light brown shalwar camise. There was an almost regal look about him. He could have been a deposed monarch hiding out in the hills. A *patou* was thrown over his shoulder and he carried a walking stick in his left hand. He smiled warmly, greeted us both with a firm handshake, then stepped aside to let us pass.

We took off our shoes and entered.

The light was flooding into the room. Thin cushions lined the floor near the walls and a metal pail of cool, clean water had been left in a corner. Niches in the walls contained books for the first time, instead of Kalishnakovs and rocket launchers.

Aziz was the local teacher.

'Where is Yahgobeh Guffarr?' he enquired, referring apparently to a friend of Abdul Muhammad's.

'Pashtun Zorgan.'

'Ah,' he said, nodding and then turning to me. 'Sit down, friend. Monda hasteed? You are tired? I shall bring tea.'

He left the room and returned later with a tray bearing three glasses, some lumps of sugar and a large stainless steel teapot. He set it down on the floor and poured the tea. As I took the first glass, I realised he was staring at me oddly. It was not an uncommon response. Even though my appearance was certainly Afghan in many ways, most people usually clicked eventually. I was used to it, but in this instance there was something more intense about his reaction. I decided to take the bull by the horns and use Hariff Khan's letter for the first time.

His mouth opened slightly as he read it. Abdul Muhammad I noticed, was smiling to himself in the corner and keeping quiet. Aziz looked at his friend, then back to me, and quietly asked:

'Parlez-vous Français, monsieur?'

I nearly dropped my tea.

'Français!'

The situation was truly bizarre. While I explained to him in Farci that my command of the language was definitely '*un peu*' and pretty awful, he held forth in a flood of excited French about Paris and the years he had spent there. Abdul Muhammad wanted to sleep, so Aziz and I went outside to a small, grassy knoll beside his house to talk.

His story was remarkable and I listened with fascination. This much I understood.

In 1946 he had walked to France with a book under his arm, Gautier's *Les Jeunes France*, given to him by a traveller. He couldn't read it, but he was determined to learn how. In Paris, the owner of a printing shop near Montparnasse offered him a job. He worked hard and studied the language. After ten years he eventually gained promotion. He rented an apartment, found himself some friends amongst his neighbours, even a woman to share his bed. There were many good times and his eyes glistened as he remembered them. Sadly one year there was also trouble – he wouldn't tell me what – and he had been forced to leave for Marseille.

But Marseille turned out to be a poor substitute for Paris. Unable to go back there, the lure of his own country became strong. Eventually he returned to Afghanistan to set up a printing business in Herat. He also married the daughter of an old family friend and raised a family. He saved his money and dreamed of one day going back to Paris. Then came the Soviet invasion. His wife and son were tragically killed in the early years, when the Soviet custom of carpet bombing was most common. There was little reason for carrying on. He had retired to this valley to teach.

He was without doubt an amazing and very likeable old fellow, but also just occasionally a little odd, or so it seemed. There was something about him that was very different from the people I had encountered so far in Afghanistan, or anywhere for that matter. At the time I simply put it down to his years away, but that night, after he insisted we eat with him and spend the night in his house, I watched with amazement as he performed an act of faith-healing.

Abdul Muhammad had complained of an aching back, as if Aziz were his local surgeon, but Aziz had responded by laying both his hands on the afflicted area for some time, hardly moving, sometimes hardly touching. I sat there in the light of a single oil lamp, transfixed more by the fact that this was happening here in a war zone than by the actual feat itself. Exactly what effect this had on Abdul Muhammad was uncertain, but the next morning my travelling companion was up and about like a man released from the very shackles of gravity.

By then it was difficult for us to leave. In a short space of time I had grown very fond of the strange old man. Aziz was lonely, for people and for contact with the outside world, but the pressures of time meant we had to go all the same. Abdul

Muhammad was due in his own village and this was on my way also. Still, it was hard to say goodbye. I called him 'Monsieur Aziz, le bon homme', and he laughed out loud to hide his sadness. There were even tears in his eyes – it was all so strange. Was I leaving an old friend, or someone I had only just met? For the life of me I couldn't decide which.

We gathered up our things and he walked us slowly to where the path ran by his house. Abdul Muhammad went out in front and I was about to follow when Aziz took my shoulder. He said he was an old man now, walking with difficulty. Perhaps when I was in Paris he would see it again through my eyes. It struck me then as a very curious statement to make. Not just because of where we were, in the middle of a remote and war-ravaged country, but because it was to someone going in the opposite direction. Paris could not have been further from my mind.

I walked away and he stood in the field outside his home, whistling the Marseillaise and waving until we were almost round the bend in the valley. But for a long time afterwards, long after we had lost all sight of his home, I swore that I could still hear him whistling.

Eventually Abdul Muhammad returned to his home and I joined a procession of villagers, some on horseback, others on foot, who were going to the marketplace of Dahntenghi. Nothing about the landscape changed drastically. The mountains didn't get any lower, the heat during the day didn't lessen, but I did feel that the miles and the days were beginning to pass more smoothly. It was as if I had unconsciously shifted down a gear and found my own rhythm. I would often walk ahead of the group, sometimes a mile or two in front and then sit on a rock to watch them approach. It helped to make me feel that I was more in control of my own direction, and no longer completely at the mercy of others.

In Dahntenghi, amongst lines of wooden sheds and dried mud storerooms hidden deep within a ravine, Jamiat mujahedeen watched over a bazaar that sold a huge variety of goods, from powdered dyes to livestock, combs to clothing. When they weren't doing this they used jeeps to launch lightning raids against the distant airbase of Shindand. The only side-effect was that occasionally the airbase returned the visit. Two days before my arrival a pair of MiGs had shot up the place and blasted a hole in the side of the mountain directly above the village. According to the local commander, they had been trying to start an avalanche.

But here as in other places, Hariff Khan's letter was my passport to travel. After staying the night with the fighter-traders of Dahntenghi, I went further on up the ravine to Gorgeh, Robat, Saghar, Panjumlang, mostly small villages but which were often staggering in their beauty. After a day of two of walking across bleak terrain, the sight of tall, leafy poplar trees rising up above a village in a well-watered valley, the fields of golden wheat yet to be harvested, the tiny fruit orchards, the goat herds up on the hillsides in the evening – these things were always tremendously heartening.

Then it would be a case of finding the village leader or local Jamiat commander to hand the letter to. Understandably, not every reception was warm and friendly at first. But after a time, once a few questions were answered, points clarified about my home and religion – the important thing was to have a religion – then even the wariest ones came round in the end. Quite often their stamp or signature on the back of the letter was seen in later villages as a seal of approval.

In the name of God, they would say, if Hussein Khan in Menoch Queeya trusted him, then so can we.

In this way I went from place to place, walking every day, usually all day, with a villager or mujahed as company.

Beyond Panjumlang, and the deep and winding valley of the river Ferah, the land opened out into a broad, sun-baked landscape of undulating hills for perhaps fifty miles. Then there would be yet another range of mountains, running down from central Afghanistan like the outstretched fingers of an open hand. During the day, the heat was always intense, the sky was cloudless, the wind was dry and hot. But at least it was quiet and free of war. Since the Soviet withdrawal, this was an area under the complete control of the mujahedeen.

Dogs represented my greatest fear. Approaching a nomad's

camp or a remote village was an especially uncertain and perilous venture, for they were always guarded by big, black, bristling mastiffs or a collection of common but no less ferocious mongrels. Nearing a village called Yukan, I was set upon by two such snarling beasts who had slipped their chains to come at me from behind. Wielding a heavy stick I managed to crack one of them on the skull, sending the dog tumbling back and causing its cohort to think twice about getting too close. It lunged back and forth at the tip of the stake, jaws snapping and teeth bared in a hellish growl, until someone from the village arrived to call them off. Three-headed these animals were not, but Cerberus by comparison was just a kitten.

However, after more than two weeks of walking, it was in Yukan that I began to feel closer than ever to Pakistan. It was a milestone passed. Some of the mujahedeen spoke Pashtu, a language not entirely dissimilar to Pakistan's Urdu, and everyone took *Nars*, a green powdery tobacco-like substance which was held under the tongue for several minutes, then spat out discreetly into a special pot. It possessed an almighty kick that could floor the uninitiated, while the shiny round tin it was kept in doubled as a mirror. In Herat, *Nars* was seldom seen, but then that was probably due to supply rather than demand. It was thought of not as a drug, but as a cure for battle fatigue and nerves, and God knows they needed something.

The commander of Yukan was a fine horseman and an excellent shot, even at full gallop. A Spanish pistol was at his waist, bandoliers criss-crossed his broad chest and he carried a whip with a silver handle, but never used it. He offered me one of his horses to the next village but I told him I preferred to walk.

'Why?' he roared teasingly. 'Can't you ride?'

I lied. 'Of course,' I said.

'Then show me.'

On his finest stallion I trotted carefully to a stream and back again, and when I dismounted, he and his men were doubled up with laughter.

'Now I understand why you wish to walk,' he said, and with that, the commander leapt onto the horse himself, raced back to the stream, cleared it beautifully, spun the animal round with hardly a touch on the reins and returned in similar fashion.

I walked on, south-east through a land littered with the remains of ancient forts: the protection racket of the old Silk Road. At every defile stood a broken but still commanding tower of sun-baked mud, to which traders and travellers alike would have once paid their fee. In return the forts kept the trading routes open and free of unofficial pirates.

There was still a long way to go, I told myself; still a few hundred miles, I thought. Although it was no use relying upon an Afghan for accurate details on distance. If I asked how far it was to our destination, to the next village say, I would be told four or five hours. But six hours later there would be no village in sight; in fact there would be nothing but empty land for miles around. Twelve, sometimes fourteen hours later, yes, then a village would appear. It was better to accept that a day's journey would take just that – one day, from dawn to dusk.

At night there was nearly always somewhere to shelter, either a mujahedeen fort at the highest point in a valley, or a nomad's black felt tent with reed stalks for walls, or a small mountain village where more than once I had to drag myself away from offers to stay longer – two days, two weeks, a month.

There were frequent disputes over money. I offered to pay and my offers were turned down. In the end I was allowed to leave something for the children, in case medicines were needed to cure an illness. The hospitality, at times, was remarkable, even though these people had suffered so much for so long.

One old man, a tall, thin fellow with a gaunt face, took pity on me and tried to stuff a few Afghan rupees into my bag. When I refused the money he gave me his string of prayer beads.

'There are ninety-nine beads,' he said. 'One for each of the names we know for God. There is another name – the one hundredth – but it is kept a secret from man.'

At a village called Char Deh, I was asked to sing at a wedding. The young bride had arrived on horseback from another village, resplendent in colourful head decorations, anklets and bracelets. All the men strutted about in their finest gear, pistols in their belts, at least one bandolier across their chests. The scene was set. The local minstrel had just finished crooning a love song, the sun was dipping into a brilliant red sky, a cool wind had come up and it was a beautiful evening, until they asked me to sing. I let loose with Dylan's *Comes a time*. They held out for a few bars, then started clapping wildly. It was a polite way of saying stop.

The father of the groom had a load of grain ready to be taken to the markets, three days away in Piesang, and I was anxious to join the cavalcade of men, camels and donkeys. If Commander Azizullah Afzali in Herat was right, then Piesang was connected by road to Kandahar, and Kandahar was within spitting distance of the border. The names of these places were like music to my ears. It was hard to believe I had come so far.

The father's name was Haji Behzok and his hair was completely white. He wore a white turban of silk and white shalwar; everything about him was white except for his mood. That, at the time of our meeting, was as black as pitch.

'Thieves!' he bellowed. 'They will steal the grain and the animals too if we are not careful.'

On the last trip to Piesang, a band of renegades had set an ambush and made off with everything. It was thought they came from the Helmand Valley, far to the south, an area well known for its bandits and cutthroats. One man in particular was held to be responsible for a number of such raids. They said he was crazy; a modern-day Assassin. This time, the convoy would be armed and prepared.

The old man raised his arm and pointed to a dent in the solid line of mountains on the horizon, the last real mountain range before the plains of Kandahar and the Pakistan border.

'If they attack,' he said, 'it will be in that valley.'

We set off in the morning and walked through a country disrupted by gulches and dried river beds, where the camels outnumbered the people by twenty to one. A herd of at least two hundred beasts watched us go by, while the herdsman lay down on the hill opposite, his back to the wind, wrapped up in a full-length felt coat with inordinately long sleeves. The valleys were long and wide, and bowl-shaped at the top end. The occasional jagged peak rose out of a bed of its own erosion, and towering whirlwinds of dust danced a crazy jig across our path.

At the end of the day we had travelled fifty miles or more and the mountains were upon us. The camels were hobbled and the donkeys corralled. We dined on bread alone. I slept on the bare ground, wrapped in my *patou* like the others, without the warmth of a fire for fear of attracting unwanted attention. The loose end of my turban I wrapped tightly round my face to shut out the wind.

Sleep did come, but only fitfully. Before dawn we were up again and quickly away, stopping only for morning prayers. There was no water to be had for the ritual ablutions every Muslim must perform before prayer. Instead, the men used the clean earth to wash in; a curious act, but one which I knew to be within the bounds of Islamic law. In the pecking order of pure substances, earth is second only to water.

Beside the mouth of the valley stood the remains of an old Christian mission house. Its bell, still intact after all this time, rang out woefully as the wind grabbed and pulled at the rope. Further on were three wooden crosses in the ground – the missionaries no doubt, but their names had long since been wiped away by natural forces.

We followed a steep path up through a forest of boulders and immediately the tension increased. At one place, the ground was stained a deep red, where a sack of dye had split open. The track zigzagged over a scree slope and down into a grey-stoned hollow scattered with olive trees. At the far end a mighty vertical cliff face had been cleft in two by the meekest of streams, and by its banks was a tiny shepherd's cottage.

The shepherd was sitting in the sun on a rock near the water. He was a wizened old man with clouded eyes. His sheep were fat-tailed but skinny, and they flocked round him like children when he called.

'Who's that coming?' he shouted anxiously, gripping his staff.

'We are from Char Deh,' came the reply.

'Going where?'

'To Piesang with grain, God willing.'

The shepherd looked relieved.

'Ah, then you are sent by Haji Bahzok. Tell me, the eldest son, has he married yet?'

'By the grace of God, two days ago.'

'Allah protect them, and you,' he said.

We squeezed through the gorge and into a tight valley that gradually widened and opened out for a while as it curved downwards. Our path zigzagged through a dry thicket of short stumpy trees which leaned in the direction of the stream. In winter with all the snow-melt, the volume of water would increase dramatically and the stream would become a river, crashing through the gorge. The debris of the season could still be seen washed up high onto the hillsides like a spring-tide mark. But by the afternoon, the valley had narrowed again and the descent was quite steep, so I knew we were dropping down onto the plains.

Like the time before, the night was spent in the open, though the valley floor was littered with boulders that helped block the wind. Overhead, a tiny satellite moved slowly across the heavens on its effortless course and then vanished behind a ridge.

FORTY-SIX

I woke to the sound of an explosion like the distant crack of thunder. Far below us in the night, perhaps even as far as Kandahar, trouble was brewing.

The men looked anxiously at each other as the animals were hastily prepared. Then we left, eager to be out of the mountains before first light.

For the few remaining hours of darkness our caravan edged its way slowly downhill, criss-crossing the stream many times in order to find a safe path. The camels protested loudly at this apparent lack of sympathy for their situation. They protested at anything and everything. Camels are the agitators of the animal world.

We kept passing the ruins of tiny hamlets, mere shadows some of them. In places, all that remained of the homes were piles of hardened earth, slowly melting into the ground. A few walls were still standing. The tail end of an unexploded rocket could be seen protruding from one of them, evidence that this destruction was not from natural causes. It was a cautionary reminder that once again we were entering the domain of war.

The wind at our backs was bitter. Even with the *patou* to wrap myself in it was cold, though it was less than comforting to know the usual blinding heat would eventually be in force by noon. The only consolation was that providing we had no trouble, this day would be the last of the journey to Piesang.

And surprisingly, it was.

I had expected a march of ten or twelve hours. Instead, the valley turned a sharp corner only a few hours later and there to my unrestrained delight was the village surrounded by miles of rolling open country. The mountains fell back behind us. The sun was a shimmering red ball above the far eastern horizon. Never again would a simple community of mud huts appear so wonderful.

The first order of the day was breakfast, then business. The goods were unloaded but left in a pile outside the head trader's house, a place that doubled as the local inn. The animals were taken to the stables for feeding. We gorged ourselves on fresh bread and pieces of goat's meat, washed down with tea and a kind of sugar known as *dislimmer* in Farci but *permit* in Pashtu.

There were others who had arrived at the inn before us as well. Traders mostly, and a few mujahedeen. Someone asked about the explosion we had all heard in the night.

'Aircraft,' came the perfunctory reply, and we were shown a conical-shaped hill behind the village where a mujahedeen fort was situated. The raids came once a week, as regular as clockwork.

Afterwards, while the others tended to their goods, I began inquiring about the chances of there being a truck going to the border, and was pointed in the direction of the head trader. He was a tall man, elegantly dressed with the rings on his fingers denoting position and wealth. It seemed he was everything to everyone. He was Jamiat commander to the mujahedeen, middleman to the sellers and friend to the buyers. He was local chief and inn keeper, mayor, mullah and settler of domestic disputes, but most importantly, he organised the transport. The truck, he said, was due tomorrow.

But tomorrow came and with it no sign of a vehicle. The head trader was stoical. 'Tomorrow,' he said again with a shrug.

I resigned myself to a longer stay in Piesang than was first thought. Delays I was used to, but being so close to the border, just a few days by truck, that was harder to take. The second night, however, was to see the arrival of someone who would share the wait.

It was dark, we had just a single lamp, and I was sitting with some friends on a broad rug outside the inn, when two men on horseback appeared. The older one spoke in Farci. He had with him a 'doctor' he said, who was going to Pakistan – a *'feringhi* doctor' no less.

They dismounted and there was some fuss over a bag. It was big and bulky, and looked very heavy. They dragged it into the head trader's house before coming out to sit with us. Greetings were exchanged. We all stared at the doctor. His face was red and peeling and he looked exhausted. He let the old man do all the talking.

'Yes, by the grace of God,' he said, 'we have come from Laulash in the Faryab province . . . No, he is from the land of France . . . I'm not sure, I think near America . . . That is right, God willing, to Pakistan . . . The horses? Yes, one is to be sold here . . .' and so on.

The French doctor was seated next to me. He had red hair and fair skin. I pitied him for that. Under the Afghan sun he had fried. I caught his eye and smiled, unsure of what to say, but he looked clean through me and then turned his head. I was just another inquisitive Afghan face after all: staring, questioning, intruding, sometimes annoying. His response didn't anger me. I was surprised more than anything, perhaps even a little pleased.

'Parlez-vous Anglais?' I asked smugly.

He nearly dropped his tea.

He was part of a French team of nurses working for Médécins sans Frontières. His name was Benoit and he was thirty-three. He had joined MSF in France after hearing a radio commercial advertise the need for skilled volunteers in Afghanistan. During the summer break from medical school, he had taken the plunge. Now he longed to be back in France. A fresh fruit salad was his heart's single greatest desire.

'Eh bien,' he said. 'But now, please excuse me. I am tired.' And with that he stretched out and went to sleep.

The truck came the next day and we left in the early afternoon. It was an old Mercedes, loaded to the gunwales with sacks of grain, pieces of a broken motorbike, oil drums and huge rubber tyres, not to mention about fifty traders and armed mujahedeen crammed into every available space. It was hot and humid, and highly uncomfortable. The dirt road through the hills and out onto the desert was rutted and pock-marked with various holes and humps, all of which we took at speed. Slowing down brought clouds of dust down upon us, aided by a strong following wind. Within an hour, everyone was covered in a fine white dust, beards, clothes and skin, making us look like extras from a zombie movie. The advantages of travelling by truck became less and less, and I was beginning to miss not having two feet on the ground.

The afternoon wore on, however, punctuated by the occasional prayer stop or the need to fill up our leaking radiator. Once while we were trundling across a wide open stretch of desert, a tremendous racket suddenly erupted from the front of the truck. Men were shouting, arms were waving, as we saw hurtling towards us the unmistakable outline of a Soviet MiG.

The jet banked as it roared past at three hundred feet. The pilot was taking a better look to consider whether or not we were worth the trouble, like a well-fed cat eyeing an easy prey. He was so close as he shot by I could see him in his cockpit. Fortunately he didn't come back.

But the incident caused us to pull over and lie low for a few hours, in case of any further aerial activity. Helicopters were especially feared, as were the airborne troops they sometimes carried. The Russians had long ago perfected the tactic of flying in with all guns blazing, landing and then offloading the soldiers to mop up any remaining survivors. The fact that the Russians were no longer present didn't seem to relieve the tension.

All this time Benoit kept himself to himself more or less, and that was fine by me. His baggage was his main concern, and woe betide the person who even so much as looked at it. He said it was just a bag of old clothes, but it was far too heavy for that. I was inclined to believe he had invested in a few old carpets and was fearful of losing them to some sticky-fingered thief. The burden was not only the weight of his treasure. The things he carried were riveted onto his mind, so that at times he seemed to think of nothing else.

At sunset we drove on for another few hours, arriving at the banks of the mighty Helmand River well after dark. Spanning the black, fast-flowing water was an iron bridge, built by the Americans before the war, and only recently captured from the government. Electric lights, the first I had seen in months, lined the road on the near side and illuminated a row of huts that buzzed with activity, a crossroads in the middle of nowhere. Spare machine parts were sold, along with general stores and food.

I had a sense of encroaching civilisation.

We stayed just a short while, then bumped and lurched our way across the bridge and along the river. The hill country away to the west was bathed in a ghostly white moonlight. The dark patches were trees denoting a waterhole or stream, and no doubt a village. Wherever there is water, there is life.

On the outskirts of a place called Sangin we stopped and climbed down to sleep in the sand. It was judged unwise to enter at night, when triggers were lighter than usual, and so there we lay listening to the river gurgling past somewhere in the darkness until dawn made it possible for us to enter.

But Sangin was already on the move as we drove in. Life was obviously fast here, and the sprawling bazaar was the town it seemed. It was like a big city in miniature. Instead of well-dressed business people out to make a killing, there were Afghans, dressed to kill and doing business.

Sangin's collection of shoddy metal shacks and mud houses

was also a main target for bombardment for some reason, and there were many shattered buildings as proof of the fact. A graveyard the size of a football pitch stood beyond the bazaar at one end. Opposite, a scrap metal yard was piled high with the junk of war – jagged sections of exploded bombs and rockets, pieces of trucks, cars and other vehicles. Someone was possibly making a very tidy sum of money.

We picked our way slowly through the people, veered round a watermelon market and came to a stop outside a Jamiat-i-Islami *komiteh*. There was a dirty brown tarpaulin raised up for shade and a rug was spread out underneath. Seated on this was the usual band of heavily bearded, swarthy mujahedeen.

'Salaam Aleikum,' a middle-aged man spoke from the doorway. He came forward, smiling tentatively, and shook my hand.

'Aleikum Salaam,' I replied before introducing myself.

'And I,' he said. 'I am the Commander Rahmat Tula Ahmaneh. Welcome.'

Like the head trader in Piesang, if there was something you needed, you came to Rahmat for it. He was another jack of all trades with his finger on the pulse of his town, who offered his services for a small fee. In my case, I needed information.

'There will be no Jamiat truck going to the border for a few days,' he said in answer to my question. 'Perhaps for a week.'

When Benoit heard this news he sat on his haunches and stared glumly at the ground. Something in me began to feel genuinely sorry for him. He suddenly seemed very alone and out of his depth.

I asked Rahmat again if there was any other way.

'With mujahedeen? No,' he said.

Then he paused mid-breath, and wrapped a smile round his discoloured teeth.

'But there is a taxi.'

FORTY-SEVEN

The taxi, I soon discovered, was a Toyota jeep driven by a dark-skinned desperado with one eye. For five thousand rupees (about US$15), he said he would make the journey to Pakistan, although his sincerity was undeniably suspect. In the end, however, there was no other alternative.

'Two days,' said Rahmat cheerfully, as we helped Benoit load his sack into the back. 'Only two days to the border.'

But an hour later, two days began to seem like an eternity, as for the fourth time we became bogged down in soft sand. The vehicle was soon unstuck again, thanks to our efforts and those of the four villagers who had joined us on the trip, but it was our slow, staccato pace which proved most frustrating. I was used to walking: movement that is continuous, flowing and independent of anything or anyone else, where a rhythm is struck and the traveller is lost in his thoughts. In a vehicle I expected to achieve speed at least, and a subsequently greater distance covered. Yet it was not until late afternoon that we crawled up to the outskirts of Kandahar city.

Children were playing in a turquoise river when we arrived, and the older ones were diving from a bridge into the central current, eventually emerging fifty yards downstream. Markets selling spare automotive parts, watermelons and even ice-cream in one instance, lined both banks. Behind them were rows of poplar trees and again, behind these sun-baked houses that followed the twists and turns of the river into the government-controlled parts of the city.

The screams of the children and the existence of such fairground sweets made it hard to believe that this was still Afghanistan. I half expected a stray mortar shell to whistle overhead and land in the middle of it all, just to confirm that this was still a dangerous place. Happily nothing like this did happen, and when we stopped to repair a puncture, I waited on the bridge with a glass of melted ice-cream in my hand, watching the fun until the repairs were completed.

A few extra fare-paying passengers crammed themselves into the back before we left, one of them a woman who was all but covered in a heavy felt shawl. Only her nose and eyes peered out from underneath. She must have been incredibly hot, even at this late stage of the day.

Out past the city on the road again, we passed several burnt-out vehicles – ordinary cars by the look of them, including a jeep such as ours. They seemed to have been in convoy and most probably fell foul of an aerial attack of some kind. Holes the size of dinner plates were punched through the roof and sides, and the doors hung open, dangling from their hinges. I asked our driver if the attack had been recent.

'Long time back,' he said, waving a hand in the air. 'Three, four – no more, five days ago.'

He took both hands off the wheel and held up the same number of fingers for everyone to see. Five days ago wasn't enough for my liking and it was a great relief to know that darkness was once again almost upon us.

Eventually our headlights were masked, leaving only a thin strip of light to show the way. Several times we were bogged down again in patches of fine desert sand and we suffered another puncture to add to our troubles, but at least the engine ran smoothly and with every hour that passed, the border drew closer.

The stars came out, bright and clear as always, and it must have been close to midnight when the driver decided it was time to stop for the night. The area around us was hard and flat except for a dry river bed nearby. The jeep was hidden beneath the bank and we lay down in the open, wrapped in our *patou*. For one split second, before submitting to the weariness that ached in my bones, I thought a tracer bullet had flashed by overhead. But in the end it was only a firefly.

Back into mind came the night I first entered Afghanistan with Hezbollah. So much had happened since then, so much had changed. What of Nebi Mohandaspoor and Karim, of Commandant Haji Qary Ahmad Ali and Nasur Ahmad Najar? What were they doing? Were they in fact still alive? I tried to picture them but for some reason, perhaps through tiredness and the strain of the past week, their faces refused to come into focus.

In the biting cold of early morning our journey continued upon a rocky road. Everyone was woken suddenly in the pre-dawn darkness by a fierce argument between the husband of one of the women and the driver. She had complained that he was eyeing her up all the time, which naturally sent her husband into a blind rage. It was soon found out however that the driver's wayward glass eye had been responsible all along. Tempers cooled as we drove on, but not by much.

Then, at sunrise, we entered a small insignificant village. The jeep stopped outside a tea house which was one of a long line of open-fronted stores. Thin pancakes of bread were being baked at the front. I climbed out of the jeep just as the others, besides Benoit, jumped down and disappeared. The driver dumped Benoit's sack on the ground and was about to tear off in a huff when I grabbed him by the arm.

'Where are we?' I demanded in Farci.

He yelled back in Pashtu. 'Chaman, of course!'

Getting shouted at twice in the same morning certainly wasn't his idea of fun.

'Chaman?' I said with greater composure. 'The border town, in Pakistan?'

'The border. Yes! Here is the border.'

He looked guilty.

'But what side is this?' I asked.

'Afghanistan here! There is Pakistan!' and with that he ducked into the cab and drove off.

The direction in which he had indicated before making good his hurried escape was beyond the last line of stores at the end of the street. A few figures, shrouded in the ubiquitous *patou* were coming from the same direction. A dawn mist hung in the air. I had a horrible sinking feeling in the pit of my stomach.

'Oh my God!' I said to myself. 'You idiot!'

All this time, I had envisaged crossing the border at some

other place, a secret route through the desert perhaps, in the dead of night, with the mujahedeen, thereby avoiding any Pakistani border guards who would ask me for the Pakistan visa I didn't have. A single impatient act back in Sangin now bore serious implications. The protective umbrella of the mujahedeen had been left behind.

Walking to the end of the street I caught sight of the uniformed policemen, the barbed wire and the grey concrete block building that was the Pakistan border post, the scene of my worst nightmare. They would ask for my visa. My reply would be that I didn't have a visa. They would tell me to go back and get one.

Go back! Where to? Herat? Or Kabul maybe?

I glanced over my shoulder. Benoit was sitting happily, drinking tea and eating bread. His sack weighed a ton, there was no way he could carry it far. But then if he had a proper visa he wouldn't have to.

At that moment I noticed a young man sitting in front of a tent, dismantling and cleaning a Kalishnakov with practised ease. His clothes were old and frayed at the edges, but neat all the same. Instead of a turban he wore a colourful Pakistani cap with the front cut away in a V-shape. The sides and top were inlaid with tiny round mirrors that glinted in the morning light. The instant he saw me approaching, he got to his feet and smiled uncertainly.

'Salaam,' I said, and shook his hand.

He spoke Pashtu at first, but then seeing that I was having difficulty understanding he switched to Farci. I was overjoyed to hear he did in fact belong to a mujahedeen group, although the name of it was unfamiliar. We sat down anyway and as he poured out a glass of tea, I explained to him who I was, where I had come from and the nature of my predicament. It was a little difficult to describe the latter, but he seemed to grasp it without too much trouble. Then I produced the letter from Hariff Khan and this was met again with the same calm air of understanding. All my prayers, it seemed, had just been answered, until he produced a block of hash from a pocket of his waistcoat and proceeded to roll himself a morning joint. Within a few minutes his eyes were red and gleaming, and he was staring off into the distance.

'Look,' I said. 'This is important!' The urgency in my voice startled him back to life and his smile melted.

'Is there a way of getting past the border guards from here?'

He blew a puff of smoke lazily into the air. 'We have a way,' he said.

'How then? By foot?'

'No, not walking,' and he put his hands onto an imaginary steering wheel in front of him. 'We drive.'

'How often?' I asked.

'Today, tomorrow . . . every day Pakistan. When do you want to go?'

'Today.'

'Then we go.'

Why I had decided to trust someone who was stoned out of his brain was beyond all reason, but then he was my only chance. I went back to Benoit and told him about the plan, but he waved me off and complained of fatigue. He would cross the border in his own time and not be pushed into any hasty decisions.

Back at the tent my friend was lighting up another joint and preparing to spend the rest of the day in a psychedelic haze. He had, however, already made the transport arrangements. Parked outside was a gaudily decorated jeep, with such colourful trinkets attached to it that would have better suited a circus wagon. At a fairground it was the perfect camouflage, but in the middle of a dust-brown desert?

Too tired to object I climbed into the back and a tarpaulin was draped over me. There was just enough room to lie down and peer through a gap at the world outside. I was trying hard to believe that everything would be fine. I was trying even harder not to think about the border and the consequences of capture, when the driver revved up the engine and with a crunching of gears we shot off down the street, onto an asphalt road, and straight towards the Pakistani police.

I buried my head in my hands and groaned.

All of a sudden I was thrown to one side as the jeep swerved violently to the right, bumped over a ditch and when I looked again, we were driving out across the open desert parallel with the borderline. Through my peephole the Pakistani police were visible behind us, going about their usual affairs with cool indifference. At any moment I expected to hear the shouting of voices, the crack of rifle shots and the zip of lead through the air. But against all the odds, it seemed, nothing happened. After several kilometres of bouncing around in the back and clinging on for dear life, we made a sudden left-hand turn, followed shortly afterwards by another. When the asphalt road was back underneath the jeep, incredibly it was the Pakistani side we were on. The ugly concrete border post was behind me and so too were the police. Directly ahead lay the border town of Chaman.

It was an oasis full of people and gaudily painted vans and trucks, and best of all – peace.

FORTY-EIGHT

'You're alive!' Elisabeth says. 'Thank God.'

The soft voice of my girlfriend in London crackled down the line, distant but not so far away. I had managed to get through the tangle of operators and we talked about everything and anything frantically, before the money ran out or the phone went dead. Some weeks ago she'd had an idea, she said – why didn't we meet up again in Paris? It would be almost springtime, the first green shoots would be appearing on the branches, it would be like starting all over again.

I smiled and told her it sounded like a wonderful idea. We agreed on the time and the place, a tiny park near the Rodin Museum, and for the moment I chose to ignore the twenty thousand kilometres that still separated us.

From Chaman I journeyed north to Rawalpindi and attempted to book into a place with all the mod-cons: a roof, running water. The manager looked at my passport and shook his head with all the gravity of a headmaster. The absence of a visa was again a major concern and I could tell he was considering making a phone call to someone I'd prefer not to meet.

I pried my passport from his stubby fingers and headed for the less auspicious surroundings of the central bus station. As it turned out, the place there didn't mind turning a blind eye to my predicament. I was taken to the second floor and given a room with no door, an iron bed, a bucket for a bathroom and orange walls. The empty doorway afforded me a view of the local market through a gaping hole in the opposite exterior wall. As I sat on the bed, the noise from the bedsprings startled a gecko that appeared suddenly on the ceiling. It moved into the hallway onto a patch of green paint and quietly changed colour to suit its new environment.

Two chameleons, I thought, sharing the same room.

A few days later, in pursuit of legality, I found the Australian embassy in Islamabad, who bundled me off to Internal Affairs, who then promptly deported me to China. I was given a severe warning from an incredulous official, whose gasps of disbelief at my audacity gave him a bad case of the hiccups. What followed was an order to leave the country within ten days.

All in all, it was a good deal. Ten days in the cool, crisp Himalayan mountains of Northern Pakistan could not have come at a better time. Although I did not realise it, I was exhausted, mentally more than physically. I needed a place to unwind and a tiny, white-stoned hut in the high-altitude village of Pasu was the perfect place.

Once there I was able to collect my thoughts and take long walks up to the Batura Glacier, where the long stretches of its icy road ended in a sheer blue wall. I had managed to buy a second-hand army coat from a bazaar in the town of Gilgit to the south, and this now became my outer skin. I could wrap myself in its wool and pull the fur-lined hood down tight over my face, then find a rock ledge in the sun to watch the apricot sellers bring their harvest to market. Perhaps it was this reflective mood that triggered something in my memory, casting my mind back to those last days in Afghanistan, for as I curled up and tried to doze, for some reason I couldn't stop thinking about Aziz: the curious old man who spoke excellent French and lived on his own in the Qasa Murg.

I remembered sitting outside with him on the morning I was to depart, watching him cup his hands round the unopened bud of a wild flower.

This, he said, was good for the plant. 'Regardez! La fleur est ouverte!'

But the flower, to my eyes, was still as tightly closed as before.

'Why is it good?' I had asked.

Smiling, he told me I knew why already, and that my hands were like his: full of magic.

I thought about this for a long while before I slept . . .

He was sitting on the grassy knoll by the side of his house, where the spring bubbled up out of the earth and where the wild flowers grew. They were still in bud. In a week, maybe less, the grass would be covered in a bright blue bloom.

I knew this was a dream, and I knew that on a rock in a valley somewhere I was still asleep, but it didn't seem to interfere with what was happening. I walked barefoot across the hard stony ground, oblivious to any discomfort this might have caused, and approached his house from down the side of a hill. In the field below there was a tree with small yellow flowers, and a flock of strange white birds nesting.

Aziz looked up and smiled when he saw me coming. He wasn't surprised, just happy. It was almost as if he had been expecting me.

'Welcome back,' he said.

I waved but said nothing in reply. I simply went and sat down beside him. It felt good after so much time spent walking. It felt as if I wouldn't have to walk another mile, because here was the end of my journey.

'So, how do you like my garden?' he asked, and in doing so, reached down and plucked a flower bud from the soil. He held it gently, cupped within long slender hands and fingers, until the petals suddenly curled back and the flower opened out completely.

I stared at him.

'You know how,' he said, interrupting my thoughts. 'You know so many things my friend, yet you refuse to acknowledge them. Faith and knowledge is all about remembering what you already know.'

In that moment he was not at all from this world. He took the flower and gave it to me. The instant it touched my palm the petals folded up tightly, blue disappearing within green.

'See, you have already forgotten why you came here,' he said.

He was laughing at me, I knew – shaking his head like a despairing teacher at a slow student's progress.

'Untrue!' I protested, but Aziz wasn't listening.

'Come,' he beckoned. 'We have little time. There is something I want you to see.'

He led the way back to his little house and we went inside to the scantly furnished main room. The sunlight slanted in through a single window onto some books on a shelf. A pail of water sat in the corner; supposedly it was there to keep the air from drying out. There were thin mattresses along the walls and a kilim on the floor. It was just as I remembered it, but for one extra thing. Mounted on the far wall was an old clock set into an elaborately carved wooden frame, its face browned with age. The room was suddenly filled with the gentle rhythm of kept time: tick-tock, tick-tock, never missing a beat. I stood mesmerised in the room's centre, wanting to speak but unable to find the words. I was looking at the exact same clock I had seen on my bedroom wall long ago, in another dream perhaps, even though I had been awake, that night my father died.

'Faith and knowledge,' said Aziz.

'What do you mean?'

'You think you came here to find something, but in fact it was to prove what you already know: that there is no separation in death, that your father is very much alive though not in this world, that you can always be in touch with him, even as we speak.'

'He is here?' I said, swallowing the lump in my throat.

Aziz's dark eyes levelled at mine and a single tiny streak of colour appeared on the flower bud.

'Very near, my friend,' he said.

We went back outside and he plucked the open flower from my hand and placed it gently back in the soil. I looked up at the sky to see an army of huge anvil-headed clouds, thirty thousand feet high, rolling in over the mountains.

'Do not be afraid!' I heard him say.

A cold wind came swirling down the valley and a blast of sand and grit stung my face. In that moment I felt my father's presence again, very strong and clear. I looked over my shoulder and there he was, where he had always been: standing right behind me. The smile was still the same, instantly recognisable: the one thing I would always remember about him. The hair was as red as ever. I saw him reach out a hand towards me.

'Do not be afraid!' came again the voice of Aziz from behind.

I took a single step forward towards the solitary figure and in so doing, the house, the valley, and everything within it melted away into a question mark blur of cornflower blue.

I woke up with a start and suddenly remembered, aged nine, sitting in a dinghy that bobbed up and down on the windswept waters of New Zealand's Mangawhai Harbour. My father stood on the pier holding in one hand the length of rope which tied us together. He was waiting for my sister to come down from the beach house, and as a joke of sorts, he started to let the rope slowly slip through his fingers. The wind tugged at my little vessel and blew it further away from the pier, out towards the middle of the channel where the faster current hastened my journey. The odd thing was, at the time it seemed as if I was the one who was stationary, and that it was my father who was swiftly receding from view. There he stood, growing smaller and smaller until the line went taut – me on one end, him on the other, each of us an island, yet still connected.

I caught my breath and sat still, not wanting to put undue pressure on the strands of thread that kept us from complete separation. If they broke, in my child's mind I thought that it was he who was in danger of being lost to the sea.

But that rope had held. I could now see it had tied us together and held us firm all these years, to the point where neither of us was moving forward. It had become a restraint, and like the pilgrim who finally reaches his destination, I began to realise what I had come all this way to look for was found. On that narrow mountain ledge, I did something I had never really properly done before. I cried. Grief fell onto the hard stone, onto the tiny alpine flowers that grew in the cracks, and then flowed away.

Yet another memory came flooding back – of a warm summer's day as we swam out from the shore, me clinging to his neck and looking down onto his broad, freckled back. On that strangely prophetic day he had spoken of letting go.

'The sea will carry you son, if you let it.'

My arms stopped flailing. The gulps for air turned to slow, measured breathing. I rolled onto my back upon that elevated rock, spread my arms and legs out wide and let go of the pain and anger that is loss.

'Keep your head back and you won't sink,' he would say, strong arms under my shoulders.

I let go of the sadness that was his empty place at our table, and of his absence amongst the lines of parents at every finish line.

'Don't be afraid, I still have you,' he would say.

I let go of the father-and-son events I could never attend, and the jealousy I directed at people who knew him better than I did. I let go of the questions because I no longer needed the answers. I stayed this way for quite a while, until I had completely set us free.

His arms fell away from beneath me. Suddenly I was floating, twelve thousand feet up.

EPILOGUE

The cellphone rings in my office and it makes me jump. I can see the name flashing on the screen is someone I don't need to talk to right now, so it rings a few more times before being silenced by my cellular secretary. I return to my laptop. Half a minute later the phone rings again. Happily, a different name: it says LIBERACE and I answer the call, trying to remember which friend in London gave Elisabeth that nickname.

'Hello you.'

'How goes it?' she says, sounding tired. I picture her at the window seat: feet up, slender musician's fingers round a mug of tea, blonde hair like a young girl's. This is the woman who rings me up at the office and brightens my day with tales of perfect arm circles at junior swimming school, and of butterflies that hatch to a chorus of childish wonder, small voices shouting with glee.

'Aw, you know. Busy,' I say.

'Too busy to talk?'

'Never,' I say. 'Are the children asleep?'

'One down, one fighting it.'

'Don't tell me, it's Isobel, right? She should be exhausted after last night. What time did she wake up?'

'Oh, three thirty or thereabouts.'

'Bad dream?'

'Not a bad dream I think. I mean she wasn't crying, she was just wide awake.'

I thought of the cold and made a mental note to buy a better radiator for her room, maybe one with a timer and thermostat.

'Poor kid,' I say. 'She's probably freezing.'

'Well,' she replies with a smile. 'Not everyone shares your affinity for the cold.'

Siberia was rushing past the window, all snow and silver birch, a blur of white as the train clattered by. The sun was low and the light filtered through the branches into the carriage. It was minus thirty degrees outside, but when I shut my eyes and let the warm rays of sunlight flicker across my eyelids, I could have been anywhere.

A couple of months before, I had done the exact same thing on an early morning bus approaching the Chinese town of Kashgar, just over the border from Pakistan. The trees were leafy poplars then, slowly turning from green to gold by the side of a dusty dirt road, and the sky was a bright, high-altitude September blue.

So much time had slipped by.

I had ambled across China, keeping to the lesser known areas and finding quiet places to hole up in and rest for a few days. The memory of Afghanistan was still very strong: of Herat city and the long walk, of Aziz in his mountain valley and all the strangeness surrounding that time, and of the last few uneasy days before crossing the border. There was also a promise I had made to Nebi long ago in Seoshan.

The *Shurevi* capital of Moscow had seemed a long way off then, but in western China a black market ticket for the Trans-Siberian Railway had fallen into my hands: Beijing to Berlin, via Moscow, for just forty dollars. Suddenly, my journey's end seemed a good deal nearer.

The frontier between Europe and Asia is marked by a stone obelisk. It stands overlooking the track on a low hill. Exactly how long it has been there, no one can say. Yet the thought of crossing the great divide bears all the characteristics of a momentous occasion. I first entered Asia over a year ago in Istanbul. It seems fitting to exit over the plains of the Soviet

Union. I wait all morning by the window, looking out for a low hill and a large oval rock. At last it passes, and I see this moment through my camera lens. I have a photograph, of a grey, slightly off-centre piece of landscape, the shape of which will not be clearly seen. Yet I will know that here is the border between West and East, the greatest of all borders that still separate men from their dreams.

Vladik had been to West Germany 'on business', and he pointed to the fashionable leather jacket he wore as proof. He was in his early twenties, a student of rocket science at Moscow University. He came up to me on the platform of Moscow central station. For five dollars American, he said, I could stay at his apartment. For seven I could buy a tin of black caviar. For three, a bottle of Russian champagne. For nothing, he announced with a slap on my back, he would show me round the city.

If Vladik were ever to apply these principles of Western capitalism to his studies, then every household would soon have its own ballistic missile.

His apartment was small, but warm and comfortable. Snow had piled up on the window ledges and drowned his potted plants. Every year, however, in the spring, they came back from the dead and flowered. He told me this represented the resilience of the Russian spirit, then he threw back his head and laughed loud like a mocking bird.

In the evening, a friend by the name of Uri came round to drink away his sorrows. A bottle of vodka appeared, the same brand I had seen once on the blood-stained floor of a government fort in Korskack. His girlfriend had left him and he signalled his troubles, and his desire to get drunk, by flicking a finger against his throat.

When the second bottle was half empty, I asked the two of them about Afghanistan.

'A shitty place,' slurred Vladik.

'Damn shitty place, damn!' echoed Uri.

'This was our Vietnam I think, yes?' Vladik said. 'Stupid

shitty damn war! You must realise we knew little about it. The government tell us nothing. Only recently they tell us: it was mistake. Very big mistake! But it is over. I am glad it is over. I am very glad we are finished with that damn stupid shitty place. Finished!'

'All over. Finished!' repeated Uri sadly, but I could tell he was still thinking about his girl.

In the morning, nursing a hangover, I caught the subway to a McDonalds. A long line of hungry Muscovites shuffled forward, collars raised against the biting wind. Most of them would get inside in time for lunch.

A heavy snow shower began as I made my way down Marx Prospect towards Red Square. A spectacular cold front was sweeping in from the north and behind it, a band of icy blue sky. By the time I reached the cobbled square, the sun had appeared beneath the clouds. Half the city was covered in sunshine, half in falling snow.

The Kremlin, 'the house of my enemy' as Nebi had put it, was busy with the frantic departure of long, black, bullet-proof limousines that roared out from the gates, across the square in front of St Basil's Cathedral, zigzagging dangerously up a side street like frightened animals doing their best to avoid capture.

I walked up to Lenin's tomb where a few others were watching the stiff, sober-faced guards on duty. There was one soldier standing nearby, smartly decked out in a fur hat and a long, grey-green army coat. About his waist was a broad leather belt, attached to which was a steel bayonet, gleaming with a parade-ground polish. I felt the bottom of my bag. The identical knife was there, its edge still keen but the shine long since gone. Had its owner once marched past here, on his way to Afghanistan and death? How had he died? I couldn't help but wonder.

Well, I thought to myself. This is it. Here is the end, punctuated by one final and lasting irony.

Only I was to be very much mistaken. Turning to go I heard voices from over my shoulder, men's voices speaking a language that was all too familiar. There were three of them. All had darker than olive skin, all had black moustaches and closely cropped hair, all were Afghan government soldiers – on leave from Kabul – come to see the place from which their orders had once come. They stood shivering as the guards about Lenin's tomb were changed, transfixed by all the pomp and ceremony, and no doubt feeling how far removed it was from the plight of their own country. What on earth, after all, had the Kremlin wanted with Kabul?

We stood and talked for a few minutes beneath the Kremlin walls. They were as surprised to meet me as I was to see them. They were polite, but cautious, and our conversation was the same. It ended amiably enough.

But the promise to Nebi was fulfilled. The circle was complete. There were no loose ends to clear up any more, save for one.

I left Red Square, the cathedrals, Lenin's tomb, the sober-faced guards outside the Kremlin, and walked down to the station to catch the last train to Paris.